The Miles Between Us
Jackson Falls Book 6

Laurie Breton

I have to once again give thanks
to my critique partner and niece,
Patti Korbet, who shoots from the hip
and always gives me wise counsel. *Mwah!*

*This, my thirteenth book, is dedicated to my father,
gone these many years, but alive forever in my heart.
You never got the chance to read any of my work,
but you were an avid reader, and I'd like to think
you would have been proud of me.*

Love you. Always.

BOOKS IN THE JACKSON FALLS SERIES

Coming Home: Jackson Falls Book 1
Sleeping With the Enemy: Jackson Falls Book 2
Days Like This: Jackson Falls Book 3
The Next Little Thing: Jackson Falls Book 4 (A Jackson Falls
MINI)
Redemption Road: Jackson Falls Book 5
The Miles Between Us: Jackson Falls Book 6

ALSO BY LAURIE BRETON

Final Exit
Mortal Sin
Lethal Lies
Criminal Intent
Point of Departure
Die Before I Wake
Black Widow

prologue

HE'D been driving aimlessly for an hour. Too fast, but that was nothing new. It should have helped to cool his anger, driving fast through the velvety darkness, with the windows open and the radio blaring, the night air threading fingers through his hair.

Except that it hadn't. The fury was still there, festering in his gut, twisting and knotting his insides until they felt like a box of snakes. That damned Irish temper. The MacKenzies weren't known for mincing words or for backing down. They were jackasses, and proud of it, with hair-trigger tempers that could ignite with little provocation. He'd inherited that temper from a long line of MacKenzie forebears, and he'd passed it on to Paige. The jury was still out on Emma; his youngest daughter was strong-willed, but she seemed to have a cool head and an even temper.

It would probably make her journey through life one hell of a lot easier than his.

Rob gripped the wheel harder, his shoulders aching, his muscles taut with tension. Arguing had been futile. They hadn't resolved a thing. His wife might not possess the famed MacKenzie temper, but Casey was about as malleable as a chunk of granite. The woman refused to back down, refused to admit that he was right. He loved her, but at times, he wanted to throttle her. This was one of those times.

Tires squealing, he took a hard right turn onto yet another anonymous blacktop road. He was hopelessly lost. These twisting back roads made no sense to a boy raised on the streets of South Boston. He'd lived in Maine for three years, but he still didn't have a clear picture of the lay of the land. It all looked the same to him. Trees, trees, and more trees, interspersed with fields and pastures and crumbling nineteenth-century barns. Casey, who'd grown up here, knew intimately every acre of land from Jackson Falls to the New Hampshire state line. He could spend the rest of his life here and never absorb what came so naturally to her. What was the saying he'd heard? *Just because the cat has kittens in the oven, it doesn't make 'em biscuits.* He was an outsider. No matter how long he lived here, no matter that his wife and his daughter had both been born here or that he paid substantial property taxes, he would always be viewed with suspicion.

The road curved to the left. He stepped on the accelerator, felt the quick response of the engine, the rush of adrenaline as he steered into the darkness with no idea of what awaited him on the other side of that curve. It chapped his ass that she didn't give enough of a damn about him, about Emma or Paige, to listen to reason. He wasn't the villain in this piece. He was just a guy who loved his wife, a guy who was trying to build a decent life with her.

A guy who didn't want to lose her.

He rolled into the straightaway and started down a steep hill, wheels humming against the pavement. They'd always been so connected they could finish each other's sentences. But the last few weeks had created a rift in the tightly-woven fabric of their relationship, had opened a vast gap between them that he had no idea how to breach. And, damn it, he was tired of fighting. He just wanted his life back.

The radio was playing an up-tempo Tom Petty song, a little too bouncy for his foul mood. His attention temporarily diverted from the road, Rob punched buttons until he found WTOS, the Mountain of Rock, where George Thorogood was belting out a song about being bad to the bone.

There. That was more like it.

When he returned his attention to the road, the doe was standing directly in front of him, frozen in time and place, her eyes glowing in the reflection from his headlights. Rob hit the brakes so hard the car fishtailed. He gripped the wheel with both hands and veered to the right to avoid her. His right-front tire dropped off the pavement to the soft shoulder. The deer bounded away into the woods. Cussing, still moving too fast, he yanked the wheel to the left and over-corrected.

Time seemed to slow as, tires screaming, the car lost control. He had a single instant of clarity, a single instant of knowing he was going to die, a single snapshot of Emma's face in his mind, before he reached the opposite shoulder.

And the car went airborne.

PART I: THE LOSS

Rob

New York City
Six Weeks Earlier

IN the isolation booth, Kitty hit a high note, and Rob leaned back on his tailbone, then closed his eyes to better appreciate its rich vibrancy. That voice, that bloodied-and-torn been-to-hell-and-back voice, should have made Kitty Callahan a star. But for some inexplicable reason, fame had eluded her. Most of the record-buying public had no idea who she was, but every professional musician from New York to L.A. was familiar with Kitty. She'd made a career of singing backup vocals on dozens of albums and a steady stream of road tours. He'd been exceedingly lucky that she'd had this one day free in the middle of a three-month tour, even luckier that she'd been willing to use her day off to fly from Seattle to New York because she, and only she, possessed the sound he was looking for.

He'd paid her way, of course. While the record company hadn't given him *carte blanche*, he still had an expansive budget for this album they'd wooed him into producing for Phoenix Hightower, the latest teenage pop star. It might be a kiddie pop album, but if Rob MacKenzie was attaching his name to it, then it was going to be a damn good kiddie pop album. And damn good meant Kitty Callahan on backup vocals.

Rob opened his eyes, took a slug of lukewarm coffee, and exchanged glances with Kyle, the sound engineer. Kyle grinned, gave him a thumbs-up and, nodding in Kitty's direction, said, "Nice pipes. Not to mention easy on the eyes. I'd do her in a New York minute."

Studying the slender blonde on the other side of the glass, Rob remained silent, in part because he was a happily married man, and in part because a million years ago, in a different lifetime in some alternate universe, he and Kitty had been lovers. It hadn't been serious; they'd never been an item. They'd simply been friends with benefits who, in between marriages, one-night stands, and various relationships with other people, got together every so often for dinner, a movie, and a sleepover.

Their relationship was ancient history. It had happened back in his wild and crazy rocker days, back when he was still touring, back before the love of his life finally opened her eyes and realized they belonged together. Before Paige and Emma, his beautiful daughters, came into his life. Before he gave up the booze and the endless array of female companions, put a ring on Casey's finger, and chopped off his tangled mane of hair to become the domesticated family man who now looked back at him every morning from the bathroom mirror.

Back in the day, he'd had a preference for blondes, and he sometimes wondered about the psychology of that. Had it been an attempt at self-preservation, a way of distancing himself, heart and mind, from the dark-haired goddess with whom he had an inexplicable and unshakable bond? The woman who, for nearly two decades, had been his gold standard for measuring other women, all of whom invariably fell short?

The woman who'd spent thirteen years married to his best friend?

It was a moot point now. Time marched relentlessly on, and the only constant was change. Danny had been dead for six years, and Casey was his wife now. But once in a while, something—like hearing Kitty sing—would stir those old memories and the past would creep up silently behind him and bite a chunk out of his ass.

The studio door opened, and he swiveled around to see who had the audacity to breach its staunch barrier while he was recording. Sheila, the front desk receptionist, shrugged her shoulders in apology. "Sorry to bother you, Mr. MacKenzie," she said, in her nasal Brooklyn accent, "but I have a call for you. She says she's your sister-in-law, and it's an emergency."

His insides liquefied. Shoving back his chair, he said into the mic, "Take a break, Kitty. I have a call. I'll be right back."

He sprinted down the corridor, past a half-dozen closed doors. Studio C. Studio B. Studio A. Breaking the corner a half-step ahead of Sheila, he snatched up the telephone receiver that sat on her desk. Breathless, he said, "Hey."

"Thank God I found you," Trish Bradley said. "I didn't have any idea how to reach you. I had to track down Colleen in Bermuda and ask her where you were. It was either that, or find a

Manhattan phone directory and start calling every recording studio in New York."

Colleen Berkowitz, his wife's sister and his invaluable right hand, was honeymooning in Bermuda with her new husband, Harley Atkins. If Trish had interrupted their honeymoon, this had to be serious. "Trish?" he said. "What's wrong?"

"I'm at the hospital. Casey had another miscarriage."

"Shit," he said. "Not again." His brain flooding with visions of gruesome and bloody death, Rob sank onto the corner of Sheila's desk. Rubbing his forehead with the fingers of one hand, he said grimly, "How bad is it?"

Trish hesitated for an instant too long. "I don't know."

Her reticence exponentially increased his fear. "Goddamn it, Trish, how bad?"

"It's bad. I won't lie to you. I found her on the kitchen floor in a pool of blood—"

He muttered an oath.

"Emma was in the playpen, wailing, and—"

"Where's Emma?" he demanded. "Who's with her now?"

"She's fine, hon. Ali has her."

He exhaled a hard breath. "Tell me." He'd thought he was terrified the last time, but that fear had been nothing compared to this. The last time, he'd been there with her, and in spite of his fear, he'd calmly and quickly taken control of the situation. This time, he was four hundred miles away, and utterly powerless. Powerlessness wasn't something he wore well. "Tell me," he repeated. "How much blood did she lose?"

"I don't know. A lot. Sweetie…she was unconscious. I tried to revive her. I couldn't."

A heavy weight, like that of a wrecking ball, settled itself atop his chest, squeezing his lungs until they were about to burst.

"Rob?" she said. "Are you still there?"

He took a ragged breath. Cleared his throat. Said, "I'm still here."

"I'm not trying to scare you. I just think you should be…"

"What?" he snapped. "Prepared?"

"I'm sorry." She was crying softly now. "I don't know how this will turn out. Yes, I think you should be prepared for any eventuality."

"Like hell I will." He turned to Sheila, motioned for a pen and paper. Said into the phone, "Give me the number you're calling from." He wrote it down, repeated it back to her. "Don't move away from that phone until you hear from me again. I need to be able to reach you. I'll be on the next flight out."

"I'm not going anywhere. Bill's here with me, and we're staying put for as long as we're needed. If one of us has to leave, the other one will stay with the phone."

"She'll be fine," he said. Was he trying to convince Trish, or himself? "She will. You want to know why?"

Through tears, Trish said, "Why?"

"Because she wouldn't leave me." And with trembling hands, he hung up before she could respond.

* * *

He spent twenty minutes on the phone with the airlines, arguing because there wasn't a seat available anywhere. The best anybody could give him was standby; the next available seat was tomorrow morning at 3:50 a.m. He could walk to Maine faster than that. Nobody gave a damn that he had a family emergency and needed to get home, and their lack of empathy was maddening. Finally, realizing he was wasting precious time, he snarled, "Thanks for nothing," and slammed down the phone.

He picked it back up again and dialed the concierge desk. Lenny answered immediately with a cheerful, "Good morning, Mr. MacKenzie."

Lenny was a minor god who, besides knowing all the best places to eat and having the instincts of a more stylish Radar O'Reilly, was capable of performing miracles at a moment's notice. Lenny was one of the reasons he always stayed at this hotel when he was in Manhattan.

"Lenny," he said, "I'm checking out early. My wife's had a medical emergency and I can't find a flight home. I need a rental car, and I need it yesterday. Is that something you can help me with?"

"Absolutely. What kind of car would you like?"

"I don't care, as long as it's fast."

"I'll have it in fifteen minutes," Lenny said. "Ten, if traffic cooperates."

"Bless you. You're a good man, Lenny."

While he waited for the rental car to arrive, he packed. It didn't take long. He always traveled light: his studio guitar in a padded case he could sling over his shoulder. A briefcase that held sheet music, pencils, a stack of CDs, spare guitar strings. A backpack containing a few changes of clothing and his toothbrush. Casey had spent years quietly but determinedly augmenting his wardrobe, hoping to improve his fashion sense. She'd finally arrived at the conclusion that there was no hope. He wasn't as clueless as he'd been two decades ago, when he'd found paisley and plaid to be perfectly acceptable traveling companions. He knew how to dress up if and when it was required. But he was most comfortable in worn jeans and a cotton shirt, sleeves rolled up, unbuttoned over a faded concert tee.

Downstairs, Lenny was waiting. The dapper black man held up a shiny set of car keys. "Green BMW," he said, "with a five-speed stick, because you look like a stick-shift kind of guy."

"I'm now adding *mind reader* to your list of exemplary skills."

Lenny grinned. "Just sign here, and you can be on your way."

Rob scrawled his signature, took the keys, and clasped hands with Lenny. "You are the man," he said.

"Have a safe trip, my friend. I hope your wife recovers quickly."

"Thanks. That makes two of us."

The BMW was parked at the curb. Rob nodded to the doorman, opened the passenger door and tossed in his backpack, his briefcase, then took the time to wrap the seatbelt around his guitar, which had cost more than the annual budget of at least one third-world country and was a primary source of his income.

He buckled himself into the driver's seat and took stock. Tachometer, leather seats, A/C, CD, moon roof. And, tucked into its own little nook in the dashboard, a mobile phone. He picked it up, examined it thoroughly. He'd been toying with the idea of getting one of these gadgets, but the technology was in its infancy, and from what he'd heard, they only worked in certain places. The place where he spent most of his time, a rural property tucked into the mountains of Western Maine that his wife was determined to turn into a sheep ranch, was highly unlikely to be one of those places. So he'd believed there was no point.

Until today. Now, thrust into a crisis situation and trapped in a car, hundreds of miles from home, with no means of communication, he suddenly understood. Once this crisis was resolved, he'd be heading to Radio Shack to pick up a cell phone for each of them.

As an experiment, he punched in the number Trish had given him and hit the send button. To his surprise, it worked. "Still no news," she told him.

"I have a rental car with a phone in it. I'd give you the number but…" He looked around, turned the phone over in his hand, opened the glove box, but it held nothing except the owner's manual. "I have no idea what it is. I'll call you again from the road."

He opened the briefcase, took out Don Henley's *Building the Perfect Beast*, and popped it into the CD player. Slipping on his Oakleys, he started the engine, checked his side mirror, and pulled out into Manhattan traffic.

It was hot, it was crowded, and it was slow, and being at a standstill gave him too much time to think dark thoughts. While Henley sang about the boys of summer, Rob tapped his fingers impatiently on the steering wheel. He could lose her. He could end up raising Emma alone.

The unthinkable possibility struck terror into his heart. He'd told Trish that Casey wouldn't leave him, but his words were nothing more than false bravado. Whistling as he passed the graveyard. There were no certainties in this world. Life, with all its warmth and vibrancy, could be snuffed out in an instant. While he sat in a Lower Manhattan traffic jam, surrounded by horns honking in protest at those inconsiderate motorists half a block ahead who refused to sprout wings and fly over the gridlock, the woman he'd loved since he was twenty years old could be drawing her final breath.

I think you should prepare yourself for any eventuality.

No. No way in hell. Not after it had taken them this long to come home to each other. They'd gotten a late start on their happy ending. It couldn't be stolen away from them now. He wouldn't allow it.

Frustrated by unmoving traffic, exhaust fumes, and the whims of fate, he popped out the Henley CD and replaced it with Marvin Gaye and Tammi Terrell. *Your Precious Love*, with its bluesy, sensual rhythm, was one of the songs they liked to dance to, in their bedroom, in the dark. Just the two of them, holding each other close, wrapped in a rich tapestry of emotion as they experienced the music with all their senses.

The wrecking ball settled more heavily on his chest. He closed his eyes and let out a hard breath. When he opened them again, the car ahead of him had moved forward several inches. Resisting the urge to call the hospital again, he revved the engine and watched the tach climb, before easing up on the pedal and seeing it drop again.

It was too soon. He'd told her it was too soon. They'd argued about it. When she'd had the last miscarriage, they'd been warned by two different doctors that they should wait at least a year before trying again. She'd lost a lot of blood, her body needed time to recover from the trauma, and she wasn't twenty years old any longer.

But her biological clock was ticking, and she was hyper-aware of that approaching midnight hour. When Casey Fiore MacKenzie made up her mind about something, she stood as solid as Gibraltar. He could argue until his breath was spent, but nothing, and nobody, could make his wife back down.

So in spite of the yellow caution lights flashing inside his head, he had let her get pregnant again. He couldn't blame this on her, because he was as guilty as she was. It took two to make a baby, and when they lay together in the dark, skin to skin, with nothing between them but the magic they created together, birth control was the last thing on his mind. He'd failed her, horribly, and if she didn't make it through this, he would blame himself until his dying day.

The sun was high overhead by the time he was finally out of Manhattan and on the open road headed north. He opened the moon roof and, with the wind in his hair, the stereo cranked, and one eye scanning his mirrors for blue lights, he stepped down hard on the accelerator and wove aggressively in and out of traffic. He'd learned to drive on the streets of Boston, had honed his skills on the congested freeways of Los Angeles. He was a Masshole, and proud of it. And right now, the only thing that mattered was getting home to her as quickly as possible.

In southern Connecticut, he approached the place where Danny had died. Shortly after his death, obsessed fans had set up a makeshift memorial on the grassy embankment at the scene of the accident. Every so often, the state DOT would clean it up, remove the flowers and the love letters and the record albums. But it was pointless. Within a week, it would start piling up again. Death had rendered Danny Fiore larger than he'd ever been in life.

And damned if he wouldn't love the attention.

Since the last time Rob was here, somebody had spray painted in neon green letters on the huge boulder that had stopped Danny's car the words: FIORE LIVES!

Driving past this place always stirred up all the old angst. The guilt, the pain, the anger, the uncertainty. The question he'd tortured himself with for six years. *If you had the chance to bring your best friend back from the dead, what would you do? If it meant you had to give up the woman you loved, would you bring him back? Or would you let him rot?*

There was, of course, no right answer. Rob loosened the muscles of his hand, picked up the phone, and called Trish again. "She's out of surgery," Trish said. "We just talked to the doctor."

He wiped a sticky palm on his thigh. "What'd he say?"

"She's not out of the woods yet. She lost too much blood. They almost lost her."

His insides, already in crisis mode, knotted so hard he feared he might pass out. "If I hadn't found her when I did," Trish went on, "she wouldn't have made it."

He opened his mouth to speak, but his voice failed him. Rob cleared his throat and managed to say, "Prognosis?"

"The doctor said he's guardedly optimistic."

Anger was easier than terror to elucidate. "What the hell does that mean?"

"I'd say it means she's one lucky woman. They're keeping an eagle eye on her to make sure she doesn't start hemorrhaging again, but the doctor seemed to believe her chances are good for a full recovery. But it'll take time. She'll be weak and tired for a while. She won't bounce back too quickly from this."

Spying a tiny opening between a Volkswagen Jetta and a fuel truck, he darted into it. "Thank you," he said. "For finding her in time. For everything. That woman's my life."

"I know that, honey. And you don't have to thank me. I've loved her since she was a little girl. It would kill me to lose her."

"What about future pregnancies?"

"He didn't say. I imagine that's something he'll want to talk over with the two of you."

"I can't go through this again. Last time, I thought it was a fluke. A coincidence. She'd had two healthy pregnancies since the first miscarriage all those years ago. But there's obviously some kind of issue. This is the second time in less than six months. It's not worth the risk. Somehow, I have to make her understand that this is it. That we're not trying again."

"Good luck with that."

"She's stubborn, but so am I."

"Oh, I hear you. I just know how much of a jackass she can be."

"Not half the jackass I can be."

"Good. My money's on you. I have a new phone number for you. Once she's out of Recovery, they're putting her in Room 219. You can call us there."

"Hang on." Steering with his left hand, he opened the briefcase with his right, took out a pencil and a piece of scrap paper. He propped the paper against the steering wheel. "Go ahead." He scribbled the number. Said, "I'm making good time. I should be there by suppertime."

"Take your time. Bill and I will hold down the fort."

* * *

The next time he called, a raspy but intimately familiar voice said, "Hello?"

At the sound of her voice, all the knotted areas in his body loosened. Until now, he hadn't realized how tightly wound, how utterly terrified, he was. His wife sounded like roadkill, but she was alive, awake, and answering her own phone. Softly, he said, "Hey."

"Hey." Even in her weakened state, Casey managed to infuse that one syllable with pure warmth.

"How you doing, sweetheart?"

"I've had better days."

"I'm on my way, babe. I couldn't get a flight. I had to drive."

"I know. I also know that you're driving way too fast."

He glanced at the speedometer, tapped the brake pedal, decelerated down to 94 mph. Said, "I'm not driving that fast."

"You're a terrible liar, MacKenzie."

She knew him too well. "Look," he said, "I need to get home to you."

"And I need you to be here. But I don't need you to kill yourself on the highway because you're too stubborn to slow down. I already lost one husband because he wasn't smart enough to drive at a reasonable speed. If anything happens to you—"

"Nothing'll happen to me. I'm an excellent driver."

"You're a terrible driver. You're only excellent when you think I'm watching. Where are you?"

"On 495. Somewhere around Haverhill."

"And you left New York at what time?"

Somehow, even through the phone line, she managed to convey the image of dark eyebrows raised in disapproval. *Busted.*

"I plead the Fifth."

"That's what I thought. I'm so sorry, Flash. Another baby gone."

While she'd been facing imminent death, he hadn't allowed himself to think about the baby they'd lost. Now, disappointment and grief rose in his chest. He'd wanted that baby, too.

"Don't you worry about me," he said gruffly. "You're all that matters."

"That is so not true. You matter very much to me. And I'm tough. I've been here before. I lived through it. I'll live through it this time, too."

"I know, but—"

"Just come home to me in one piece. I need to hold you. Promise me."

He slowed down to a sedate 79 mph, a speed which, on 495 circling around Boston, was likely to get him mowed over by some psychotic trucker. "I promise."

"Good. Now hang up the phone. You shouldn't be talking and driving at the same time. And I need to sleep for a while. I'll see you in a few hours. Drive safely. That's an order."

And she was gone.

Casey

THE sun pooled like a warm puddle of honey on the polished floor tiles of the hospital room, dust motes dancing in midair. She'd sent Trish and Bill home. As expected, Trish had objected, quite vehemently. But she'd stood her ground, and Bill, understanding his sister's need to be alone, had ushered his wife out of the room. When they disappeared down the corridor, Trish was still squawking like a peahen left out alone in the rain.

In a couple of hours, Rob would be here. He was somewhere north of Boston, undoubtedly traveling at the speed of light. She would hold on until he got here. It wasn't as though she had a choice. Somehow, she would survive until he walked through that door. Then, if she needed to disintegrate, she could do it in the safety of his arms.

But for now, she was alone. Groggy from the anesthesia and distracted by a dull, nagging ache in her lower abdomen, Casey turned onto her side and adjusted the scratchy hospital bed sheet. She closed her eyes, felt the warm sunlight on her face, saw its red haze behind her closed eyelids. She slept, and dreamed of Katie, squealing with laughter as she ran in slow motion through a field of poppies, a human dynamo with flowing blond hair and Danny's blue eyes. She woke to the ringing of the telephone, and lay there, disoriented, for a moment before she remembered where she was and reached out to answer it.

"Hey," her sister said. "Are you okay?"

Okay was a relative term, one that could be debated endlessly. Not sure how to answer, she said instead, "How did you find out I was here?"

"Trish called me. You were in surgery, and she didn't know how to get in touch with Rob."

"I'm sorry. She shouldn't have bothered you."

"Rob would have strangled us all if she didn't. You almost died. And you sound like you've been swallowing gravel. Why is your voice so hoarse?"

"It's from the surgery. Breathing tube. It'll wear off in a day or two."

"I think we should come home."

"Don't be ridiculous. The last thing I need is for Harley to stop speaking to me because I destroyed his honeymoon."

"Harley thinks you walk on water. The only reason he married me was so he could have you for a sister-in-law."

"Right."

"You think I'm kidding, don't you?"

"I'm clearly alive and functioning. I have competent doctors. Nurses who watch over me obsessively. And Trish hovering over me, the quintessential mother hen."

A movement at the doorway caught her eye. Rob stood there, his lanky body propped against the frame, his face ashen, eyes sunken, hair poking in forty different directions, as if he'd been running his fingers through it. Mirrored sunglasses dangled from the neck of a faded blue tee shirt that had seen better days. Her sister continued talking, but Casey didn't hear a word she said. The pain and grief in those green eyes slammed into her with brute force. The last time he'd looked this gutted was the day they buried Danny.

She glanced at the clock, silently counted the hours, and eyed him with brows raised. He shrugged, but not with his customary insouciance. This clearly wasn't the time to critique his driving habits. He'd made it home in one piece; that was what mattered. "I have to go," she said into the phone. "Rob just got here. I'll see you next Tuesday."

And she hung up without waiting for a response.

He stepped away from the doorway and crossed the room. Pulled a chair up to the bed and sat. She opened her arms and he dropped his sunglasses on the bedside table, leaned over the bed, and they melted into each other. His warmth, his scent, the tickle of his breath on her skin, filled the emptiness inside her. This was what she'd needed, what she'd waited for. Casey combed fingers through his messy hair, reveled in the scrape of beard against her face. A little sloppy, a little unkempt, he needed a haircut. A shave. And still, he was the most beautiful thing she'd ever seen.

With his head cradled against her breast and her fingertips tracing his features, he studied her through soft green eyes. "You okay?" he said.

"I will be. You?"

"I am now."

"I'm so glad you're here." A single hot, salty tear, forming beneath her left eyelid, threatened to spill and betray her.

"You gave me one hell of a scare," he said.

"I'm so sorry."

"If I ever lost you—"

"I know."

She knew because the road ran both ways. The connection between them couldn't be explained by any conventional means. He was friend, lover, husband, soul mate. All of those things, yet none of them came close to describing their bond. It was so much more than any of those concepts. So inexplicable that she'd long since stopped trying to explain it, even to herself. They were *Rob-and-Casey. Casey-and-Rob.* He was hers, and she was his. They belonged together. It was that simple, and that complex.

"What happened to Trish and Bill?" he said. "She promised to stay here."

"They left an hour ago. I threw them out. You know how Trish hovers. She was sending my blood pressure skyrocketing."

He lifted his head to study the numbers displayed on the softly beeping machine beside her bed. Settling back against her breast, he said, "I know you don't want to hear this, but—"

"Then don't say it." She closed her eyes against a sudden sharp pain beneath her breastbone.

"I have to say it, babe. I think it's time we quit trying for another baby."

Raggedly, she said, "And admit defeat?"

"What this is doing to your body…Jesus, Casey, you could've died. You came so damn close that I'm still shaking. And what about the heartbreak—for both of us—every time we lose another baby?"

"What about the heartbreak if we give up? We agreed we wouldn't put a limit on how many kids we had. Why are you changing your mind now?"

"I'm not changing my mind. I'm scared. Damn it, you have me, and Emma, and Paige. Aren't we enough? Don't we have a good life? Aren't we happy, the four of us?"

"Of course we have a good life." With a fingertip, she traced the line of his eyebrow. "Of course we're happy. But I'm not willing to stop at one. I thought you wanted more kids."

He sat up abruptly, leaving her empty-armed and bereft. Picking up her hand, he brought it to his mouth and placed a kiss in her palm, then folded her fingers around it. "You know better than that. You know I wouldn't bat an eye if you said you wanted to adopt a dozen Russian orphans. But we're talking about your life here, babe. I'm not ready to be widowed."

"I don't want a dozen Russian orphans. I just want your baby. *Our* baby."

"So do I, sweetheart, but it doesn't seem to be working out for us."

She turned away from him. Outside the window, the sky was a brilliant blue. "I can't do this right now," she said. And that damning tear dribbled from beneath her eyelid and rolled down her cheek.

He sighed. "I'm sorry. I should've kept my mouth shut."

"You had something to say, and you said it. I'm just not ready to hear it."

"We don't have to talk about it today. I'm not trying to be thoughtless. We can talk about it another time. There's no rush."

Turning back to him, she said, "My answer won't change."

"We'll figure it out." He lifted the corner of the bed sheet and used it to wipe the trail of dampness from her cheek. "Together. Okay?"

She nodded. "Have you seen Emma yet?"

"I came directly here. I needed to see you first."

"Will you please go pick her up? She was there. She saw what happened to me. Trish said she was wailing like her little heart was broken. She must be terrified. She needs her dad."

"And her mom. Do you want me to bring her in to see you?"

"They don't allow kids under twelve on the ward."

"I know. Do you want me to bring her in to see you?"

Of course. How could she have forgotten? Rob MacKenzie, with his zillion-megawatt smile and boyish charm, could talk his way past the archangels and walk directly into heaven. "Yes," she said. "Please bring her in. I need to hold my little girl."

Rob

EMMA'S wailing, at a heretofore-undiscovered decibel level, carried through the open windows and across the yard to the driveway. He heard her as soon as he got out of the car. There were two other babies in the house—Ali had recently given birth to twin girls—but his daughter's cry was unmistakable. "Mum mum mum," she wailed. *"Mum mum mum mum mum."*

Rob closed the car door and approached the old farmhouse where he and Casey had lived for the first two years of their marriage. She and Danny had bought the place a few months before he died, and living there had been difficult for Rob. He'd felt Danny's presence everywhere, had seen him around every corner, opening up old wounds and allowing them to fester. It wasn't healthy for him, or for his relationship with his wife, and he'd finally realized that if they wanted their marriage to work, they needed to move away from the memories and focus on the future instead of the past. So they'd built a new house, one without any ghosts, and sold this one to Casey's nephew Billy and his wife, Alison.

At the kitchen window, the curtains parted, then fell back into place. Ali must have heard his car. When he entered the shed, she was waiting at the open kitchen door with a wailing Emma in her arms and relief stamped on her face. "Thank God," she said over Emma's screaming. "I didn't know what to do. She's been inconsolable."

"Poor kid."

At the sound of his voice, Emma swiveled her head around. With a choked sniffle, she said, *"Da!"* and held out her fat little arms.

"Hey, Miss Emmy Lou Who." He took her from Ali, bounced her in his arms. "I hear you're having a bad day."

His daughter snuffled and hiccupped and, with a sigh, pressed her warm little body hard against his chest. "Da," she said, playing with a button on his shirt.

He kissed her patchy duck-fuzz hair. "It's okay, baby. Daddy's here now."

"Unbelievable," Ali said. "She's been screaming for hours. One look at you, and she goes silent."

"Such is my amazing effect on the female of the species."

"Right. I'm just glad you're here. No matter what I tried, it didn't work."

"I'm sorry. I know you have your hands full with the twins."

She waved him off. "Don't worry about me. I'm a human dynamo. How's Casey?"

"Stable. Stubborn. Alive and beautiful. Waiting to see Emma."

When she crinkled her nose, all the freckles drew together, giving her the appearance of a ten-year-old boy. "I thought the hospital didn't allow kids under twelve on any of the wards."

He just looked at her, and Ali rolled her eyes. "Never mind," she said. "I forgot you have magical powers."

"I'm a wizard," he said. "Has she eaten?"

"Not since lunch, and even then, she picked. She was too upset to eat. I still have to feed the twins, and Billy's not home from work yet. I was just about to give her a cracker to get her through until supper."

"I'll take it from here. Car seat?"

He expertly buckled Emma into the car and walked around to the driver's side of the Beemer. His daughter, gazing wide-eyed around the interior of the unfamiliar car, said, "Hoo."

"I hear you, kiddo. Hoo, indeed." He buckled his seat belt and started the engine. "Are you hungry? Want something to eat?"

"No!" It was her first, and favorite, word. She'd quickly learned its power, and wielded it with the enthusiasm and effectiveness of a pirate wielding his broadsword.

"No?" he said, pulling out onto Meadowbrook Road. "No crackers? No grapes? No Cheerios?"

"No!"

"Okay, then." He flexed his fingers on the steering wheel. "You want to go see Mom?"

"Mum."

"Is that a yes?"

"Da."

His finely-tuned parental ear automatically differentiated this "da" from her previous "da" and understood she meant yes. He supposed the kid wouldn't starve to death if she went a little longer without eating. She'd been through a traumatic experience. What she needed right now was to see her mother, to know that Casey was fine.

"Okay, kiddo," he said, "the hospital it is."

Technically, they were probably between visiting hours, although most hospitals had relaxed their policies in recent times. Ditto for kids being allowed to visit. Although it had been standard procedure since the beginning of time to allow only visitors over the age of twelve, most family-friendly hospitals had eased back on that rule in recent times. But County General, a small rural hospital, was a little behind the times. Their medical care was outstanding, but they stubbornly adhered to administrative policies that had become obsolete at least a decade ago.

He wasn't worried. For some inexplicable reason, the nurses grew giggly and flirty every time he walked by. He'd always had that effect on women, and he'd never been able to figure out why. It sure as hell wasn't his looks. Now, take Emma—sweet, beautiful Emma, with her big green eyes and those tufts of yellow duck fuzz all over her head. There was somebody guaranteed to melt the heart of even the hardest nurse. But him? With his scrawny ankles, his bony knees, and the hair he still couldn't seem to tame unless he cut it every month? His attractiveness to women was a mystery he would probably never unravel. But he wasn't above taking advantage of it. He knew he could walk into his wife's room with Emma in his arms and nobody would even question him.

At this time of day, the parking lot was sparsely populated. Rob pulled into an empty space, got out, walked around and took Emma from her seat. She studied him solemnly through wide green eyes. Even after more than a year, it was still a shock to look into their daughter's face and see both of them looking back. She had his coloring, his eyes, his strong jaw. The rest of her was all Casey. Through the magic of biology, she'd inherited the best of both of them. But Emma was her own person, with a strong personality that already displayed itself on a daily basis.

He blipped the locks and said, "Give Daddy a kiss?"

His daughter leaned forward and, with absolute trust, smacked her soft little lips against his. All six-plus feet of him melted into a soft puddle of goo. How had he lived four decades without experiencing this kind of love? He'd missed this with Paige. She'd come to him fully formed, fifteen years old and furious with the world. He'd made mistakes in his life, and Paige had paid the price. He was older now, and one hell of a lot smarter. This time, with Emma, he intended to do things right. He owed it to her, and her love was all the reward he needed.

He walked through the main entrance, Emma in his arms, and moved swiftly and purposefully across the lobby to the elevator. They rode in silence to the second floor with a young nurse who played peek-a-boo with his daughter while shooting him surreptitious and curious glances, as if trying to place him. It was doubtful that she'd even recognize his name; she wasn't much older than Paige, and kids weren't listening to his brand of music anymore. She'd probably seen him in an MTV video she was watching with her mother, back when she was nine.

On the second floor, he passed the nurse's station, nodded politely in response to the embarrassing chorus of greetings, and paused at the door to Casey's room. Apparently he wasn't the only one flouting convention; perched on the edge of his wife's bed, his red-haired sister Rose looked as comfortable as if they were at a garden party. Casey glanced up, saw him at the door, and pleasure lit her face. "There's my baby girl," she said, and Emma, at sight of her mother, began struggling to get away from him.

He crossed the room and deposited his daughter in her mother's arms. "Guess we know where I stand," he said. "Hey, Rosie." His sister offered her cheek, and he kissed it.

"Hey, brat," she said. "I need coffee. Come help me find it while Emma visits with her mom."

Rose was uncharacteristically silent as they walked together down the corridor to the vending machine. He popped in a couple of quarters and watched the paper cup fill with steaming sludge. Rose offered it to him, but he shook his head. His sister shrugged, said, "Let's go out on the patio," and he followed her.

They found a café-style table bathed in dappled early-evening sunlight, and Rose, being Rose, went directly for the jugular. "You can't let her get pregnant again," his sister said. "It'll kill her."

"I know that, and you know that. Maybe you'd like to try telling her that."

"Jesus Christ, Rob, grow a pair. Put your foot down. She'll listen to you. She thinks you hung the moon."

"She may think I hung the moon, but Casey has her own agenda, and if I get in the way, she just bulldozes over me."

Rose's eyes, MacKenzie green like his and Emma's, narrowed. "This was too damn close, Rob. If Trish hadn't come along when she did, you'd be planning a funeral right now."

"Twist the knife a little harder, why don't you?"

"I'm looking out for your welfare! And hers! And that sweet little girl's! What would Emma do if she lost her mother?" His sister, who excelled at aggression but hated being vulnerable, shook her head and turned away from him. But not before he saw the tears in her eyes.

He leaned over the table. "Do you think I don't know any of this? Do you think I'm not scared shitless?"

She swung back around. "Then do the right thing! Get a vasectomy. Put the issue to bed."

"It's not that easy. I can't do that to her."

His sister snorted. "Why not, for the love of God?"

"Because Danny did it to her, and it destroyed their marriage!"

Rose's eyes clouded, and she wrinkled her forehead. "I don't understand."

"After Katie died, Danny decided to be a dick. He went behind her back and had a vasectomy. When she found out, she left him."

"That's why they separated? I thought it was because of Katie. So many couples, if they lose a child, have trouble holding it together."

"There was that, too. But it was the vasectomy that tipped the scales. That's why I can't do that to her. Don't you think I'd get snipped tomorrow if I could?" He drummed frustrated fingers on the tabletop. "I won't betray her trust like that."

Rose sipped her coffee and considered. "Of course," she said, "there's always celibacy."

It was his turn to snort. "As if."

"I'm just weighing the options."

"Yeah? Well, you can toss that one out. Been there, done that. Don't plan to do it again in this lifetime."

Rose snorted. "You haven't been celibate since you were twelve."

"Seventeen, for your information, Ms. Smart-Ass. And I have. After Danny died. For two frigging years."

Rose's eyebrows went sky high. "No way. My brother, the rock star? The one with a girl in every port? No way in hell."

"Two years," he repeated. "Two of the longest, loneliest years of my life. And I'm not a rock star. I'm a professional musician."

"Semantics," she said. "Nothing more than semantics. I don't get it. Two years? Why?"

"Because!" he snarled. Then he sighed, leaned his elbows on the table, and rubbed his temples in an attempt to dislodge the headache that hadn't been there five minutes ago. "Because," he said, "I was waiting for her."

* * *

Without Casey here, the house echoed with emptiness. His wife was everywhere. In the ceramic floor tiles ordered direct from Italy, in the stained glass windows that showed up in delightfully unexpected places. In the smell of freshly-baked bread that permeated the air. Even in the colors they'd painted the exterior. Casey told everyone who'd sit still long enough to listen that they'd designed, planned, and decorated the house together, but in all honesty, it had been her baby from start to finish. He'd done little more than give his approval to her ideas. He trusted her implicitly, and what did he care, anyway? He just wanted to be with her, in a place they could call their own, a place where she hadn't slept with Danny, a place where the memories belonged to just the two of them. If she wanted to paint the living room ceiling purple, he wouldn't care, as long as she was happy.

He made macaroni and cheese for Emma, the kind that came in a box with a foil packet. It was quick and easy, and she usually loved it. But tonight, she picked at it fitfully, still traumatized, still unable to understand why her mother wasn't here. He'd had one hell of a job peeling her away from Casey when it was time to leave the hospital. By the time he managed to separate them, his wife and his daughter were both in tears.

"Just one more bite," he urged, as Emma vigorously avoided the spoon he was trying to tempt her with. "Just one more bite, Emmy."

"No!"

"Aren't you hungry, kiddo? I know you want your mom, but she can't come home until the day after tomorrow. You need to eat."

"Mum! *Mum mum mum.*"

Oh, boy. He'd just reopened the can of worms he'd been desperately trying to keep the lid on. "Shit," he said.

"Sit," Emma repeated.

If Casey was here, she'd be giving him the Death Glare right about now. She was adamant about him cleaning up his language around Emma, who was already beginning to repeat everything he said.

"Bad word," he said. "Bad Daddy." Emma looked at him as though he were spouting Martian. To illustrate his point, he slapped his own hand. "Bad Daddy," he repeated. "No naughty words in front of Emma."

His daughter stared at him with the absolute certainty that he was deranged. "Mum," she said, and a fat tear trickled down her cheek.

This situation was rapidly deteriorating. He thought about calling Paige, putting Emma on the phone with her sister, but then he'd have to answer questions he wasn't ready to answer. And it might make things worse instead of better. Emma still didn't get the concept of how a telephone worked, and she'd probably be looking for her sister once she heard Paige's voice. She'd suffered enough trauma today. Besides, he didn't want to ruin Paige's camping trip. She'd been there since Saturday with her friend Tina's family. He had the phone number for the campground, but he'd probably scare the kid half to death if he had the office track her down with a message to call home. Besides, there was no point in spoiling her week by telling her that Casey had lost the baby. When she came home would be soon enough to give her the news.

So he was on his own. He took Emma out of her high chair, washed and changed her, and cleaned up the remains of her supper. When he was done, he tried rocking her in Casey's favorite Boston rocker. That usually did the trick. But Emma squalled and squirmed and refused to close her eyes.

The phone rang. He rose, propped Emmy on his hip, crossed the kitchen to the wall phone, and answered it.

"What in bloody hell are you doing, disappearing like this?" said an all-too-familiar voice. "We have a record to finish, in case you hadn't heard."

Phoenix Hightower, teen idol and all-around pain in the ass, had been a London guttersnipe with a modicum of talent when he was "discovered" and turned into a pop star a couple of years ago. He had a pretty face and great hair, a sweet, girlish voice, and a truckload of attitude. Teenage girls adored him. Record company executives feared him. He'd sent more than one record producer into meltdown mode.

And right now, he was all Rob's.

In resignation, he said, "Hey, Phoenix."

"Hey, Phoenix? That's not an answer, mate."

Bouncing his daughter on his hip in an unsuccessful attempt to silence her, Rob squared his jaw and said into the phone, "I had a family emergency."

"This is very unprofessional behavior," Phoenix said. "And what's that god-awful, bloody noise?"

"That god-awful, bloody noise is my daughter." And if Phoenix Hightower wanted a picture of unprofessional behavior, he needed only to look in the mirror.

"Well, for the love of Christ, shut her up."

On his hip, Emma continued wailing. "Was there something you wanted, Phoenix?" he said. "Because I really don't have time for this right now."

"I want you back here. You disrupted my plans. I need to be recording tomorrow."

"Not gonna happen, buddy. I told you, I had a family emergency."

"What sort of family emergency?"

"Not that it's any of your business, but my wife had a miscarriage this morning."

With utter disbelief, Phoenix said, "And you went all the way home to—wherever the hell home is—for something like that?"

"Home is in Maine. And yes, I did. I suppose you think I should've blown it off?"

"I've never heard of Maine, and you need to think about your priorities."

Rob's eyebrows went sky high. With a calm he was far from feeling, he said, "This *is* my priority. There are times when family comes first. This is one of those times."

"I need that album finished on time."

"It'll be done on time. I already talked to the record company. Who gave you my home number, anyway?"

"The record company's run by a bunch of wankers. I need this done now. I have things I need to be doing, places I need to go, and the longer this drags on, the more of a time squeeze it places on me. I have a tour coming up. I need time to get ready for it."

A headache sprang to life beneath his right temple. "Phoenix," he said, "how old are you?"

"I'm seventeen. Why?"

"I presume this means you've never had a wife, or a kid, or even, I suspect, a serious girlfriend you really cared about?"

"What's your point?"

"My wife just lost a baby. We lost a *child*, Phoenix. A child we had hopes and plans for. A child we're currently mourning. In the process, my wife almost died, too."

"Sorry. But she obviously didn't die. So why are you there instead of here?"

Jesus, Mary and Joseph. Rubbing at his temple, he said, "This might surprise you, but the world doesn't revolve around you."

The kid actually laughed. "My world does. It's not my problem that yours doesn't. You work for me, and—"

"Hold it just a minute, kid. I don't work for you. I work for the record company. Maybe you should take it up with them."

"Maybe I will. Maybe I'll order them to fire you for walking off the job."

One could only hope. "Are you unhappy with my work?" he said. "Do you have a problem with it? Because if you do, I have no problem with tearing up my contract and walking. There are plenty of producers out there. I'm sure you and your friends at the record company can find somebody else to finish the album. Eventually."

"Whoa. I didn't say I had a problem with your work. Just—"

"Fine. Then I'd like to suggest that you take a step back, retract the claws, and try to acquaint yourself with the concept of compassion. I'll be back in a few days. In the meantime, put on a pair of dark glasses and a wig and spend a few days playing tourist.

Take a boat ride to the Statue of Liberty. Ride the escalator to the top floor of Macy's. Pretend you're on vacation."

"I don't need a bloody vacation! What I need is—"

"Goodbye, Phoenix."

The kid was still sputtering when he hung up the phone.

It took him a moment or three to recover from the steaming mass of sheer audacity that was Phoenix Hightower. That wasn't even the kid's real name. His real name was Russell. He'd been dubbed Phoenix by his manager, who'd thought it sounded more appropriate than Russell for a future teen idol. "Can you believe that, Emma?" he said. "That goddamn—I mean, bleeping—little monster? Talking to Daddy like that?"

Emma studied him through tear-filled eyes, but her only response was a whimper.

So he let it go. When he found out who at the record company had given Phoenix his unlisted home number, heads would roll. But for now, he would let it go and focus on his daughter instead of that condescending British twit. He turned on the stereo, found an oldies station, and began dancing his daughter in swooping circles around the kitchen, singing with Doug Fieger of the Knack as he danced. This was his favorite thing to do with Emma, and usually it elicited peals of delighted laughter, especially when he sang off key with great gusto, butchering the lyrics. Sometimes, she even tried to sing with him in her charming, non-musical way. But tonight, Emma was having none of it. Tonight, *My Sharona* wasn't her cup of tea.

The song ended, and he said, "This isn't working, is it?" Sobbing, her eyes wide with accusation, his daughter just stared at him. "You want to go for a ride?" he said.

She bobbed her head up and down and, through her sobbing, said with exquisite clarity—at least to his ears, "Car?"

Emma never failed to surprise him, never failed to delight. With fatherly pride, he said, "That's an offer I can't refuse," and grabbed his keys.

It was getting late, but the lights were still on at Trish and Bill's house. Together, they greeted him at the door. He handed over his daughter to her adored Uncle Bill, then allowed himself to be enveloped in a warm, motherly hug from Trish. "How are you doing, hon?" she said when she released him.

"I've had better days." It had finally caught up to him. The exhaustion. The stress. The terror.

"Ice cream," Bill said to Emma, opening the freezer door and pulling out a carton of Häagen-Dazs. "Drizzled with chocolate syrup. Sound good to you, Emmy?"

"Kee," she said. "Kee."

"Works every time," Bill said, closing the freezer.

"Little brat wouldn't eat anything for me," Rob said.

"Uncle Bill has the magic touch," Trish said. "He's been spoiling the grandkids for years."

"I never met a kid who'd turn down ice cream." Bill took a spoon from the drawer and adjusted his wire-rimmed glasses with a knuckle. "How's my sister doing?"

"I talked to the doctor before I left. They're keeping her an extra day, just to be safe. As long as everything goes okay tomorrow, they're releasing her Sunday morning. She's coming home with some strict rules, and they're giving her iron supplements to boost her blood. Right now, I'm counting my blessings. This could've been so much worse."

His stomach growled, and a frown crossed Trish's face. "When was the last time you ate?" she demanded.

He opened his mouth to answer, realized for the first time that he hadn't eaten all day. He'd been too focused on Casey to think about food. "Breakfast," he admitted. Breakfast had consisted of an Egg McMuffin, eaten at God only knew what time, and washed down with a cup of black coffee. No wonder the exhaustion had crawled inside his brain and left him drained and empty.

"Sit here." Trish pulled out a chair. "How do you like your eggs?"

"Right now," he said, "I'm so hungry I could eat the damn things raw. But over easy will do."

"Coffee? Tea? Beer?"

"I'd love a cold one."

Emma and her Uncle Bill retreated to the living room with their ice cream, and Rob nursed his beer and watched Trish bustle about the kitchen. Damp curls ringing the edges of her upswept hair, his sister-in-law swung a cast-iron frying pan onto the stove and lit the burner. His grandmother had owned one of those pans. She'd called it a spider, and the food she'd fried up in that spider, swimming in lard, was one of his fondest memories from childhood.

Trish moved to the fridge, took out a package of bacon and three enormous eggs. Beneath the blond curls, she had a sweet face, softened and enhanced by the twenty extra pounds she carried. When he'd first met Trish Lindstrom Bradley, he hadn't been sure he liked her. Trish had made knowing everybody else's business her life's work, and she wasn't shy about expressing her opinions. Sometimes, her assertive and overly maternal demeanor grated on him. Tonight, he found it comforting. When she plopped a huge plate of perfectly fried eggs, bacon, and toast in front of him, he almost wept. "Anything else I can get you?" she asked.

"Ketchup? And coffee, if you don't mind." After the day he'd just gone through, he would have loved to ask for another beer or six, but he had precious cargo to transport, and with Casey away, he needed all of his faculties. So he settled for coffee instead, generously poured ketchup over his eggs, and wolfed down the meal as though he hadn't eaten in six months.

When he was done, he set down the fork, sighed in satisfaction, and wiped his mouth with a napkin. "Thank you," he said. "I had no idea I was so hungry."

"You have to take care of yourself," Trish said. "Casey and Emma need you right now. When will Paige be home?"

"Sunday."

"Good. Casey'll be running on empty for a while. Paige should be a big help to both of you."

"I swear to God, Trish, I've never been so scared in my life. If I lost her—" To his acute embarrassment, tears sprang to life behind his eyelids. It was the exhaustion, he told himself as he leaned forward on his elbows, hands covering his eyes in mortification.

Trish patted his forearm. "I'm so sorry about the baby, hon."

"I keep thinking." He drew in a long breath. "I keep thinking that it would've been another little girl like Emma. And it breaks my heart to think she never even got a chance. And then I think—" He paused to look over at her, unable to continue for an instant. "The same thing could've happened with Emma. You know? And my blood runs cold. We're so lucky to have her. I never realized how much."

She took his hand in hers. Squeezed it. "But it didn't happen with Emma. She's right here with us, precious and beautiful and every inch your daughter. I know you're grieving for the baby you lost, but you have to focus on what's right in front of you. Casey, and Paige, and Emma."

"Yeah. I know." When she released his hand, he wiped his eyes on his sleeve. Cleared his throat and combed long, bony fingers through his messy hair.

"Casey wants more babies," she said.

"Yes." He picked up his fork, idly dragged the tines through the egg yolk that was rapidly congealing on his plate.

"What are you going to do about that?"

He dropped the fork back onto the plate. "You know what, Trish?"

"What?"

"I don't have a freaking clue."

* * *

Back home, he got Emma bathed and dressed for bed. She'd finally quieted down, but she still wouldn't sleep. He turned on the bedroom TV, and with Emma lying on his chest, cuddling with her favorite blanket, he stretched out on the bed. There was nothing on TV worth watching, and he flipped channels with growing disillusionment. Finally, he gave up, traded the remote for the bedside phone, and called Casey's hospital room.

"I hate this house when you're not in it," he said when she answered.

"I know, babe. Are you okay?"

"I'm lonely. And sad. And a bunch of other things I can't even put into words."

"Me, too," she said.

There was silence on the phone line between them, but it was a comfortable silence. Just knowing that she was there, at the other end of that line, was a comfort. "How's Emma doing?" she said.

"She's missing you. She finally stopped crying after Uncle Bill bribed her with ice cream. But she doesn't like being here without you any better than I do."

"I'll be incarcerated in this lovely establishment until Sunday. Why don't you pack up Emmy's gear and make a quick trip down to visit your folks?"

"Tonight? It's a three-hour drive."

"It's still early enough. They'd be thrilled to see you, Flash. And Emmy. You know how they dote on her."

It hadn't occurred to him, but the idea was greatly appealing. With one exception. "If I do," he said, "you'll be all alone tomorrow."

"Believe me, I'll have visitors. Probably more than I want. In between, I could use some alone time. And I think you could use some Mary time."

She was right, of course. Casey had a way of seeing through the bullshit and zeroing in on whatever was beneath all the bluff and bluster. There were times in a man's life when he needed his mother, if only as a sounding board and soft shoulder. "Are you sure you don't mind?" he said. "I hate to leave you." Especially at a time like this, but he didn't want to say that.

She read his mind anyway. "I'm not in any danger. I just need to rest and recuperate. They're holding me because they know my definition of rest isn't the same as theirs. It's very hard to overdo it in a hospital bed. But there's no reason you shouldn't go down to Boston and enjoy a little time with your family."

"I'll think about it." He paused, shifted himself into a more comfortable position. "Phoenix called me."

"Oh?"

"He wanted to know why I thought being with my wife in her time of need was a higher priority than recording his frigging album."

"Oh, for the love of God. What did you tell him?"

"I told him the world doesn't revolve around him."

"And how did that go over?"

"He laughed at me. The little bastard."

"How disrespectful."

"That's our Phoenix. Gotta love the kid. Generally I just laugh it off, but tonight, his utter inability to put himself in somebody else's shoes got to me. The guy lacks empathy. I think he's a sociopath. Like Ted Bundy."

"A serial killer in the making?"

"Don't make fun of me. I'm serious."

"I know you are, my darling. That's one of the reasons I love you."

* * *

He debated whether or not to call his mother, finally decided he didn't want to surprise her by showing up at her door unannounced at some ungodly hour. On the other hand, he didn't want to go into details over the phone. "Hey, Mom," he said when she answered.

"Well, if it isn't my long-lost son." Her Irish brogue always said *home* to him in multiple lovely shades of color. "About time you remembered you have a mother. How's the wee one? Am I going to see her again before she graduates from college?"

"She's fine. Growing like crazy. As a matter of fact, I was thinking about coming down tonight, if you wouldn't mind making up the crib for Emma."

"You know you're always welcome, any time." There was a brief pause. Then, "What's wrong?"

Like Casey, his mother had that sixth sense, that built-in radar that honed in on the tiniest note in his voice, the most minute body language. "Nothing's wrong," he said.

"You were never any good at lying, my son."

"Everything's fine," he said. "I just feel like visiting my mom. You have a problem with that?"

"Mind your mouth or I'll have to take you over my knee. You may be taller, but I'm still in charge. I'll get the crib ready and freshen a bed for you." Another pause. "I assume Casey's coming with you?"

"Not this trip. And stop prying."

"I have to pry. Otherwise, I'd know nothing, since none of my children ever tell me anything. Is something wrong between you and Casey?"

"We're fine, Ma. Stop worrying."

"I'll stop worrying when I know there's no reason to worry. Until then, I'll carry on. I'm Irish. It's what we do best."

It was nearly midnight when he reached South Boston, where he was greeted by a light summer rain infused with the intoxicating scent of his mother's blooming roses. Emma had fallen asleep shortly after they left home. Fearful of waking her, he carried her into the house, car seat and all. His parents waited, their faces somber, concerned. "I made tea," his mother said. "Crib's in the room at the top of the stairs. Since you don't need a double bed, I thought you'd like your old room."

"Thanks, Ma." He kissed her on the cheek, clasped hands with his dad, and carried Emma up the stairs. The poor kid was so wiped out that she never woke up, not even when he untied her pink sneakers and removed them. Once she was settled, he pulled the covers up to her chin and then stood watching her, tiny and innocent and perfect, his heart flooding with a love so deep and strong, it nearly brought him to his knees.

He quietly closed the door—as far as it would close—and took a look around. The upstairs hallway was still the same hideous gold color it had always been, the carpet threadbare and thin. The house was creaky, the roof saggy, the floors so crooked you could go bowling without even throwing the ball. Just drop it and watch it roll. But this was home, in a way that no other place had ever been home. He'd spent the first twenty-two years of his life in this house, and that upbringing would always be a part of who he was. He'd been lucky. He'd grown up in a home filled with love and family and wonderful memories, with two parents who loved each other, who still loved each other after forty-plus years of marriage. And yes, he knew he was romanticizing it, conveniently forgetting the times when they'd lived on soup for days on end because there hadn't been enough to feed a family of nine kids. But as a boy, he'd never given a thought to that kind of thing. He'd been too busy living. As far as he was concerned, he'd had an idyllic childhood. That was what he wanted for his own kids.

He'd missed the boat with Paige. Those lost years were something he could never get back, and he would spend the rest of his life regretting them. But Emmy symbolized love and hope and a bright, shiny future. Even starting as late as they had, in their mid-thirties, he and Casey had talked endlessly about what they expected from their life together. They'd spent her entire pregnancy making plans for the family they intended to raise. They'd agreed to eschew boundaries, to let biology determine how many children they would have. They hadn't expected that bright and shiny future to be tarnished by loss after loss.

His parents were waiting downstairs. "All right," his mother said briskly, "why are you here and why isn't Casey with you?"

"Casey's in the hospital," he said. "She had another miscarriage."

"Goddamn it," his father said.

"Oh, Robbie," his mother said. "I'm so sorry. But Casey's all right?"

He sat down in a chair and stretched out his legs. "She is now. It was touch and go for a while. Too damn close. I was in New York, working. If Trish hadn't found her…" He ran a hand over his face, scrubbed back his hair, let out a sigh. "I was so damn scared."

"Of course you were! But why aren't you there with her?"

"It was her idea for me to come here. She knows how much I hate being in that house alone, and the hospital's holding her until Sunday. She did a few mental calculations and decided I needed the two of you right now more than she needed me." Beneath the table, he worked off his sneakers and wiggled his toes. "And of course, she was right."

"Of course. When has she ever not been right?" His mother poured hot water over a tea bag and set the teacup in front of him.

"Thanks," he said, and took a sip of hot, bracing tea. He closed his eyes and leaned back his head, grateful for home, for his parents, for the simple comfort of a cup of hot tea at the end of a very long, very bad day. "Listen, Ma," he said, opening his eyes and turning his head in her direction. "Do you still have Great-Grandma Sullivan's ring?"

"Of course. I promised it to you three years ago. I've just been waiting for you to ask."

"Our anniversary's coming up soon. I've been waiting for the right time to give it to her." He took a sip of tea. "I think now's the right time."

"Oh, so you think, do you? I was starting to wonder if you were planning to wait until your fiftieth. Sometimes men can be so stupid." And she got up from the table and bustled out of the room.

He narrowed his eyes, set down his cup. Fighting back a smile, he said, "Tell me something, Dad. The way she bullies all of us, how have you managed to put up with her all these years?"

"I don't know," his father said. "Maybe for the same reason Casey puts up with you?"

"Ouch."

"You might have taken your looks from me," Patrick MacKenzie said, "but in every other way, you're the spitting image of your mother. Stubborn, willful, outspoken. A little too impulsive, a little too rash." Patrick lifted his own teacup and saluted him with it. "But in spite of all those sins, my son, you and your mother are redeemed by virtue of the fact that you both have a heart as big as all outdoors, and you both wear it proudly on your sleeve."

Rob lifted his teacup, touched it to the one Patrick still held high. "Amen," he said.

Casey

THEY stopped at Dunkin' Donuts on the way home from the hospital. Rob cautiously handed her a cup of decaf, then took his own cup from the girl at the drive-thru window, mumbled his thanks, and set it in his cup holder. Without speaking, he pulled away from the window, circled the building, and waited for a Dodge Ram to pass before pulling out into traffic. "You're quiet," she said.

"Sorry." He removed both hands from the steering wheel, stretched his fingers, and returned them to the wheel. "I'm just thinking."

She took a sip of decaf. "About?"

"I have to go back to New York. I have an album to finish. Those fat-cat record executives don't have a sense of humor. Time is money, and the meter's ticking. Plus, I lost Kitty on the one day she was available, and now I have to try to reschedule."

"And it's all my fault."

"Hey." He shot her a glance. "What happened wasn't your fault. Shit happens."

"Yes," she said, and took another sip of coffee. "It does."

"I want you to come with me."

"To New York?" She raised an eyebrow. "What about Emma? And Paige?"

Upon hearing her name, Emma, who'd been babbling contentedly in the back seat, went silent.

"We'll take the girls with us."

"Paige has school. She's starting her senior year soon. She can't miss that."

"School doesn't start for a few weeks. I may be finished by then. If I'm not, she could probably stay for a while with my sister. Or Trish."

"I don't know. We're in the middle of construction. Things could go wrong. I might need to make decisions—"

"You'll be a phone call away. Besides, Colleen can make decisions as well as you can. She'll live without you for a few weeks. I want you where I can keep an eye on you."

"Damn it, Rob, I don't need a babysitter." Darkly, she added, "And you certainly don't have to worry about me getting pregnant again if you're not around."

"I don't know, babe. What about those hot guys at the bowling alley? Those shirts? Those shoes?"

"Although tempting, I'll have to pass. I'm off the market. Permanently."

"I'm being serious here. You just gave me the worst scare of my life. I thought I was about to lose you. I just want you near me for a while, okay? I'm not ready to be hundreds of miles away from you right now. I need you sleeping beside me at night."

She let out a hard breath. Wasn't that the same thing she needed? "What'll you do if you can't get Kitty?"

"I don't know. I don't really want to go with anybody else, but I might not have a choice." He considered her question at length. "Her tour will be finished soon. If I can't get her to New York before we wrap the recording, maybe I can bring her to the house for a day or two. I'm already planning to do the mixing at home."

"I am not having that woman in my home!"

He swiveled his head and gave her a long, appraising look. "I thought you liked Kitty. Have I missed something?"

"Do I have to spell it out for you?"

"I guess you do."

"The two of you—" She quickly checked on Emma, who'd gone back to babbling. Casey lowered her voice. "—used to have a relationship."

"I'd hardly call it a relationship. Not the way you mean. We were friends."

She opened her mouth to counter his argument, remembered Emma in the back seat. "With benefits."

His response wasn't what she expected. His face split in one of those zillion-megawatt grins, the one that was capable of melting even the hardest of women into a hot, bubbling mess. "You're jealous," he said, with obvious glee. "Hot damn, Fiore, you're jealous of Kitty!"

"She had carnal knowledge of you, Flash. Way before I did."

"A lot of women have had carnal knowledge of me."

"Don't remind me. And it's not the same at all."

"How is it different?"

"With a few exceptions, I didn't know any of them personally. Or even know their names. They were just notches on your bed post. I know Kitty."

"And you've always liked her."

"The woman has seen you in your birthday suit. Multiple times. Don't you think that might make for slightly awkward dinner table conversation?"

"I don't see why it has to. Kitty and I are ancient history."

"The very idea of the two of you together makes me want to wrap my fingers around her neck and squeeze until she stops gurgling."

He raised both eyebrows. "Who the hell are you, and what have you done with my sweet, beautiful wife? Jesus Christ, Casey, she's a nice woman."

"She's a nice woman who used to sleep with my husband. I don't think I'm being unreasonable when I say I'm not comfortable bringing her into our home."

"Fine by me. So if we see her in New York, you won't be rude to her?"

"Come on, Flash. Have you ever known me to be rude to anyone? I may be a mess right now, but I'm not about to verbally gut any of your friends."

She reached out a hand and laid it atop his, resting on the gearshift. He threaded fingers with hers, brought her hand to his mouth, and kissed it.

In the back seat, Emma was making *vroom-vroom* car sounds. "I know you're feeling like roadkill," he said. "I know things will be hard for a while. I know you're grieving. So am I. But we'll get through this. Together."

Her chest contracted with guilt because he'd reminded her, in his subtle way, that he, too, had lost that unborn baby. That she wasn't alone in this. That while it might have been her body that expelled its precious cargo, his emotional investment was as real as hers. What he didn't understand, what he couldn't see, was that it wasn't grief she was feeling right now. It was numbness.

"Yes," she said, curling her fingers around his. "We'll get through it together."

And knew her words for the lie they were.

* * *

She'd only been gone for two days, but the house felt different. Strange. Foreign. Not like her house at all. The granite countertops, the Italian tiles, the hardwood floors, felt wrong. Even her mahogany four-poster bed seemed odd, as though its dimensions were off by a half-inch here, two inches there. The strangeness pulled and tugged at her, messing with her head, leaving fingers of anxiety curling up into her throat.

"Why don't you lie down?" he said. "Rest for a while?"

"I spent the last two days lying in bed. I want to get back to my life."

"You need to take it slow. You heard what the doctor said. It'll be a while before you bounce back."

Bouncing was the least of her worries. It would be enough to shake off this otherworldly fog that had her feeling as though she didn't fit in her own skin. "I need to putter. Wander around the house, the yard. Get the smell of the hospital out of my head. Will you keep an eye on Emma for a little while?"

"Of course. But—"

"Rob. Please. Don't hover. I need this."

He let out a hard exhalation of breath, those green eyes of his troubled, and nodded. She gave him a faint smile to acknowledge his acquiescence, but didn't touch him, too afraid that the strangeness would extend to his touch. The thought terrified her. "Thank you," she said. "I'll be back in a few minutes."

The sound of hammering grew louder as she approached the construction site. The drywaller's van sat in front of the building that would house the spinning and dyeing rooms, as well as her office. The hammering came from the barn, where workers were spreading tar paper over the roof before tacking down the shingles.

She stopped first in the main building where, trowel in hand, a lone worker was mudding the drywall. An ancient, white-speckled transistor radio, perched on a folding chair, played the Moody Blues. *Knights in White Satin*. The man looked up and they acknowledged each other. "It's coming along nicely," she said.

"Ayuh. It is. You oughta check out your office."

The walls were smooth and white, ready for paint, the floor tiles new and shiny. The baseboards and window trim were already in place. Casey walked to the window, drinking in the view of endless mountains that would be so distracting she'd probably never get any work done here.

When she'd had her fill of the view, she bade farewell to the drywaller and moved on to the barn. On this hot summer day, it was too warm inside, no air moving anywhere. Once the livestock arrived, the building would be climate controlled. Warm in winter, cool in summer. Casey checked out each corner, each stall, every inch of storage space. Turned on the water taps and confirmed that they were running properly. This was a huge undertaking, one she'd been so enthused about. Today, she felt only an apathy that was so unlike her. She blamed her waning enthusiasm on lack of sleep. Maybe Rob was right. But if he was, then why did the apathy seem to squeeze, like spray foam insulation, into every crevice of her life?

She returned to the house, where she found that Rob had been a busy boy in her absence. "I have everything set up," he said. "Colleen will be home on Tuesday, we'll drive down to New York on Thursday, and I can be back in the studio by Friday. Our hotel reservation is made, and I thought we'd drive down in your car, so I made an appointment for an oil change on Monday morning. I've talked to Trish and Rose, and if Paige doesn't want to come with us, she's welcome to stay with either of them. I'm hoping she'll come, though. I think the studio atmosphere would be good for her. Plus, that would give us a built-in babysitter for Miss Emmy Lou Who. I might just want to take my best girl out dancing some night, and I know I can trust Emma with her big sister."

"Wow. You have it all figured out, don't you?"

"What's that supposed to mean?"

Her words had come out more pointed than she'd intended. Clearly, he'd heard the resentment in them, and clearly, he was trying to figure out why it was there and where it was coming from. Rob was just doing what he always did. Her husband was a go-getter who didn't let any grass grow under his feet. She'd never minded it before. As a matter of fact, it had always been one of the things she admired most about him. But not today.

A dull ache flitted across her forehead. "Nothing," she said. "Where's Emma?"

"I put her down for a nap. She was getting fussy."

"I'm going for a drive."

He didn't like it. She could tell by the way his nostrils flared and his breathing quickened. He didn't need to say a word for her to know what he was thinking.

He said it anyway. "You just got out of the hospital."

"And I'm perfectly capable of driving a car."

"Let me get Emma up. I'll take you anywhere you want to go."

Touching his hand to soften her words, she said, "No. I need to be alone."

So he let her go. Rob MacKenzie was a smart man. He knew it was useless to argue with her. Besides, considering her mood, it was just as well that she was going off alone.

It was a beautiful day for a drive, sunny and warm, with very little humidity, a perfect Maine midsummer afternoon filled with buzzing bees and nodding daisies. She didn't realize where she was headed until she found herself turning in at the cemetery gate. But it made sense in some parallel-universe way. Casey parked the car at the top of the hill and got out, breathed in the fragrance of ripe summer as a breeze lifted and tangled her dark hair. She passed Danny's grave without pausing, kept going until she reached a simple rectangular stone topped by a carved marble lamb. Beneath the lamb were the words BELOVED DAUGHTER.

She'd spent the better part of a decade avoiding this gravestone. For a long time, she'd come to the cemetery regularly to talk to Danny. He was a good listener, and sometimes, she just needed somebody to listen. But those cozy visits had come to an end when she realized how unfair it was to Rob. She belonged to him now. She wore his ring now, slept in his bed, loved him deeply, knew him as well as any woman could know a man. It wasn't fair to him that she should still visit regularly with her first husband. So she'd stopped visiting Danny.

But she'd never before come here to talk to Katie. It was too much like ripping the bandage off a wound that had never scabbed over. If she never stood here, never looked down on that BELOVED DAUGHTER, she could hold Katie in her mind, in her memory, and somehow convince herself that none of it was real. That her daughter still lived, still breathed, still laughed, in some alternate dimension. Casey Fiore MacKenzie wasn't a religious person, but she held firmly and desperately to the belief that one day, she would see Katie again.

"I failed you," she said. "I'm so sorry that I failed you."

She'd failed not just Katie, but those three unborn babies as well. She pictured them now, lined up like dominoes, those sweet, tender souls that she'd somehow managed to fail in the most horrible of ways. Maybe those lost babies were the penance she had to pay for letting Katie die. Because her daughter's death had been her fault. What kind of mother would go off on a business trip, three thousand miles from home, and leave her five-year-old daughter in the care of her father? Certainly, Danny had loved Katie as much as she had. Losing her had nearly destroyed their marriage. But he'd been consumed by his career, so Casey was the one who'd nursed their daughter through ear infections and chicken pox and scarlet fever. While Danny was off playing rock star, she had breastfed Katie, potty-trained her, taught her to tie her shoes and drink from a straw. She had a mother's instincts, an intuition that Danny lacked. It wasn't his fault, what had happened. If she'd been home where she belonged, instead of in New York with Rob, being wined and dined by a big Broadway producer, she would have rushed her daughter to the hospital hours earlier. Early enough to save her.

But she hadn't been home where she belonged. The one time in her life when she'd put her own career ahead of her daughter, the one time when Katie needed her most, she'd been in New York, celebrating a new business partnership with filet mignon and champagne. Because she hadn't been there to recognize the signs, she and Danny had lost their daughter. And the guilt was crushing.

It was why she was overprotective of Emma. She knew she was, and so did Rob. The fact that he'd never called her on it was testament to his love and understanding. But the truth was there, hovering in the air between them, like a firefly that briefly flared, then disappeared in the darkness. She tried to temper it. She didn't want Emmy growing up in a bubble. That was no way to raise a child. But sometimes it was hard, especially when she kept flashing back to all the mistakes she'd made with Katie.

She tried to imagine what Katie would look like now. She'd be thirteen years old, and undoubtedly a head-turner, for she'd taken her looks from Danny. Would she still have the same sunny disposition, her smooth surface buffeted by the occasional storm cloud? Or would she be dark and angsty, a drama queen, like Paige had been when she first came to them?

It was pointless to speculate. The past couldn't be changed. Katie was lost to her, and she'd accepted that truth eight years ago. That was the only way she'd managed to survive. With the stoicism that was bred into her, she'd said her good-byes and moved on, deliberately ignoring the bad and focusing on the good: Rob, love of her life; Paige, daughter of her heart; and Emma. Beautiful, sweet Emma. She focused all her energies on the little girl who needed her now, and had closed the door on the one who needed her no longer.

So why had this miscarriage unlocked all that negative energy and sent it swirling around her like a miniature tornado?

She'd managed so well all these years. Sometimes a week or two would go by when she wouldn't even think about Katie. And then something—a little girl's laughter, a snippet of song on the radio—would bring back a rush of memory so strong it sent her reeling. But she always recovered. Always managed to hold herself together. What else could she do? Life went on, no matter how much something might hurt. It was a truth she'd learned at the age of fifteen, when she lost her mother, and everything in her life had changed. You kept on going. You raised your chin, threw back your shoulders, and put one foot in front of the other. You continued moving. Because standing still was the worst thing you could do. If you stood still, the demons might catch up to you.

And nobody wanted the demons to catch up.

* * *

When she got home, Rob was on the porch swing, feet propped on the railing, bony ankles crossed, the swing moving with glorious indolence. His gaze followed her as she approached the house. She paused to deadhead a wilted marigold in the flower bed that lined the walkway, then climbed the steps and crossed the porch to him.

"Hey," he said.

"Hey." She sat beside him and drew her legs up under her. He raised an arm and she scooted closer to his side, her cheek cushioned against his bicep. He pressed a kiss to the back of her head and said, "Feeling better?"

She ran a finger down the soft flesh of his inner arm, elbow to wrist. "I went to visit Katie."

"Oh," he said, his tone rife with meaning.

"I'm sorry I was snotty to you."

"I have broad shoulders. You've just been through hell. And your hormones are all messed up. Give it a little time. Things will eventually settle down, and you'll start to feel more like yourself."

"I need to see Emma. Come with me?"

Hand in hand, they climbed the stairs to Emma's bedroom, where the shades were drawn against the bright midday sun. Still holding hands, they stood by the side of their daughter's crib and watched her breathing. Her features softened by sleep, Emma lay on her stomach, arms flung haphazardly, her knees bent, her round little rump pointing heavenward.

"We did this," Casey said, leaning her head against his shoulder. "We made her. You and I."

He wrapped his arm around her and said, "We did."

"It still takes my breath away. The miracle of life. The fact that she's half you and half me. Don't you think that's amazing?"

"I do. I look at her and I see you. Then she changes expression, and I see me. She looks like Paige, and my sister Meg. Then I look at a picture of your mother, and I see a resemblance yet again."

"She's the amazing, ultimate expression of the love I feel for you."

He lowered his head and, his breath warm on her ear, kissed her temple. "You worry about her, don't you?"

"I can't help it. After so many losses...I'm not the same person I used to be. I've learned, through experience, just how cruel life can be." In her sleep, Emma grimaced, those pink rosebud lips drawing together in an expression of distaste. Casey gently brushed her knuckles across her daughter's cheek, and Emma flinched. "You understand, don't you? Why I need another baby? Why I'm so unwilling to quit?"

"I'm trying, babe. I'm trying to understand."

"It's the miracle. It's that inexpressibly sweet baby scent that I draw into my lungs, that hot rush of love when I see her smile.

That fierce and primal protectiveness that means I'd kill anyone who tried to do harm to her. It's looking into her face and seeing you looking back. It's watching the two of you, walking hand in hand through my flower garden, picking a fistful to bring to me. It's an addiction, like heroin. I need that feeling, that overwhelming, incomparable feeling of love that I can't get any other place. And for some inexplicable reason, I need it over and over again. Which is why I can't give up. I can't stop trying."

He pulled her closer, and she pressed her cheek to his chest, where his heart beat strong and steady. "We'll talk about it again," he said, "when the time's ready. But for now…you'll come to New York with me?"

She closed her eyes, exulted in his warmth, his tenderness. And let out a sigh. "Yes," she said. "I'll come to New York with you."

PART II: THE MILES

Casey

NEW York City, the Big Apple, the city that never sleeps, was a loud, congested, smog-filled kaleidoscope. Five years had passed since the last time she visited this city she'd once called home, and although time had wrought changes, some things never changed. Yellow taxis still whizzed past slower vehicles, missing them by inches. City buses still lumbered along from stop to stop, spewing exhaust in their wake. Impatient motorists still honked at other drivers a half-second after the light turned green. Panhandlers still stood on corners, and discarded candy bar wrappers still littered the gutters. What was that French saying? *Plus ça change, plus c'est la même chose.* The more things change, the more they stay the same. That perfectly described New York, where the players might come and go, but the energy level never faltered.

She'd always loved that energy, had thrived on it, but for some inexplicable reason, this time around, it drained her. The city felt hostile, suffocating. Every time she stepped outside, she was surrounded by people in a hurry. Rude, pushy people who looked right through her as they shoved past, intent on their own agendas and oblivious to the fact that she stood there, a living, breathing human just like them. They gave off high-stress vibes that left her jittery and unsettled and desperate to go back indoors, where none of this madness could touch her.

Being Casey, she stubbornly refused to let the anxiety control her. Instead, she forced herself to go out, even though her insides were screaming at her to hide in a safe, comforting place. While Rob spent long hours in the studio, she and the girls visited Macy's, the Empire State Building, the Statue of Liberty. They explored Times Square, Central Park, the Museum of Modern Art. One rainy afternoon, she took them to see a matinee performance of *Cats*. Another day, they ate lunch in the dining room at the Hotel Montpelier, where she and Danny had once worked, so long ago that she could barely remember being that young.

She spent a morning with Rob in the studio, but her heart wasn't in it. The music didn't feel the same. She didn't understand the stuff teenagers were listening to these days. As far as she was concerned, Phoenix Hightower's music was little more than canned, electronic noise. She knew Rob felt the same way, but he was being paid well to produce, and that kind of money went a long way toward tolerance. Paige, on the other hand, was slightly star-struck at the prospect of meeting the pop idol. It made sense that the girl was deep into the current music scene. This was her era. She would be a high school senior in a few weeks. Someday, she would look back fondly on the music from this decade and wonder why her own kids listened to such awful stuff. It was the way of the world, the passing of the torch, the circle of life. Casey was a dinosaur, a throwback to an earlier time when pop music made sense, both lyrically and melodically, to her ears. So she packed up Emmy, left Paige there with her father and Phoenix, and returned to the apartment.

Peace. Quiet, blissful peace. Three days into their stay, Rob had managed to find them a furnished sublet just a few blocks from the studio, on the sixth floor of a 1930s-era Art Deco building with an elevator and a doorman and broad casement windows that, after dark, transformed a mundane view of Midtown into something wondrous. If it had been just the two of them, the hotel would have sufficed, but it was too much to expect the girls to be happy cooped up in a hotel for a month or more. This two-bedroom apartment, furnished right down to the towels and silver, was a perfect temporary home for their family. All they had to do was bring in a crib, a high chair, and their clothes, and, *voilà! Chez* MacKenzie.

She put Emma down for a nap, then ran herself a bubble bath. The tub wasn't as big or as comfortable as the one at home, but it was deep, the water was hot, and the bubbles were satisfying. Best of all, she didn't have to interact with anyone, didn't have to think or feel. Here, in the hot, sudsy water, alone in the bathroom of her sixth-floor apartment while Emma slept in the next room, all she had to do was breathe in and breathe out, and let the frantic world rush by six stories below.

She closed her eyes and sank deeper into the bubbles. Rubbed her temple, wondering where this staggering exhaustion had come from. Last night, Rob had told her she was pushing too hard. "Remember what the doctor said?" he'd scolded. "You need to give yourself time to recuperate."

He was probably right. Since they'd arrived in Manhattan, she'd barely given herself time to breathe, let alone recuperate. It would probably behoove her to slow down, but idleness didn't sit well with her. She needed to be busy, needed to be doing something, needed to feel useful. Didn't want to be dependent on anyone else. But this exhaustion was so complete, she wasn't sure she had the energy to drag herself out of the tub.

The miscarriage certainly could—and probably did—account for the exhaustion. But not for the lethargy. Not for the ennui, or the apathy. She was a woman of strong convictions. Never, in thirty-seven years, had she felt indecisive about anything. If you asked for her opinion about something, she always had one. Always cared deeply, one way or another.

But this was something entirely outside her frame of reference. Yes, she'd carted the girls all over Manhattan. She'd done it because she felt it was what a good mother should do. Show them the sights, broaden their horizons, give them some nice memories while teaching them something. That was why she'd done it. That, and the fact that it filled up space and time in a way that sitting around the apartment, watching television, would never do. But she'd derived no joy from it. Her emotional investment in the edification of her daughter and stepdaughter was roughly equivalent to that of a paid tour guide.

In other words, she simply didn't give a damn.

And that was so not like her.

* * *

Fifteen years ago, when they were both still wet behind the ears, Rob had taught her to play the guitar. None of that fancy fingering like he played; he was a musical genius, and she wasn't a performer. She didn't need to know how to make an electric guitar cry or sing. She just needed to know how to play a few chords to accompany the melodies that lived inside her brain. For her, the guitar was a compositional tool. So Rob had taught her, on his old, third-hand acoustic, how to play C and G and D^7 and E minor. Basic stuff, and just in case what was inside her head included a note or two not covered by those basic chords, he taught her how to turn a simple chord into an augmented or diminished. That was adequate for her needs, just enough knowledge so that if there was no piano available, she would always have access to an instrument on which to try out her new tunes.

So while he and Paige were in the studio and Emma was sleeping, Casey took his Gibson from its case, along with a few pieces of manuscript paper and a couple of stubby pencils—she didn't think Rob had sharpened a pencil ever in his life—and she sat down to capture some of the music that had been playing in her head ever since the miscarriage.

To her surprise, the music flowed like a bubbling spring. But it was nothing like the songs she'd written in the past. This new work was dark and disturbing, rich and deep and discordant. Somehow, she'd tapped into some dark place she never knew existed inside her, and she was helpless to stop until the flow either bled out or stanched.

At some point, Emma awoke. Casey took her to the potty, called the deli down the block and ordered a plate of their special home-style spaghetti. After the delivery boy left, they enjoyed some cuddle time while Emma ate, then Casey parked her in front of the TV and kept on writing.

When Rob and Paige came home, she was asleep on the couch, Emma in her lap and a half-dozen new songs scattered about the room. "Hey," Rob said, taking his sleeping daughter in his arms. "Looks like somebody's been busy."

Casey stretched and yawned. "Did you eat?"

"We had pizza brought in. What about you?"

"Emma ate. I'm not hungry."

"You need to eat something. Want me to grill you a cheese sandwich?"

"I'm fine. I'll eat a big breakfast in the morning to make up for it."

He carried Emma into the bedroom she shared with Paige. Casey closed her eyes, listening to the soft murmur of conversation between Rob and his oldest daughter. He came back alone, gathered up the scattered sheets of music, and sat beside her on the couch. Slumped on his tailbone, he propped his feet on the coffee table. Brow wrinkled in concentration, he studied the music she'd written.

When he was done, he met her eyes. And said, "Wow."

"I know. It's dark."

"It's brilliant."

"I'd hardly call it brilliant."

"Are you kidding? You dug deep, babe. I'm impressed. Scared, but impressed."

"Scared? Why on earth? It's just music."

"It's music like I've never seen from you before. It's like Carole King meets Stephen King."

"That's where my head is at these days. Do you have a problem with that?"

"I'm not criticizing. I'm just...wow."

Later, in the darkness of their bedroom, he drew her to him and kissed her shoulder, worked his way to her collarbone. When she failed to respond, he said, "What's wrong?"

"Nothing. Nothing's wrong."

The silence from his side of the bed was dense and heavy. He rolled away from her, and a moment later, the bedside lamp came on. "What?" she said.

"You aren't yourself at all. What's going on?"

"I'm tired." She plumped her pillow. "I just had a miscarriage. I almost bled to death. You're the one who told me I needed to slow down."

"I told you to slow down. I didn't tell you to freeze every time I touch you."

"Don't be ridiculous."

"Is it me? Have I done something to offend you? Are you mad because I dragged you to New York with me?"

She let out a long-suffering sigh and rolled toward him. "I am not mad at you," she said. "I have a lot going on inside my head. None of it is related to you, except in the most peripheral of ways. I just need you to give me some space."

He squared his jaw. "When are you seeing Doctor Deb?"

"Wednesday. I'll fly home in the morning, see her, then fly back in the afternoon. You and Paige will have to take care of Emma while I'm gone."

"Are you sure you're up to it? Flying home and back in the same day? Isn't there somebody you could see right here in Manhattan?"

"I know her. I trust her. She knows me. Why would I want to go to the trouble of finding another doctor when we'll only be here for a few weeks? Deb's my doctor. She's the one who should be doing my follow-up exam."

Those soft green eyes studied her speculatively before he reached out, turned the light back off, and drew her into his arms. They lay together in the darkness, both of them thinking thoughts they didn't choose to share. "You know," he said, "all I did was kiss you. I wasn't trying to hump you like a dog in heat."

"You paint such lovely, romantic word pictures."

"Oh, shut up. We've been through this before. I know enough not to try anything until you have the go-ahead from your doctor."

"Sexually frustrated, are you, Flash?"

"Stop playing games. I'm serious. I'm worried about you. You've been distracted lately. Distant. Depressed. Not yourself at all."

"I'm not depressed. But the miscarriage hit me hard. I don't know why. I just need you to be patient with me while I try to work it all out in my head. Can you do that?"

"Of course I can do that. But promise me that when you see Deb, you'll talk to her about what's going on with you. Because you're starting to scare me."

"You worry too much. You worry about things that aren't real. Phantoms. This is one of those phantom things."

"It looks pretty damn real from where I'm standing."

"That's the nature of phantoms. They masquerade as the real thing, but they're made of sea smoke and half-remembered dreams. Far too insubstantial to be real."

"Why is it I don't feel better about that?"

"I love you, Flash. You know I do. But this is something you can't help me through. I have to do it on my own."

He sulked. Even in the dark, she could tell that he was sulking. The vibrations sloughing off him were clear and vivid. "Just don't pull any further away from me," he said. "Don't disappear. Because I need you. You're my true north. And you're not the only one who has to deal with this."

She reached out in the darkness and touched a hand to his cheek, brushed her knuckles along the line of his jaw. His skin was warm, the soft bristle of whiskers satisfying. "Sometimes," she said, "I feel as though I'm seeing the world through the wrong end of a looking glass. Everything that should look familiar seems small and distant. Distorted. It's very disconcerting."

"Am I distorted?"

"You," she said, "are my love. Always and forever."

He kissed the top of her head and lay back against his pillow. Just as she was about to fall asleep, she heard him say softly, "You didn't really answer my question."

Rob

THE kid was late this morning.

Rob killed a half-hour drinking coffee and cleaning up loose ends he'd been too busy to deal with over the past weeks. He worked his way through a stack of paperwork, then called Kitty's agent about setting up a time for her to come back in and record the background vocals. After that, he and Kyle spent some time playing around, overdubbing the song he expected would be the album's first single release.

An hour passed, then two. Finally, he called Drew Lawrence at the record company. "I just thought you'd like to know," he said, "that your million-dollar baby was a no-show today."

Lawrence uttered an epithet. Said, "How late is he?"

"Two hours. And I find it a little hypocritical, considering that when I took a week off because of Casey's miscarriage, he had the nerve to call me at home and demand that I get back to work because he was in a big hurry to finish this album."

"I'm sorry. Hang tight. I'll see what I can do."

Twenty minutes later, his cell phone rang. It was Luther, Phoenix's sidekick. Part bodyguard, part babysitter, and part personal assistant, the mountainous black man said in his crisp British accent, "Mr. Hightower won't be in today. He's a little under the weather."

"Meaning he partied the night away?"

Luther hesitated for a fraction of a second too long. "That's not what I said. I simply said he's not well this morning."

"Right. That's what I thought." He tapped the pen in his hand against the desk. "Listen, Luther, you're a good guy. I like you. But I don't envy you your position. How do you put up with it?"

Luther cleared his throat, and his sigh carried distinctly over the telephone line. "I'm handsomely paid."

"I'm sure you are. But is it worth selling your soul?"

"He's not so bad. Once you get to know him."

"Really? Because all I've seen is a spoiled brat."

"I suppose it would be pointless to say that there are extenuating circumstances?"

"We all have extenuating circumstances." He tossed down the pen. "You pull yourself up by the bootstraps and keep on keeping on."

"While I fully agree with what you're saying, please understand that I'm nothing more than an employee. I don't run the train. I simply try to keep it on the track and make sure all the passengers are properly cared for."

"I hear you, buddy. But if somebody doesn't do something with your passenger pretty soon, your train's going to derail. And then guess who they'll blame?"

"Thank you. You've considerably brightened my day."

"Glad I could help." He disconnected the call and swiveled his chair in Kyle's direction. "The *enfant terrible* is too hung over to work today. Looks like we get the rest of the day off."

"*Enfant terrible?*"

"Hey, it fits. Note that I used the proper French pronunciation. I learned it from my wife."

"Go ahead. I'll probably hang around here for a while. Play around with some different mixes. That's why you're paying me the big bucks."

"Hah! Right."

Out on the street, he called Casey's cell. "Hey there, my hot little *mamacita*," he said when she answered.

"Hey, yourself. You sound uncharacteristically cheerful. What's up?"

"Your husband unexpectedly got the rest of the day off, and he thought maybe you'd be interested in a hot date. Go somewhere, do something. Play tourist. Eat exotic foods. Have a drink or two. No kids included. Just you and me, my gorgeous, sexy woman."

"I'd love to, babe, but your timing is terrible. The girls and I are on the train, halfway to Coney Island. I promised them the beach, and they're getting the beach." She paused. Said, "You could always hop a train and join us."

The dead-last place he wanted to be on this sunny summer day was on a train headed for Coney Island. A little disappointed, he said, "I think I'll take a rain check. I have plenty here to keep me busy. Give Emmy a kiss for me. I'll see you later."

Even without Casey's companionship, it was a rush, playing hooky from work. Dealing with Phoenix Hightower and his antics had turned into one big headache. Funny, back when he was producing for Danny, it had never felt like work. Nor had it with the handful of artists he'd signed to his own fledgling record label in the last fifteen months. It had felt more like play, the kind of play that left him elated and made his soul sing. But Danny Fiore, and the artists Rob had signed to his Two Dreamers label, were people he believed in, artists who were deeply invested in their own careers. Artists who listened to what he had to say and who respected his opinions and his input. Even when they didn't agree, they were still willing to try his ideas on for size.

Phoenix wasn't there yet. He might not ever get there. Right now, the kid was too caught up in the fame and fortune, the parties and the drugs and the easy women, to care one whit about the quality of the material he produced. He was just taking the ride, without a thought for the future. But the future would come, as surely as tomorrow's sun would rise, and when his ride slammed into that brick wall, Phoenix Hightower would crash and burn like so many others Rob had seen over the years.

He ducked into a small bakery, bought himself a glazed doughnut, and ate it while he walked. Rob loved the quiet of home, loved raising his kids with the kind of safety, comfort, and community that a rural Maine town like Jackson Falls could provide. But at heart, he was still a city boy, and New York was the ultimate city, one loaded with novelty and excitement, a place he didn't think he could ever tire of.

He'd passed this music store a hundred times, had admired all the guitars displayed in the window just as often, had itched to take one in his hands and make it sing. But he'd always been in a hurry, always on a deadline, always headed somewhere else. Today, there was nowhere else he had to be, and today, he was going to treat himself to a little bit of bliss.

He licked the doughnut glazing from his fingers, wiped them on a wrinkled tissue he pulled from his pocket, and sauntered into the store.

It was a guitar player's heaven. Guitars of all shapes and varieties stood on stands, hung overhead, sat shoulder-to-shoulder on shelves, an abundance of rapture so magnificent that, like a kid dropped into a vat of cotton candy, he didn't know where to begin. He started at the beginning, picked up the nearest guitar, a shiny

Fender acoustic, figuring he'd work his way through them all, one riff at a time.

"Can I help you?"

He paused, guitar in hand, strings throbbing beneath his fingertips. The sales clerk, a twenty-something kid, clean-cut and eager in a white dress shirt and navy blue tie, was undoubtedly as knowledgeable about guitars as Rob was about alligators. "Just looking," he said.

The kid nodded, as though he'd said something sage and significant. "What kind of music do you play?"

He carefully replaced the Fender, moved to a shiny blue Yamaha. Picked it up, ran callused fingertips along smooth, lacquered wood and almost shuddered at the rich, sensual delight it brought him. "A little of this, a little of that."

"Country? Folk?"

"Rock. Blues. Jazz."

"A rocker. Well, then, I have this sweet little Jackson over here that you'll love. Come check it out."

Rob followed him, noted the price, took the Jackson hard-body electric in hand, ran a finger up and down one of the strings, fluttered it a little at the end. "Nice," he said. "Nice sound. Good and responsive. Easy on the fingers."

"I can give you a great deal on it. Twenty percent down, small monthly payments."

"What else do you have? A little higher end than this?"

The kid reminded him of a used car salesman, the words *higher end* sending dollar signs rolling around his head where there should have been eyeballs. "Right over here in the window," he said, "there's this very nice Gretsch." He bounced up three steps to the window display, took the Gretsch from its stand, came back and handed it to Rob. "This is real quality."

With the kid beaming like a proud papa, Rob checked it out, tested the sound, the feel. Running his hand over the smooth, glassy finish, he said, "I come home with another guitar, my wife'll be showing me the door."

"Oh, come on. Play the lady some pretty music. Woo her with it. She'll love it."

"I'm not looking to buy," he said. "I'm just looking."

"But I bet you're dying to try it out." The salesman's cheeks were pink with excitement over the prospect of a sale, and of course he was right; Rob *was* dying to try it out. His face was too damned expressive. Casey always said he wore his heart on his sleeve. It was why he was such a lousy poker player. And the kid was smart enough to know that, just like selling a new car, getting the customer into the ride was the first step in making a sale.

"Okay," he said. "I'll try it out ."

The kid, practically rubbing his hands together in glee, disappeared into the back room. He returned a minute later, carrying a wooden stool, a small amp, and a power cord. He set down the stool, the amp, and began unwinding the cord. "We just plug it in here," he said, "and here, and, *voilà*! There you have it. Now, let's see what you can do."

The guy obviously had no clue who he was, and that was exactly the way he wanted it. He preferred anonymity. He didn't want people chasing after him the way they had with Danny, because that pretty face of Danny's had been splashed across every magazine cover, every television screen, from coast to coast. Although he'd done a couple years of solo work after they split, the bulk of his career had been spent backing up Danny Fiore's soaring vocals. He'd been content to let Danny be the front man. He was much happier staying in the background, where people could enjoy his playing without paying too much attention to his face.

He settled himself on the stool, adjusted the amplifier, spun a couple of dials on the guitar, played with the tuning knobs until the strings were in perfect tune. While the clerk stood by, arms crossed and a smug expression on his face, Rob launched himself into some classic twelve-bar blues as a warm-up exercise.

The Gretsch was a joy to play. His fingers glided over the strings like hot buttered popcorn as he added in a playful riff or two, improvised a melody line. When he glanced up from the guitar, the kid, his expression changed from smug to astonished, had been joined by the girl who ran the cash register.

Rob nodded to her, closed his eyes, and lost himself in the music as he played a haunting, weepy blues melody that came from deep in his core. When he finished, he opened his eyes and saw that a couple of customers had stopped to listen. He rose, prepared to hand over the guitar, but the cash register girl said, "Don't stop! Please don't stop!" So he reclaimed his comfortable spot on the stool, closed his eyes again, and let the music wash over him.

He had no idea how long he played. Ten minutes? An hour? He played a little Clapton, a little Stevie Ray. Some of his own originals, songs he and Casey had written for Danny that had become big hits. As he played, he heard whispers coming from all around him. A couple of times, he thought he heard his name being bandied about. But he was too wrapped up in the music to register the fact that his cover was blown, his anonymity tossed to the wind.

When he finally finished, the last note still reverberating, he emerged from his fog and blinked a couple of times, surprised to remember where he was, more surprised to discover that a small crowd had gathered. Their applause stunned and exhilarated him. He hadn't been playing with any audience in mind. But now, filled to overflowing with music and feeling the love from his impromptu audience, there was an inner satisfaction that had eluded him for years. This was the reason he'd been put on this planet. How could he have forgotten?

He handed the guitar back to the sales clerk, stood smiling stiffly as people approached him, one after another, enthusiastically shaking his hand, patting him on the back, gushing their admiration: *I saw you guys at the Hollywood Bowl, man. What a show that was! Why'd you stop playing, dude? You were so damn good. You didn't need Danny. You were the one with the talent. When are you putting out a new record? When are you going back on tour? Please, make it out to my sister: D-E-A-N-D-R-A. She's gonna flip when I give it to her!*

It took a while, but he finally made his escape, slipped on his Oakleys and melted into the sidewalk crowd. He felt all weird and jangly inside. Agitated, yet at the same time, more like himself than he had in so long he couldn't remember. Where the hell had the real Rob MacKenzie gone? What had happened to that absolute certainty that made him who he was? When had he stopped being the guitar wizard and become—

Dull. Boring. Stagnant.

He'd never thought of himself as an adrenalin junkie. That had been Danny's gig. Rob had been so much more—and so much less—than that. Never one to hold back, he'd gone after what he wanted in life. First, it had been the music. And then it had been Casey. But it seemed that somewhere along the way, he'd given up the one for the other. It was dangerous territory he trod these days.

Fame hadn't mattered to him, not one bit. Nor had the money, not if you really wanted to be honest. It was a perk, one he enjoyed, but one he could have lived without, as long as he still had the music. He'd given up performing because of the bullshit that went along with the money and the fame. And he hadn't missed the bullshit. Giving it up had been a relief.

But the connection with the audience—that was a whole different thing, and until today, he'd forgotten what it felt like. The rush. The outpouring of love. The absolute understanding that flowed both ways, from the stage to the audience and back. The people, the ones who knew every word of every song he and Casey had written, every note of every song he and Danny had turned into household words. The fans who refused to stay in their seats, standing instead in a crowded, hot, overpriced venue, singing along with them as they played.

Until this moment, he hadn't realized how much he'd missed it.

Casey

THE sheet draped over Casey's bare knees professed to offer some kind of modesty, but it was false modesty at best. Hunched over on the rolling stool between her thighs, Doctor Deb said, "I'm going to palpate your abdomen. You let me know if anything hurts."

"Fine." She pretended that the photo taped to the ceiling above the examining table, a shot of two divers exploring a coral reef, was so fascinating it trumped the indignity of a pelvic exam.

"Any tenderness here?" Deb said, prodding with two hands.

"No."

"Good. Here?"

"No."

"Excellent. Everything looks good. Pink and healthy and healed. No spotting?"

"No."

"Everything okay at home?"

"Everything's fine."

"Emma doing well?"

"Emma's fine."

Deb poked a little more. "Everything okay between you and Rob?"

"Of course. Why?"

"Idle chitchat. Does this hurt?"

"No."

"Good. How are you holding up?"

"Why are you asking me all these questions?"

Deb rolled away, peeled off her gloves, and rummaged on a nearby table, returning with a packet of tissues. "You lost a baby two weeks ago," she said, handing the tissues to Casey. "It's okay if you're not okay." She patted Casey's knee. "Go ahead and get dressed and meet me in my office."

She hadn't come here prepared for the Spanish Inquisition. Casey sat quietly in Deb's office, her purse on the floor by her feet. Deb breezed in, her lab coat unbuttoned and a wavy strand of red hair escaping from the bun she'd wound it into. "I'm surprised Rob didn't come with you today," she said.

"He and the girls are in New York."

Deb's eyebrows arched. "And they left you here all by yourself?"

"I'm just here for the day. I'm flying back tonight. He's producing an album for Phoenix Hightower. He didn't want to leave me here alone. He worries."

"Understandably." Deb steepled her fingers and swiveled in her chair. "You're cleared to resume normal sexual activity. If anything hurts, stop doing it. If it continues to hurt, make an appointment to see me."

"Fine."

"So." Deb stared at her, unblinking, for so long that Casey began to squirm. "What's the game plan for birth control?"

She sat up a little straighter. "There is no game plan."

"Then we have to come up with one. Because I don't want you even thinking about getting pregnant again. Not for a long, long time, if ever. Two miscarriages in such a short time have undoubtedly wrought havoc on your body. Especially at your age."

Casey opened her mouth to protest, but Deb held up a hand to stop her. "I'm not implying that you're old, so you can get off your high horse. But you're also not twenty any longer. You have to give your body time to rest and recuperate. Six months, minimum. Never again would be optimum."

"Now you sound like Rob."

"Listen to him. He's a smart man."

Casey raised her chin. "I'm not going to stop trying."

"I do understand." Deb's eyes softened. "I spent my twenties in medical school, residency, internship. Now, here I am in my mid-thirties, working night and day to establish a steady medical practice. My biological clock is ticking like crazy. And I have no husband, no significant other, nobody waiting for me at home except my cat. I deliver babies for a living. I understand your baby hunger better than most women."

For a moment, she felt a kinship she'd never before felt with Dr. Deb Levasseur. For the first time, they were connecting woman-to-woman, instead of doctor-to-patient, and she could clearly see the pain in Deb's eyes. "Then you surely understand why I won't quit."

"There are other options. Adoption. Surrogacy. Foster parenting. You have a beautiful little girl, a lovely teenage stepdaughter. Why put yourself through this when you already have children?"

"In other words, why am I being so greedy?"

"That's not what I'm saying, Casey. I'm saying that you're a warm, loving woman with a huge heart. You and Rob have a beautiful family. I'm only suggesting that if you feel a need to expand that family, you might consider other options that won't destroy your body."

"I wish I could explain why I need another baby so much. But I can't. And as much as I'd love any child, I need that baby to be mine. Mine and Rob's. There's this hole inside me that won't be satisfied, won't be filled, until I hold another baby in my arms."

"And where does it stop, Casey? How do you know that one more baby will satisfy it?"

She met Deb's eyes with a level gaze. "I don't."

Deb picked up a pen from her desk and clicked it once. Twice.

"Listen," Casey said. "I gave up everything that mattered to me when I married Danny. It was an idiotic thing to do, but I was young and madly in love and I didn't know any better. When I finally thought I'd caught that brass ring, it was taken away from me.

"And now, I have Rob. My husband's a good man. They don't make them any better. But sometimes I think that if I let him, he'd sit down beside me at the table, cut my steak for me, and feed it to me, bite by bite. He loves me, I understand that. And I love him. But he's not responsible for my happiness, any more than I'm responsible for his. This is what I want. I can't explain why. I shouldn't have to explain why. All I know is that I refuse to be treated like a child who doesn't know what she wants. This is my life, and people need to let me follow my own path."

"I won't argue with that. However, I will urge you to be careful. Because I'd like to keep seeing your smiling face for a good, long time."

"Fine. I'll be careful. But I won't let you or Rob or anybody else dictate how I should live my life."

"All right, then. I think we understand each other. Now let's move along and talk about birth control."

"I won't use anything that I can't stop at a moment's notice. Nothing invasive, nothing that could make it more difficult to conceive when I'm ready to try again. That means no shots, no implants, no pills, no IUD."

Dryly, Deb said, "Doesn't leave us much to work with."

"I was thinking of a diaphragm."

"A diaphragm has side effects."

She wrinkled her brow. "Such as?"

"Such as pregnancy. In other words, you won't bother to use it."

"Why wouldn't I bother to use it?"

"If you'd ever had to peel one off the bathroom wall, you wouldn't ask that question. Why not an IUD? Once it's in there, you just forget about it. When you're ready, you make an appointment, come into my office, and we pull it out."

"I've heard it can take longer to conceive after using one of those things."

"No more so than the pill. And it's just as effective, if not more. Plus, you don't have to remember to take it every day. It's pretty much foolproof."

"I'll have to think it over. I'm not ready yet to make a decision."

"Fine," Deb said. "You don't have to decide today. But don't take too long. And for the love of God, use something in the meantime. Because your body is nowhere near ready for another pregnancy." Deb studied her for a moment. "Can I ask a question?"

"You seem to have done quite well at it so far."

"It just seems to me that up until you went all *I Am Woman* on me, you were a little…subdued. Not your usual pleasant, chatty self."

"I don't understand."

"Let's see if I can explain this better. 'How are you?' 'Fine.' 'How's Emma?' 'Fine.' 'Are you and Rob okay?' 'We're fine.' It's not like you. So naturally, as your doctor and your friend, I'm concerned. Are you eating? Sleeping? Having crying jags? Are you and Rob fighting? You wouldn't be the first couple to experience marital discord after miscarrying a baby."

She raised her head, drew back her shoulders, and said, "I. Am. Absolutely. Fine."

"Well, now, you see, that's what worries me. You just lost a baby. Your second one in less than six months. Most people in your place would not be fine."

"I'm a rock. I've always been a rock."

"I know that. I also know that even a rock has its breaking point."

"I'm not planning to break." She punctuated her statement by bending down and picking up her purse from the floor. "You don't need to worry about me."

"All right, then. I'll stop worrying. Just remember, my door is always open. Promise me one thing."

Casey stood, shouldered the purse, and said, "What's that?"

"If you find yourself needing help of any kind, please get it."

* * *

The apartment was empty. No Rob, no Paige, no Emma. It seemed odd, but then, lately it felt as though odd was the new normal. She could have called a taxi, but since she'd spent most of her day closed up in an airplane, it would probably be healthier if she walked over to the recording studio. It was only five blocks. She was tired, but not that tired.

Rush hour in Manhattan was not the time to take a leisurely stroll. Then again, there was never a time when Manhattan wasn't crowded, and nobody took a leisurely stroll here unless they wanted to be mowed down. Bankers and office drones and secretaries wearing flat-soled athletic shoes, their pumps tucked away in brightly-colored tote bags, streamed from office buildings and into the subway. Intent on their destinations, they rudely elbowed her out of the way, clearly irritated by this woman who had the audacity to take up a minimal amount of space on a sidewalk the locals considered their own.

Five blocks in Manhattan, even at a brisk pace, took a few minutes. A half-block shy of the cross street where the studio was located, she glanced randomly at a shop window and came to an abrupt halt. "Jesus, lady," said the man behind her, sidestepping her with a furious scowl. "You wanna go window shopping, do it when people aren't trying to get somewhere."

She flipped him the bird. It was a significant moment in her life, the first time she'd ever done such a thing. She'd thought about it a time or two, but had never had the *chutzpah* to pull it off. Rob would be shocked. Or, more likely, pleased by this minor foray outside her comfort zone.

Her act of defiance, unnoticed by its target, died a quick death when she crossed the sidewalk, threaded her way through people, and stood there, her heart melting at the display of tiny ruffled dresses, sailor suits, and snazzy pink sneakers. *Oh, Baby!* was the name of the place, and without conscious thought, she moved to the door and stepped inside.

A bell tinkled overhead, and the handsome young sales clerk, busy ringing up a customer, gave her a brief nod of acknowledgment. He had to be from somewhere else. Northern New England, or maybe the Midwest. In Manhattan, where people lived next door to each other for decades without ever meeting, a nod was almost as intimate as a marriage proposal. Casey wandered the aisles, fingering terrycloth bibs and soft, stretchy little onesies and fuzzy, multi-colored socks. The store carried designer diaper bags and fancy bottle sterilizers, and a room in the back held high-end strollers and walkers and crib mobiles that played *Baa Baa Black Sheep* when you wound them up.

Without warning, a black, yawning hole opened up inside her, the sense of loss so great it threatened to suffocate her. Was this the end of her dreams? Was it truly possible that she, who had so much love to give, would have only one child to give that love to?

Her eyes, those traitorous eyes, filled with tears. Mortified, she turned and stumbled out of the store, leaned against the brick wall of the building next to it and sobbed into her open palms.

Because this was Manhattan, nobody paid any attention to the weeping woman who could no more explain why she was crying than she could discuss, with even a modicum of understanding, Einstein's theory of relativity. Both were cloudy, amorphous, and inexplicable.

She cried until there were no more tears, and then she pulled a tissue from her purse—for she always carried tissues in her purse—and wiped her face and blew her nose, right there on the street. When she was done, she tucked the snot-and-tear-encrusted tissue back into her purse and continued on her way.

Rob was in studio D, his swivel chair leaned back, feet propped on the desk in front of him, while behind the glass, in the isolation booth, Phoenix Hightower warbled something that vaguely resembled music. She let herself in, held the door while it closed, whisper soft, behind her. Took a look around the room, wondering who all these spare people were: a huge black man wearing a suit and a stony expression, a slender Asian woman whose painted-on eyebrows gave her a look of perpetual surprise, a young man whose red eyes and messy hair made him appear either hung over or sleep deprived, and a doe-eyed teenage girl who could have been a poster child for bulimia. Moving smoothly and soundlessly to her husband, Casey rested her hands on his shoulders and whispered, "Hey."

"Hey." He leaned his head back, saw her face, and swiveled the chair around. Whispered, "You've been crying."

"It's nothing."

"It's not nothing." He leaned over the mic, pushed a button, said, "Phoenix? Take ten. I need to talk to my wife."

The kid's mouth clamped abruptly shut. With a sour expression on his face, he stomped from the sound booth, through the control room, and slammed out the door, taking all those spare people with him.

"Do I dare to ask?" Casey said.

Rob leaned back in his chair. Swiveling lazily, he said, "The big guy—Luther—is his bodyguard. Or maybe just his babysitter. No clarification on that yet. The others? They're his posse."

"His *what*?"

"You knew you'd be sorry you asked. I believe in our day it was called a retinue. Basically, it's a loosely-organized group of hangers-on who leech off the money teat, milk it dry, then move on to a new, milkier teat."

"How lovely. What'll they do when his voice changes?"

"See?" Rob said to the sound engineer—Kyle, she thought his name was. "My wife is not only beautiful, but smart, and she has a razor-sharp wit."

"I can see that. I'll just make myself scarce for a few minutes." Kyle picked up his coffee cup, nodded politely, and let himself out of the room.

"Where are the girls?" she said. "Why aren't they here with you?"

Rob drew her onto his lap. "Paige took Emma to a movie."

Fear, instantaneous and ridiculously out of proportion to the situation, slammed into her chest and swallowed her alive. "You let them out on the street alone? In Manhattan? Are you *insane?*"

"They're fine. They're just a block away. And Paige is as tough as they come."

"My God. What if something happens to them? What if—I don't know. What if they get mugged?"

"Casey."

"Or—" She scraped her hair back from her face. "Or hit by a taxi?"

"Babe."

"Or molested by some pervert in that darkened movie theater?"

"Casey!"

He finally got her attention. "What?" she said.

"For the love of Mike, woman, the girls are fine. Don't you trust me?"

Her heart still hammered, double-time, inside her chest. "I trusted Danny," she said. "And look how that turned out."

He muttered an expletive, drew her closer, and folded her in his arms. She rested her head against his shoulder. And let out a hard breath.

"You're shaking," he said.

"Just hold me. Just shut up and hold me."

For a time, they were both silent as her breathing gradually slowed, smoothed, until it matched his. He picked up her hand, kissed the knuckles. Said, "Why were you crying?"

"Nothing. I—I don't really know. It just hit me, and—you're sure they're all right?"

Tenderly stroking the hair at her temple, he said, "One hundred percent sure. Do you think I'd let anything happen to Emma?"

She took a breath, wet her lips. Said, "I'm not being rational, am I?"

"Truthfully? Not really."

"Oh, God." She drew a sharp, ragged breath. "What is wrong with me?"

"Maybe I should take you home. Cut this thing short for the day, and pick back up tomorrow."

"No." She sat up straight, smoothed her hair, pulled her dignity around her like a suit of armor. "You have a job to do, you have studio time booked, and I'm being ridiculous. I just—I want my little girl, that's all. I want to hold her in my arms and never let her go."

He took her hand in his and gently rubbed her knuckles. "The girls are due back anytime. How'd it go with the doctor?"

"It went."

"Everything okay?"

"I'm fine. Nicely healed. Fully cleared for playtime activities."

He waggled his eyebrows. "Good to know. So, did you have the Big Talk?"

She looked at him blankly, and he tucked a strand of hair behind her ear. "Don't pretend you don't know what I'm talking about. The birth control talk. What did she have to say about that?"

"Exactly what you'd expect her to say. Don't even try for at least six months. Decide on a birth control method that's workable. Don't take too much time deciding, and be damn careful in the meantime."

His eyes narrowed. So did his mouth. "She didn't put you on anything?"

"I told her I had to think about it."

"Is that a good idea? Jesus, babe, we don't need any accidents."

She sat silent, tight-lipped and stiff. "Or," he said, "maybe you're hoping for an accident."

"The clock is ticking, Flash. I'm almost thirty-eight years old. I don't have that much time left."

He leaned his head back and, staring at the ceiling, let out a pained sigh. "Did you talk about this obsession you have with getting pregnant again?"

"It's not an obsession, and I resent you calling it that."

"I'm sorry, but that's how it looks from my side of the bed."

"I don't know what you want me to say."

"I don't want you to say anything. I also don't want you to die. Because facing life without you beside me? Not a place I'm interested in visiting."

* * *

On the way back to the apartment, with Emma safely tucked into her stroller, Casey stopped at *Oh, Baby!* again. Determined to not make an ass of herself this time, she avoided the newborn department, instead marching directly to the 18-month-size clothing for girls. She thumbed through racks of dresses, with their ruffles and lace and girly, flowery prints. "Look, Emma," she said, holding up a pretty little aqua-colored number with loads of ruffles and a big, puffy bow on the bodice. "You'd look beautiful in this, don't you think?"

"Gah," Emma said.

"That's what I thought, too," Casey said. "Do you want Mama to buy you this pretty dress?"

"No," Emma said, usually her default response to any question.

"Maybe this one, too," Casey said.

"Mum mum."

"We can dress you up all pretty and surprise Daddy when he comes home."

"Da."

That sounded like agreement to her, so she bought two dozen dresses, six packages of tights, and a pair of shiny white patent-leather shoes that took her back to Easter mornings and summer Sunday school when she was a girl not much older than Emma. As she paid for her purchases, she told herself there was no rational excuse for her earlier meltdown. It wasn't as though Emma had grown up overnight. She was still a baby. And if, while she was shopping for Emma, she happened to take a peek at the newborn items as well, it didn't mean she was psychologically unstable. She liked baby clothes. Liked baby toys. Liked *babies*. What was wrong with liking babies? It didn't mean she was obsessed. Rob was, once again, blowing things out of proportion, worrying about phantoms that only existed in the darkest regions of his mind.

Back at home, she dropped the bags on the couch, left Emma's stroller in the entryway, and settled in the rocking chair, where they spent some special mother-daughter time. With Emma cuddled on her lap, Casey read *Pat the Bunny* to her wide-eyed little girl. "See how soft the bunny is?" she said. "Does Emmy like the soft bunny?"

"Da." Emma reached out a tiny hand, touched the furry creature with eager little fingers, then looked up at her mother and grinned, a grin so like Rob's that Casey found it a little disarming. It was a sure bet that by the time she was fifteen, Emma would be turning members of the opposite sex into a warm puddle of goo, just like her father still did.

Casey buried her nose in Emma's velvety-soft neck, eliciting squeals of delight. "My sweet baby," she said, breathing in the heady scent of little girl, "I haven't given you enough Mom time lately."

"Mum," Emma said.

Guilt nibbled at the edges of her consciousness. Emma wasn't the only one she'd been neglecting. She'd always been a good wife, a good mother. But lately, she'd been too encased in her own cocoon of misery, too spent, too empty, to expend any of her time or energy on Paige or Rob. She really needed to make a little more effort, even if that effort did feel like wading through a sea of molasses.

So she picked up the phone and called Rob.

After the miscarriage, he'd bought them matching cell phones. It had seemed silly to her at the time. What on earth would they do with the things? At home, tucked into the rolling hills of Western Maine, the phones barely worked. Cell towers were few and far between in Maine's rural areas. Nobody she knew had a cell phone, and she'd lived almost forty years without carting one around. Why was Rob so insistent that she needed one now?

But she had to admit that here in New York, where there were no problems with reception, the phones came in handy. With Rob working so many hours, it was nice to be able to reach him at any point in time without having to go through Sheila.

He answered on the second ring, sounding a little distracted. "Hey," she said.

"Hey. What's up?"

"Emmy and I are going through Daddy withdrawals. I thought if you could get out at a reasonable hour, I'd make a nice dinner for the four of us."

"Are you sure you're up to it? You've had a long day. Paige and I are perfectly fine having pizza brought in."

"My day just got better. Emmy and I have been shopping. And you can't live on pizza. I thought that since I've been neglecting my family lately, I'd try to make it up to you tonight. Are you game?"

"I can manage it, if you're sure. What time do you want us home?"

"Eight-thirty?"

"Eight-thirty works for me."

So she loaded Emma back in her stroller and went to the market on the next block, where she picked up fresh salad greens and a roasting chicken. Back home again, she stashed her groceries in the fridge and gave Emma a bath.

Bath time was Emma's favorite time of day. She splashed and played, poured water from one plastic teacup into another, babbled contentedly while her mother shampooed her hair and washed every inch of her with a soft terry bath mitt. Casey rinsed Emma's hair, then plucked her from the bath water, wrapped her in a soft towel, and carried her into the bedroom.

Diapered and powdered, Emma lay on the bed, giggling when Casey pressed her lips to her belly and blew a raspberry. Casey had picked out the aqua dress with the bow. The dress went on with relative ease; the tights, not so much. While Emma squirmed and fought, Casey struggled to pull them up straight and smooth.

The white patent leather shoes finished off Emma's ensemble, and Casey sat her daughter in her lap and brushed Emma's yellow, baby-fine hair. Pulling it into a topknot, she clipped it with a barrette, and the transformation was complete. "You look so beautiful, Miss Emmy Lou Who," she said. "You could pass for a movie star."

"No," Emma said.

"Oh, yes. A glamorous blonde. Daddy will be so impressed."

"Da?"

"Later, baby. Let's go set up your playpen in the kitchen. Right now, we have to cook."

Rob

AS soon as he stepped out of the elevator, he heard the music. Sheryl Crow, singing *All I Wanna Do*, from her album *Tuesday Night Music Club*. He'd bought it for Casey last Christmas. She wasn't playing it loud enough to bother the neighbors, just loud enough to be recognizable. Rob exchanged a glance with Paige, then unlocked the apartment door and held it so she could go in ahead of him.

His olfactory nerves went crazy the instant he walked through the door, teased by a smell so wonderful that at first he thought he'd died and gone to heaven. He wasn't even sure what he was smelling. Chicken, maybe, with one of those wonderful rubs that she made from her secret mix of spices. If he hadn't already been crazy in love with her, he would have married Casey Fiore for her cooking skills alone. He found her in the kitchen, humming along with Sheryl as she stirred a little taste of heaven in a large cooking pot with a wooden spoon. Her cheeks flushed, her hair messy, she looked like something cool and sweet that he wanted to pour over himself, dive into, and take a deep swim in. The table was already set, with a tablecloth and fresh flowers. She turned from the stove and said, "Hi," with a saucy smile.

"Hi," he said.

"Dinner's almost ready." For the first time in weeks, she seemed like herself: calm, competent, sexy.

In the playpen, Emma reached up her arms and bounced up and down, saying, "Dadadadadadada."

Rob bent down, swept her up, swung her high over his head, and said, "Who is this hot young chick, and what happened to my Emmy Lou Who?"

His daughter squealed in delight. He lowered her, propped her in the crook of his arm and, waggling his eyebrows, said, "You're quite the vamp in this get-up, Emmy. Something new?"

"I told you," Casey said, "we went shopping." Wooden spoon in hand, she stretched on tiptoe, past their squirming daughter, and he leaned down and kissed her. "Wait till you see the rest," she said.

"There's more?"

"Much, much more. Right, Emma?"

"Am I going to have to revoke your credit card privileges?"

"Very funny, Flash. Get yourself a drink and wait. Ten minutes. Out of my kitchen. Shoo! Paige, want to stay and help?"

He did what she said; he didn't dare not to. He settled on the couch with Emma and a cold bottle of Heineken, picked up the remote and switched on the television with the sound muted because Sheryl was still singing. Flipping silently through the channels, he settled on *Seinfeld*. But he couldn't focus on the show. Muted, the visuals gave no clue as to what the episode was about, and with *Seinfeld*, it was all about the dialogue. Besides, he was too distracted by Casey's behavior. He was probably overreacting, but this perky, enthusiastic goddess didn't quite gibe with the anxiety-ridden woman he'd seen just a few hours ago. One of these opposing twins was a Stepford wife, but which one?

Every so often, when there was a break in the music, the quiet murmur of voices floated from the kitchen. He was grateful that his wife and the daughter who'd come to him as a surprise package two years ago had bonded almost from the beginning. Paige had given them a run for their money. Penance, he supposed, for the stupidity and single-mindedness of his youth. His wife had been born with the kind of patience he lacked. There were times when he'd been ready to give up on the kid, but Casey remained cool, calm, constant in her love for his daughter.

He'd grown a few gray hairs last winter, when Paige and Mikey Lindstrom had cooked up some cockamamie scheme about eloping. Thank God they'd realized how crazy the idea was before it was too late. Now, on the verge of her senior year, she'd settled down, was gradually losing the chip from her shoulder as she evolved from resentful teenager to smart, beautiful young woman. She'd inherited some of that single-mindedness from him, but she wore it much better than he had. In his younger days, he'd been so focused on his music that the rest of his life had been in tatters. If it hadn't been for Casey, he probably would've crashed and burned years ago. She'd been his rock, the one solid thing in his life. It hadn't mattered that she was married to Danny, not back then. She was Danny's rock, too. Among many talents his wife possessed, that was arguably her greatest.

But now, he was seeing the rock begin to crack, and he had no idea how to fix it. Or even whether it could be fixed. So he sat here, beer in hand and his daughter in his lap, and brooded over it, because that was his greatest talent. He was a world-class, grand champion brooder.

A few minutes passed before Paige came to the doorway and said, "Dad? Dinner's ready."

Casey'd gone out of her way to make dinner something special. Fresh flowers on the table. A salad with fresh organic greens and homemade poppy seed dressing, followed by a roast chicken with cornbread stuffing, creamy mashed potatoes, peas, and a side dish of cinnamon-flavored pink applesauce. Nothing elegant, just good, old-fashioned home cooking. While Emma played in her potatoes with her plastic spoon and chased peas with her fingers, Rob and Paige shoveled in the first real home-cooked meal they'd eaten since they came to New York, and Casey kept up a steady stream of bright, cheery patter. She seemed so light and airy, he knew that something was off.

"While I was out," she said, "I picked up some movies. I thought we could watch one together after Emma goes to bed."

Paige raised her head. His eyes met hers, and she shrugged. "Fine by me," he said, reaching for a second dinner roll. He just wanted his wife to be happy, and if he had to sit through a chick flick to accomplish that, it was a small price to pay.

While Paige and Casey cleaned up the kitchen after dinner, he got Emma washed up and in her pajamas, read her a bedtime story, then settled her in the crib with a bottle. The women were just finishing up when he came back. "Why don't the two of you pick a movie and get it started?" Casey said. "I'll make some popcorn."

He'd eaten so much already that he wasn't sure his stomach would hold anything else, but if it would make her happy, he'd eat popcorn until it came out his ears. While the microwave hummed in the kitchen, he and Paige checked out the movies, argued a little, finally came to a compromise. Paige settled into the recliner that she'd claimed the day they moved in, and he got the TV and the VCR ready. Halfway through the previews, realizing he'd stopped hearing the sound of popping corn quite some time ago, he headed to the kitchen to see what was taking her so long.

The room was dark, lit only by a single night light. A dark figure set against its illumination, his wife stood at the sink, her head bowed, her hands gripping the counter so hard that even in this faint light, he could see the taut tendons in her wrists, the whiteness of her knuckles. "Babe?" he said softly.

She raised her head, straightened her spine. But still didn't look at him. "Casey?" he said, taking a step toward her.

His wife finally turned, and he saw the sunken eyes, the pallor. "I'm just so tired," she said. "That's all."

He muttered a curse under his breath, and she reached out a slender hand and touched his face. "I'm fine," she said. "Really."

"Like hell you are." Before she had time to protest, he scooped her up in his arms. "Change of plans," he told Paige as he carried his wife through the living room and down the hallway toward the master bedroom. Casey didn't argue, and that was what frightened him the most. The Casey he knew would have been making sassy remarks and issuing orders. This Casey was limp and compliant. The wife who was the center of his universe was disappearing right in front of his eyes, piece by piece, like the Cheshire Cat.

He sat her on the edge of the bed, knelt and took off her shoes, set them aside. Peeled off her socks, her jeans, her tee shirt. Sitting there in just her underwear, she said, "I'm so sorry, Flash. I've been neglecting you, and all I wanted was to make things festive for one night."

"Don't be ridiculous. There's not a damn thing to be sorry for. You're exhausted, physically and emotionally. You've been through hell, and today, you pushed yourself to the point of collapse. Paige and I appreciate everything you do for us, but it's more important to us that you take care of yourself."

"If that's so, then why are you taking care of me?"

"Hey," he said. "Remember that jazzy little thing they put in the wedding vows? *In sickness and in health.* Remember that?"

"I'm not sick."

"You're heartsick, babe. Add exhaustion to that, and what you have is a volatile cocktail."

"You make me sound like something that's about to explode."

Except that she wasn't exploding. She was imploding. "Come on," he said, drawing back the covers and patting the mattress. "Let's get you into bed."

Like an obedient five-year-old, she scooted into place, rested her head on the pillow, dark hair falling all around her, and he drew the covers up to her chin. "There," he said. "You get some sleep. I guarantee you'll feel better in the morning."

She ran a hand up his arm. "Are you coming to bed?"

"In a few minutes. I need to talk to Paige first. Go to sleep." He leaned and kissed her forehead, then reached to turn out the light. "That's an order."

He closed the bedroom door softly behind him. Paige was waiting in the living room, the movie on pause, her eyes wide with concern. "Is she okay?" she said.

"I don't know." He sat down hard on the couch, braced his elbows on his knees. Scraped his fingers through his hair. Lifted his head, met his daughter's eyes. And sighed. "I honest-to-God don't know."

"I don't understand what's going on. She was fine, right up until she wasn't."

"She wasn't fine. She was faking it. Eyes a little too bright, chatter a little too enthusiastic. I don't know who that woman was, but she wasn't my wife."

"Her hormones are messed up. She was pregnant, and now she isn't. I don't think it matters that she didn't deliver a full-term baby. She could still be going through post-partum depression."

"She just saw the doctor. You'd think Deb would've noticed if something was wrong."

"I don't know. She's pretty good at hiding it. I live with her, and I didn't see through that bright and bubbly façade."

"True."

"Is there anything I can do to help?"

"Just help me keep an eye on her. This is bound to pass. Eventually." He rose to his feet. "I'm going to bed. Don't stay up too late."

In the bedroom, he undressed in the dark and crawled into bed, silently, so he wouldn't wake her. But his wife wasn't sleeping. She rolled onto her side, slipped an arm around him beneath the covers, and rested her cheek against his chest. Her words slurred from exhaustion, she said, "Hey there, hot stuff."

"Hey." He gathered her closer, that warm body pressed hard against his. "I thought you'd be asleep by now."

"I'm too tired to sleep."

"And I'm the King of Siam."

She let out a sleepy sigh and said, "Yul Brynner."

"What?"

"*The King and I.* The movie?" She cleared her throat. "Yul Brynner played the King of Siam."

Her words conjured up a vague image of a broad-shouldered man with a shaved head, but he didn't think he'd ever seen the movie. "Forget Yul Brynner," he said. "You need to sleep."

"And you need to stop worrying about me."

"Like that's ever going to happen."

"I overdid today. It's my own fault. I'm probably still anemic from blood loss. It's only been a couple of weeks." She yawned, settled more comfortably against him. "Flying up and back in one day was too much for me. I should've stayed overnight and flown back tomorrow. Stupid."

"You don't have a stupid bone in your body, Fiore."

"I love you, too, MacKenzie."

"I didn't say it because I love you. I said it because it's true."

"Mmn hmn."

The silence between them was comfortable, the silence of two people who drew their sunlight and oxygen from each other's presence. After a time, deciding to dip a single toe into the water, he said, "Babe?"

"Mmn."

"There's something I need to talk to you about."

"Mmn hmn."

"You know that little guitar store down on Broadway, near 43rd?"

Silence, punctuated only by her deep and even breathing. He carefully brushed the hair away from her face and adjusted the blankets around them.

And stayed awake for a long time, pondering his future.

Casey

SHE knew she was dreaming, but the dream started out so lovely that at first, she just went along with it. Beneath a stunning blue sky, the Pacific sparkled like a polished gemstone. At low tide, the waves rolled in like champagne bubbles, mellow and harmless, popping just before they reached the shore. They were on the short stretch of beach that fronted their Malibu home, tucked in between neighboring properties that made their relatively modest house of redwood and glass look like a shack. The home to her left belonged to a famous television actor whose hit show was watched every week by millions. The one on her right was owned by the widow of a Hollywood scriptwriter who'd penned more than two dozen successful action films in his decades-long career.

They'd brought everything they needed for a fun mother-daughter afternoon at the beach: two lounge chairs, one Mommy-size, the other Katie-size; beach towels, sunscreen, beach toys. Flip-flops, bottled water, a bag of potato chips. A portable radio and a magazine. Perched sideways on her lounge chair with her toes buried in the sand and Katie propped between her knees, her tiny body humming with impatience, Casey slathered sunscreen on her daughter's shoulders, her cheeks, the bridge of her nose. At five, Katie was losing her baby fat. That sweet, round face was becoming less round as the bone structure beneath became more defined. She wore a bright pink two-piece bathing suit, her blond hair in loose braids, and a white sun hat which she kept losing—Casey suspected deliberately—in the sand. Her baby was growing up too quickly. A hard fist wrapped around her heart and squeezed. She wasn't ready for this. Wasn't sure she'd ever be ready for her little girl to grow up.

"Big hug," she said, wrapping her arms around that warm little body, burying her nose in Katie's neck, inhaling the mingled scents of salt air, sunscreen, and little girl.

"Enough, Mommy!" Katie said with indignation, squirming to escape from her mother's embrace. Casey let her go, sat watching those chubby little legs pump as Katie raced toward the water, her pigtails bouncing, her red bucket clutched tightly in her hand. Her daughter plunked down on the wet sand at the water's edge and began digging with a blue plastic shovel.

"Don't go in the water without me," Casey reminded her.

Katie glanced up, gave her a withering look, and said in a sing-songy voice, "What do you think I am, stupid?"

Casey raised her eyebrows, and Katie, being nobody's fool, returned her attention to digging. Katie was going through a stage. She was, by turns, charming, funny, and delightful. Of late, she'd also been sassy, impertinent, and naughty. This had been going on since shortly after she started preschool, where she'd quickly discovered the fearsome power of peer pressure. Casey had interrogated other mothers, who'd assured her it was temporary and that her best course of action was to ignore it. Leanne Ackerman, the mother of Katie's best friend, said, "She's pushing the boundaries. Trying to find out how far she can go with you. It's normal, and if you respond negatively, you'll reinforce the behavior. Don't give her the satisfaction. When she fails to get a rise out of you, she'll move on to something different."

"Something worse? I certainly hope not."

"Oh, hon, just wait until the teenage years. The real fun is still ahead of you."

She would cross that bridge when she came to it. In the meantime, in spite of her daughter's occasional foray to the dark side, life was pretty close to perfect. Could there be a better way to spend a lazy summer afternoon? Sun, sand, salt air. The ocean's rhythmic roar, the Monkees on the radio singing *I'm Not Your Stepping Stone*, and Katie, her beautiful Katydid, who owned every inch of her heart, playing at the water's edge.

Casey loved being a mother. Loved the damp hugs and the sticky kisses and the messy little fingers. Loved making PB&J sandwiches with the crusts cut off, loved dressing her daughter in girly, ruffled dresses, loved reading to her at bedtime from *The Cat in the Hat* and *Charlotte's Web* and *The Wind in the Willows*. She loved sitting together at the kitchen table with a pad of paper and a box of crayons, using their imaginations to create whatever they fancied. She loved perching Katie on a kitchen stool, wrapped in a red apron that was five sizes too big, and teaching her to bake cookies, just the way her mother had done when she was a girl. Danny had been her universe until the day Katie was born. How could she have foreseen the vast difference between her love for him and what she felt for her firstborn child? How could she have understood how that child would exponentially expand her universe? How could she have known that her life wouldn't truly begin until she became a mother?

"Look, Mommy! See what I can do!"

Somehow, despite her warnings, during the second when she'd been lost in thought, Katie had waded into the surf and now stood chest deep, her little arms outflung in a wordless "Ta-da!"

A dense bed of kelp floated on the incoming tide. On the horizon, storm clouds had gathered, and as she watched in horror, the wind picked up, kicking up the surf that a moment ago had been as tame as bath water. "Katie!" she shouted. "Come back here!"

In too deep to have solid footing, her daughter bobbled and swayed in the rushing surf. "Look, Mommy," she said. "I can swim!"

And, fearless, she ducked her head underwater.

Except that she couldn't swim. Danny hadn't wanted her to learn. He'd said there was no need until she was older. They never allowed her on the beach alone, and he didn't want people at the YMCA staring at her, whispering about her, because she was his daughter.

But Casey was a strong swimmer, and as a massive breaker rolled in like a shark at feeding time toward the last place she'd seen her daughter, she raced across the sand to the water, screaming Katie's name as she ran. She splashed through the shallows, reached deeper water just as the breaker slammed into her. It took her down and under, tumbled and tossed her until she had no idea which way was up. She swallowed salt water, scrabbled in the loose sand driven up her nose by the force of the water. A clump of seaweed slapped her in the face, and she gasped, took in more water. Frantic now, struggling against the undertow that threatened to pull her out to sea, she began swimming, searching desperately for the child who had disappeared right before her eyes.

But it was murky and dark beneath the surface, and her lungs were on fire, her body weakened by her desperate attempt to hold her breath. Just as the lack of oxygen forced her to breathe, the roiling sea coughed once and spit her out. Choking, gasping, she struggled to her feet and wiped the sting of salt from her eyes, felt its agonizing burn through her sinuses.

Tangled in a bed of kelp, a tiny body floated face up on the surface of the water, bobbing gently in a sea that had gone dark and flat. Eyes wide, staring but unseeing, Katie now wore a lacy white dress. A burial gown. With a cry of despair, Casey fought her way through water that had turned the consistency of Jell-O, one laborious step after another bringing her closer, closer, until she reached her lifeless daughter, swiped a soggy strand of hair away from the child's face, and realized that it wasn't Katie at all.

It was Emma.

Noooooooooo. She opened her mouth to scream, but no sound came out. She was helpless, ineffectual, powerless. But inside her head, the screaming was so loud her brain threatened to implode. Casey untangled the dead child from the kelp, took her daughter in her arms like a rag doll, and slowly, laboriously, made her way through the water to the shore. Reddish drops of sea water dripped steadily, *plunk, plunk, plunk*, from Katie/Emma's hair. A tiny splotch of red appeared on the front of the burial gown. As she watched, the spot grew larger, then began to drip, running faster, faster, until it carved a river of red in the wet sand.

Behind her, instead of the hiss of waves, there came a soft murmuring, like the buzz of a beehive in early summer. With the limp child still in her arms, she turned and saw them. Her dead babies, their precious souls instantly recognizable. While she stood rooted in place, the buzzing grew louder. Those three dead babies multiplied into a hundred dead babies. A thousand. A sea of dead babies where there once was water, a chorus of voices taunting her, judging her, terrorizing her.

"Baby killer!" a voice said, and then another, and another, like bullfrogs randomly chirping in a dark spring bog. "Murderer!"

"No!" she shouted, although she didn't open her mouth. "I'm not a killer! I'm not! I loved my daughter!"

"Your fault," the voices whispered. "*Your fault, your fault, your fault.* Baby killer!"

No. Oh, no. A wave of grief and despair washed over her, brutal, unbearable, so powerful it brought her to her knees. She knelt on the sand, her dead daughter in her arms, opened her mouth, and let the pain pour out in a shrill, piercing scream that went on and on and on.

"Casey."

The voice intruded into her dream. It was a familiar voice, but she couldn't place it, couldn't respond, because every ounce of her was focused on the utter blackness of her grief. The poison continued to pour forth in the keening of a grieving mother, until she thought surely her insides would come up next because there was nothing left to hold them in.

"Babe, wake up. You're having a nightmare."

She awoke with a gasp. Blinking in the light from the bedside lamp, she was unable, at first, to tell what was real and what was not. Rob lay on his side next to her, one hand curled around her hip, the other stroking her temple. "Emma," she said. "Emma!"

"Shh." Rob gathered her in his arms and began rocking her. "Shh," he said, his fingers gentle in her hair. "Emma's fine. She's sleeping."

"No." She struggled to escape, terror giving her a strength she never knew she possessed. "I have to see her!" She shoved him away, sat up and swung her legs over the side of the bed. "I have to make sure she's okay."

"Stay here." He put a hand on her arm to impede her. "I'll get her."

Dazed, she sat with her heart pounding, the pain and the grief and the despair still clutching her in their grip. He returned with a sleeping Emma cradled limply in his arms. For an instant, her heart rate accelerated, until he placed the child in her arms and Casey saw the rise and fall of her chest.

She brushed a damp clump of hair away from Emma's face, buried her nose in her daughter's soft little neck, inhaled the incomparable aroma of baby powder and shampoo and sleeping baby. "Oh, my God," she said. "Oh, my God."

"A bad one?" he said.

"You don't want to know." As she rocked her beautiful, perfect, very much alive daughter, Casey said, "She's sleeping here with us tonight. I'm not letting her out of my sight."

Her husband knew better than to argue. He turned out the light and wrapped an arm around both of them. And with their sleeping daughter cradled between them, her breathing soft and even, they returned to a fitful, restless sleep.

* * *

"And then," she said, "your father woke me up."

"Jesus Christ," her stepdaughter said.

They were sitting on a bench in a small riverfront park in Lower Manhattan, not far from the World Trade Center. Nearby, a group of excited Japanese tourists grouped and regrouped for a series of photos set against a backdrop of New Jersey skyline. "Did you tell Dad what you just told me?" Paige asked.

"No." Beside them, clad in a pretty yellow sundress that matched her hair, Emma sat in her stroller, squinting into the sun as she contentedly watched a tugboat chug upriver. "I couldn't talk about it last night. All I could do was hold Emmy and try to stop shaking. And this morning, in the bright light of day, it all seemed so silly and ridiculous."

"Fear's never ridiculous."

"I suppose you're right, but I just didn't want to get into it with him."

"Dad left pretty early this morning."

"He had a busy day ahead of him. You take studio time when you can get it. That week he lost really screwed up his schedule. Now he's rushing to get the job done on time."

A man walking a white Pomeranian passed them. Leroy, napping on the bench beside Paige, lifted his head and growled low in his throat.

"Mind your manners," Paige told him, and he laid his head back down on his paws and returned to napping. Paige stretched out her long legs, so much like her father's, and said, "Is everything okay between you and Dad?"

"Of course," Casey said, surprised. "What makes you ask?"

"He's been so quiet. Ever since you lost the baby. The bounce is gone from his step."

"Really?" She turned her head and met Paige's eyes.

"You didn't notice? Things have been kind of weird."

She hadn't noticed, and guilt gnawed at her. How was it possible? How could she have been so wrapped up in her own pain that she hadn't noticed Rob was struggling? "Your father worries," she said. "He can't help it. It's built into him. And he's had a lot to worry about lately, thanks to me."

"Don't be so hard on yourself. It's not like you miscarried on purpose."

"No. But I allowed myself to get pregnant, knowing how risky it was. So who else can I blame but myself?"

"The last I knew, it took two people to make a baby. I'm no mathematician, but by my calculations, that means that at most, you're only responsible for fifty percent of the blame."

"You're a sweet girl to say that."

"I'm not sweet. I'm just brutally honest."

They began walking uptown, in no hurry on this beautiful summer day when neither of them had any place to be or anything important to do. Here, in Lower Manhattan, the sidewalks weren't as crowded as they were in Midtown. They passed block after block of office buildings and convenience stores and brownstone apartment buildings. Wandered the side streets, with no particular destination in mind, until she glanced at a cross street sign, recognized the name, and realized they'd wandered into the West Village, and they were two blocks away from Wong's. She wasn't sure what drew her, but the pull was strong, as strong as the undertow that had nearly drowned her in last night's dream. "Let's go this way," she said, and turned Emma's stroller into the crosswalk. "There's something I need to see."

As she approached the corner where she'd spent so many hours waiting for the bus to take her to Midtown and the Hotel Montpelier, her hands grew sweaty and her heart rate accelerated. They turned the corner, and there it was, the big red and yellow WONG'S TEA HOUSE sign still hanging from the side of the building.

"I can't believe it," she said, moving automatically in the direction of the building. "They're still in business." To what miracle should she attribute this mixed blessing? Casey paused across the street and stared at the restaurant, heedless of the fact that she was blocking the sidewalk with Emma's stroller. Beyond the red neon "open" sign in the window, she could see customers, heads bowed over noodle bowls. Out front, a burly young man was unloading produce from a yellow truck. He hoisted a case of cabbage onto a dolly, wheeled it down the ramp to the street, then wrestled the dolly up over the curb and began rolling it in the direction of the front door.

With a wild mix of emotions churning inside her, Casey took a deep breath and raised her gaze to the second floor. She wasn't sure what she'd expected, but the sky didn't fall. Lightning didn't strike her dead. She continued to breathe, without any fatal repercussions. The apartment windows were dirty and bare. No curtains. No sign of life. Had the housing authority finally shut Freddy down? Was he between tenants? Or had he rented to some crackhead who didn't give a damn about curtains or privacy or any of the niceties of life? Not that anybody who cared about the niceties of life was likely to rent from Freddy Wong.

"You're staring," Paige said. "Why?"

Casey wet her lips and said, "We used to live here."

"We?"

"Your father and Danny and I. This is where we lived. In the second-floor apartment over the restaurant."

"You lived in that dump?"

"We were poor."

"I'll say." Paige silently gazed at the building. Then eyed her and said, "Are you okay?"

Lost in the past, she dragged her gaze away from the building's façade. "I'm fine," she said. "Why?"

"You just turned as white as the Pillsbury Doughboy."

"I'm just remembering."

"Maybe we should get out of here. It's kind of creepy. Unless you want to get lunch."

"At Wong's?" she said with raised eyebrows.

Paige shrugged. "Whatever. I just figured it's lunchtime, and we're here. How bad can it be?"

"You don't even want to know. I spent two years living upstairs over that place, and I wouldn't eat at Wong's if you held a gun to my head."

Rob

THE recording session wasn't going well.

Phoenix had dragged in a half-hour late, trailed by Luther and arm in arm with a couple of the less unattractive female members of his posse. Not that any of them were particularly attractive; it was more a matter of levels of skankiness. His blue eyes, those eyes that famously made prepubescent girls swoon, were bloodshot. With his face as pale as a cod's belly, and his customarily flawless hair looking like he'd combed it with an egg beater, the kid smelled like a combination of alcohol and tawdry perfume.

Rob eyed him long and hard, gave Luther an inquisitive look, and raised his eyebrows. "Mere employee," Luther reminded him. "Not responsible for a certain person's behavior."

The kid extricated himself from the hold of the two girls and, his attitude clearly as sour as his breath, spat out, "Let's get on with this, then," and slammed through the door into the sound studio.

"You know," Rob said to Luther, "there was a time in my life, after my second divorce, when my two favorite activities were drinking and whoring. But I didn't do it at seventeen. And I never, ever did it when I had to work the next morning."

"Point taken," Luther said. "What might you suggest I do about it?"

"Where the hell are his parents?"

"His father's dead. His mum is…well, perhaps we shouldn't discuss his mum. And, as you know, he's soon to turn eighteen, which means that even if the woman cared—which she clearly doesn't—the lad would be out of her reach."

"Ah, yes. The eighteenth birthday bash. I haven't mentioned it to my wife yet. I'm afraid to."

"One could hardly blame you for that. If there was a way to avoid participating, that evening would find me sitting in my hotel room, with my feet up on an ottoman and a cup of tea in my hand."

"You and me both, buddy."

"I don't know what you two are yammering about," said a disembodied voice, "but the sooner we get started, the sooner I can get back to the hotel and take something for this hangover." On the other side of the window, Phoenix stood with arms crossed, a scowl on his face.

"Sorry," Rob said into the mic. "You all set with your lyrics?"

Through dark glasses he hadn't bothered to remove, the kid stared blankly at him. "You take care of your little piece of this venture," he said, "and I'll take care of mine. It should work out nicely."

Since he wasn't sure how to respond to that comment, he chose to ignore it.

Nine takes later, Rob pulled off his headset and said, "Maybe we need a break."

"Don't need no break, mate. I've got this."

"You flubbed the lyrics nine times, Phoenix. Maybe you need to sit down and take another look at the sheet music."

"My mouth's as dry as the Sahara. What I need is a drink."

"There are vending machines just down the hall."

Phoenix took off his headset and trudged back through the control room and out the door. The two interchangeable groupies eyed each other, shrugged, and went back to contemplating their navels. Luther looked up from the *Wall Street Journal*, met Rob's eyes, and raised an eyebrow.

"I'll go," Rob said.

He followed the narrow hallway to an alcove that held vending machines and a couple of folding chairs, arrived in time to see Phoenix pop the top on a Dr Pepper and upend the can. The kid swilled half of it, his Adam's apple bobbing as he swallowed, before he stopped, belched, and wiped his mouth on his sleeve.

And saw Rob standing there. "What?" he said.

Rob moved loosely to one of the vending machines, dropped in a handful of quarters, and pushed a button. His drink fell with a muffled thud. He took it from the machine, popped the top, and was rewarded with a satisfying fizz. "You know," he said, studying the bright red can in his hand, "I'm not the enemy. We're on the same side here." He took a long slug of Coke and added, "We both want this album to be the best it can possibly be."

Phoenix eyed him. Said, "Right," and went back to his soda.

Rob perched on the edge of a metal folding chair. Stretched out his legs and crossed his ankles. "Okay," he said. "*I* want this album to be the best it can possibly be. And you should, if not for creative reasons, then at least because it puts food on your table."

"Don't pretend to be something you're not. It puts food on your table, as well."

"I'm not pretending a goddamn thing. There's not a hypocritical bone in my body. But the future of my career doesn't depend on this record, Phee. And I'm not in any danger of running out of money."

"So you think I am? And don't call me Phee."

"Just a word of caution, my friend. You may have a nice, fat bank account balance right now, but that money disappears damn fast, especially if you spend it on the wrong things. If your career's down the toilet when it disappears, think of how screwed you'll be."

"What makes you think I spend it on the wrong bloody things? What do you spend your money on?"

Groceries. Diapers. Heating oil for a ten-room house, in Maine, in the winter. Sheep. *Goddamn sheep.*

"Nothing extravagant. That's not the way we live. We're not pretentious people. My daughter goes to public school. I drive a Ford Explorer. My wife drives a Volvo, mostly because it's a tank, and I want to feel that my family's safe on those icy Maine roads. Nice car, and not inexpensive, but still modest compared to, say, a Ferrari. Or a Lamborghini. Or a Rolls-Royce." All of which, Luther had informed him, were among the kid's recent purchases.

"Don't be a judgmental ass. I have a perfect right to spend my money any way I choose."

"That you do, my friend. And if you take care of them, those cars will appreciate in value. I understand your love of nice cars. I drove a Porsche for years. There's nothing like the open road ahead, the top down, the wind in your hair—"

"A pretty bird tucked under your arm."

It occurred to him then that he wasn't really all that different from Phoenix. For a time, he'd had the fast car and the fast women, the booze, the parties. He halfheartedly tried to convince himself that his taste in women had been a little classier than Phee's. But he was too honest to believe his own bullshit. For a time, he'd lost his way, and he'd been quite indiscriminate about who he slept with.

Until that fateful morning when he'd waltzed through the front door of Casey's Malibu house, in search of breakfast. Casey had taken a single look, a single sniff, and slammed the door behind him.

If you think you're coming to my house looking for a handout, she'd said, *after rolling out of some skank's bed, looking like yesterday's garbage and smelling like a whorehouse, then you have another think coming, my friend.*

And she'd proceeded to ream him a new asshole.

Danny, being nobody's fool, had grabbed his car keys and his daughter, suddenly remembering an urgent errand he had in town. And he'd left them there to duke it out. The neighbors probably heard the screaming all the way to Sacramento. When it was over, she tossed him out on his ass, minus his breakfast, minus his dignity, minus his outer layer of skin.

"You can come back," she said, "when you clean up your act."

She'd probably saved his life. He'd been headed down a bad, dangerous road, a road not so very different from the one he saw Phoenix traveling now. His devastation had been total; there was nobody whose regard was more important to him than Casey Fiore, and he couldn't imagine anything worse than being cut out of her life. He spent a couple of weeks licking his wounds, and then, infinitely smarter, he pulled himself up by the bootstraps and put his wrecked life back together.

Tough love. Sometimes, it was the only way you could save someone from himself.

"You're right," he told the kid. "I don't have any right to judge. But I can tell you from experience that you should be careful. Think before you jump, because if you land the wrong way, the only one you'll hurt—if you're lucky, that is—is yourself."

Phoenix didn't bother holding back his yawn. "Are we finished with today's morality lesson?" he said. "Because if we are, we might consider getting back to recording. But don't let me stop you if you've more to say. I find it quite entertaining."

At that point, he gave up. The kid was a lost cause. It wasn't up to him to try to save the obnoxious brat. If Phoenix Hightower was determined to tank his career and his life, that was his business. It wasn't Rob's responsibility to give a damn, just because nobody else did.

It irritated the hell out of him that he did give a damn.

This time around, on the tenth take, the kid finally got through the entire song without making mincemeat out of the lyrics. Rob and Kyle exchanged high fives as the song wound to a close. The vocals sounded as good upon playback as they had originally. The kid actually had a strong voice. He was no Danny Fiore, but he could sing. And he was young enough so that, even hung over, his vocal ability wasn't affected. Give him decade or two, and he'd find recording after a night of debauchery to be a little more of a challenge.

"Great job," Rob said. "Now, I'd like to try something different."

"I can barely contain my enthusiasm."

"Shut up and listen to me. I want to record you singing some background vocals that we can overdub. You singing over yourself. Sort of an echo, when you reach the chorus. At the part where it says 'for you' I want you to harmonize with yourself. 'For you, for you, for you.'"

The kid looked at him blankly, still wearing the sunglasses. "Oh, joy," he said.

"As a matter of fact—" The wheels in his head began spinning at breakneck speed. "I think we could overdub you harmonizing all the way through. Give the damn thing a little meat. Because right now, it's not much more than cotton candy."

"I have no bloody idea what you're talking about."

Irritation warred with enthusiasm. This would really make a difference, add a little richness, a little quality, to what amounted to nothing more than another forgettable pop song, indistinguishable from all the other forgettable pop songs the kids danced to.

Enthusiasm won. "I'll show you," he said. "Trade places with me."

So they traded places, and while Phoenix sat silently in the producer's chair, arms crossed and a bored expression on his face, Kyle ran the track and Rob sang the harmonies that had originated inside his head. When they were done, Kyle played back the recording. "See?" Rob said. "See what a difference it makes? Before, it was bland and colorless. Now it pops."

On the other side of the window, Phoenix stared at him blankly through those irritating sunglasses. And then he took them off and hung them from the neck of his tee shirt. The kid leaned and said into the mic, "You're a better flippin' singer than I am, MacKenzie. What in bloody hell are you doing producing for me when you should be making your own records?"

Rob blinked, opened his mouth to respond. Then closed it when he realized he had no idea how to answer.

Because he realized, for the first time ever, that it was a damn good question.

Casey

THAT night, as they were preparing for bed, she said to Rob, "You won't believe this. We were walking around the Village today. Did you know that Wong's is still in business?"

Through a mouthful of toothpaste, he said, "I didn't know that." He spat into the sink, rinsed his mouth, spat again. Swiping at his face with a towel, he added, "And I could've died a happy man without ever knowing."

He stepped away from the sink and she took his place. Uncapping the toothpaste, she said, "Paige was ready to eat there."

"Jesus Christ on a popsicle stick. I hope to God you said no."

"Of course I said no. I've long since lost my taste for cockroach-flavored eggrolls."

She finished brushing her teeth, put her brush and the toothpaste away, washed her face, and followed him into the bedroom. When they were situated under the covers, she laid her head on his shoulder and said, "Paige is worried about you."

"Oh?"

"She told me today that since I lost the baby, you've lost your bounce."

"Paige said that?"

"She did. I know she doesn't always show it, but she loves you."

"Ah, hell. It's not just the baby. That's a big part of it, but this job is getting to me. Working with Phoenix gives me stress on top of stress. I'm usually such a laid-back guy." He absently stroked her bare shoulder with his thumb. "Remind me not to ever again take on an outside job, no matter how hard they beg."

"You'll be finished soon, won't you?"

"I can only hope. We hit some snags in the last few days, and it only put us further behind. The minute we're done recording, I'm out of here. I plan to find a good sound engineer, somebody who's a whiz at mixing, make the guy an offer he can't refuse, and finish this puppy in my home studio."

She closed her eyes and drifted.

"I still have to connect with Kitty," he said. "We've been playing phone tag for the last week."

Casey opened her eyes again. Said, "Why does that woman's name irk me so much?"

"I have no idea. You've peacefully coexisted with her for fifteen years, and never once during that time did you snap like a pit bull. Now, every time I mention her name, I can see the hackles rise on the back of your neck."

"You should be grateful that I care enough to be jealous."

"I love you, too, babe. But I think you're going overboard. Kitty's no threat to you."

"Says you."

In the silence, the bedside clock ticked once. Twice. "That's not the only place you're going overboard," he said.

Stunned, she opened her mouth to respond. Closed it. Finally said, "Maybe you'd like to clarify that statement."

"Look, I'm not trying to criticize, or tell you what to do. But…all that stuff you bought for Emma. Don't you think it's just a bit of overkill?"

"Overkill?" She sat up, turned on the bedside lamp, and stared at him.

He squinted in the sudden brightness. "You bought the kid two dozen dresses, Fiore. *Two dozen*. That's twenty-four dresses—"

"I know how many two dozen is!"

"The way she's growing, she'll outgrow half of them before she gets a chance to wear the damn things."

"What difference does it make how many dresses I buy for our daughter? It's my money I'm spending. And it's certainly not as though I'm breaking the bank. Why should it matter to you?"

"*Jesus, Mary and Joseph*. It's not the damned money. You know better than that. Between the two of us, we have more money than God. That's not the issue. The issue is that you seem a little…out of control. And it worries me."

"I don't see it."

"That's what worries me. And don't look at me like that. Don't be offended. This isn't criticism. This is—"

"It certainly looks like criticism to me!"

"—concern. Nothing else."

"Let me live my own life, MacKenzie. Don't try to hogtie me, because it'll backfire on you, and I promise you'll regret it."

"So now, you're pissed."

"Of course I am. You're insulting, and I don't appreciate it!"

"Fine. You want to be mad, you be mad. But since you're already mad, we might as well get into it, right here, right now. One, you bought the kid more dresses than she can wear in a month. Two, you're having nightmares so bad you won't even talk to me about 'em. Three, you're crying over nothing. Four, you went apeshit when I told you I'd allowed Paige to take Emmy to the movies. Five, you were hanging around outside Wong's. What the HELL were you doing in that neighborhood? Six—" He paused, took a breath. "Should I go on?"

Her skin felt as if it were stretched too tightly over her face. Had her staunchest supporter abdicated? Had he somehow turned on her? A wave of despair washed over her, and she drew the blankets more tightly around her to ward off the sudden chill. "Because I don't want to say something I'll regret later," she said, "I'm going to pretend I never heard that remark."

And she switched off the light, turned her back toward her husband, and pulled the pillow over her head.

* * *

In the morning, he was gone before she woke, gone without a kiss, without a note, without giving her time to process last night's squabble. He'd taken Paige with him. His daughter loved hanging around the studio, and Rob never had to ask twice. There was no sign of breakfast. No frying pan on the stove, no dirty plates in the sink. They must have eaten out before heading to the studio.

By the time she'd showered and dressed, Emma was stirring. Her daughter's face lit up the instant she walked into the room. "Good morning, baby girl," she said. "How's my Emmy today?"

Emma stood in her crib, her chubby little hands clasped tightly to the rail, bouncing up and down with eager enthusiasm. "Mum mum mum mum," she said, her second favorite word, right behind "no." A pink crease from sleeping on wrinkled bedding marched across her left cheek. Her stretchy yellow sleeper, splashed with red and brown teddy bears, was damp and aromatic. Her little arms came up into the air, and Casey scooped her up and buried her face in Emma's belly.

Emma's peal of laughter melted her heart. "Ew, stinky," she said. "Let's get that diaper changed, poopy-girl, and then we'll have breakfast."

"Da."

Emma kicked and squirmed and wiggled while she changed the smelly diaper, cleaned and powdered her daughter's sweet little bum. Then she carried the baby to the kitchen, where she scrubbed both their hands thoroughly before she strapped Emma in her high chair.

Today was a good day. She didn't have a lot of those, so she shoved her tangled thoughts aside and focused on her time with Emma, on the delight her daughter's facial expressions brought her, on the fun of watching Emma's intrepid attempt to pick up Cheerios with her sticky little fingers. Childhood moved so rapidly, and every day brought new changes. She couldn't afford to miss any of those days, because they were building memories that would last a lifetime. Especially if Emma turned out to be her only child, she needed to cherish those memories, hang onto them with every ounce of her strength.

But last night's quarrel with Rob had left a sour taste in her mouth. They'd always quarreled, often good-naturedly, sometimes vehemently. This was different. This was their own personal Tower of Babel. They were at opposite poles and speaking different languages, and simply couldn't get through to each other.

Yet she wanted to get through to him. Wanted desperately to make things right, to take their relationship back to where it was before the miscarriage. From the beginning, things had been so good between them. Maybe too good. After her long, troubled marriage to Danny Fiore, she'd been so giddy with love, so overwhelmed by her discovery that Rob MacKenzie was the man she'd been meant to spend her life with, that she'd been blind to the reality of how to keep a good marriage on track. Maybe on some level she'd believed that once you found your soul mate, everything just fell into place, and there'd be no work involved.

If so, she'd been utterly wrong. Like a growing flower bed, marriage, even a good, solid marriage, took a great deal of work to maintain. It had to be fed and watered, pampered and pruned and given just the right amount of sunlight or it would wither and die right there on the vine.

The thought struck terror into her heart. If she lost Rob, she wasn't sure she'd be able to go on. All marriages went through rough spells. Sometimes they ended. It was a fact of life. But their marriage was supposed to be different, immune to the slings and arrows of everyday life. Their relationship was special, wasn't it? She'd always believed it was, believed they had something that other couples lacked. Rob MacKenzie was so much more to her than just a husband. He was air and water and sunlight. And, like a delicate flower, without him she would perish.

She had to make more of an effort. She had to snap out of this craziness, and start living a normal life again.

But she didn't feel normal. She felt so far from normal that she couldn't locate the place on a map. If only she could find a way to unburden herself, to make the overwhelming sadness dissipate. But every time she had a good day, every time she thought she'd tamed the monster, every time she let down her guard, the melancholy would return, like a heavy, wet, woolen blanket, all scratchy and smelly and miserable. She needed to make Rob understand what she was going through, but how could she, when she couldn't understand it herself?

While Emma banged her plastic spoon against the tray of her high chair, Casey picked up her cell phone and called her husband. He didn't answer right away, and she wondered if he was busy, or possibly avoiding her. "Hi," he said cautiously after the fourth ring.

"Hi," she said.

"What's up?"

"I didn't like the way we left things last night. And this morning, you were gone when I woke up."

"I can't really talk right now."

Emma banged her spoon and sang tunelessly. Casey's fingers tightened on the phone. "You're mad at me."

"No, no. I'm just…there are people here."

"People. Not the usual people?"

"Correct."

"Record execs?"

"Also correct."

She let out a breath. "Then I'll make this brief. I'm sorry about last night."

"Me, too."

"I know this—whatever it is—has been hard on you. I don't mean for it to be."

"I realize that."

"So we're okay?"

"Absolutely. Talk later?"

"Talk later. Love you."

"Ditto. Always."

She felt marginally better, although things still seemed a little stilted between them. Her behavior had been odd lately, no question about it. On the other hand, three years ago he'd stood before her in a white tux and a red cummerbund, held her hand in his, and promised to cherish her until one or both of them was dead. There should be a little wiggle room, shouldn't there? A little play in the steering wheel? A little tolerance for oddball behavior?

As she washed the breakfast dishes, bathed and dressed Emma, and vacuumed the living room carpet, her mind kept drifting back to yesterday, when she and Paige had stumbled upon Wong's Tea House. She'd been thinking about that moment ever since. Last night, she'd spent hours lying awake, alternately stewing over the squabble with Rob and obsessing over the empty apartment above that smelly Chinese restaurant. She couldn't explain why she was so drawn to it. Her life there had been somewhat less than charmed. It was a past she thought she'd come to terms with, yet her instincts were telling her that her old life, and her old apartment, held the key that would unlock the craziness inside her.

"Come on, Emmy," she said. "Let's go for a nice walk in the sun."

So she packed her daughter in her stroller, took spare diapers and a sippy cup and a bottle of water, and headed out. The streets were crowded; the subway was worse. All those sticky, sweaty bodies crammed together like crayons in a box. Alone with Emmy, she fought her aversion to the crowds, maneuvered the stroller on and off the train like a pro, and emerged back into the sunshine. After the damp, airless heat of the subway, where people were squeezed together so close she thought she might faint, the Village felt airy and open. Gripping the stroller tightly, she headed at a rapid clip toward her old neighborhood.

Rob wouldn't approve. She knew this without being told. Rob was not the kind of person to wallow in the past. Neither was she. It was one of the things that made them so compatible, this similar outlook on life. They both believed in making lemonade out of lemons. It was pointless to waste time sitting around feeling sorry for yourself when there was work to be done, when the only acceptable way out of a dilemma was to choose a new path—even if you had to go the *eeny-meeny-miney-mo* route—and follow it.

So why was she drawn back to a time and place in her life that had been so difficult in so many ways? A time when she'd endured so many body blows, it was a miracle she'd survived?

If there was an answer to that question, it was locked inside her, and the key, she felt certain, lay somewhere on that short block of mixed commercial and residential real estate in the West Village where she'd spent her early twenties.

New York, in the late Seventies, had been an exhilarating place. As musicians, they'd lived and breathed the local music scene, which was eclectic and exciting, and ran the gamut from folk to rock, from disco to punk. CBGB's and Max's Kansas City were the hot spots, where bands like the Ramones, the Talking Heads, Blondie, and Patti Smith played. It had been an amazing time for anyone who loved music, even more so for those who wrote and played it. Although she'd never been into partying, she'd spent a fair amount of time in the clubs, hearing bands both new and old, famous and obscure. And although she was married to Danny, she did most of her clubbing with Rob. They were, after all, musical collaborators and partners. Times were hard; the three of them had lived from paycheck to paycheck, barely making ends meet. But the music fed them in a way that money never could. They lapped it up, like kittens with a saucer of warm cream, and the music they absorbed in those salad days of the late Seventies heavily influenced the music that expanded and exploded their careers throughout the Eighties.

Times were different then. The travesty that was the war in Vietnam still hung, a dark shadow, over the nation like a bad dream. The anti-war protests were over, but the effects of the war were long reaching. Returning soldiers, instead of receiving a hero's welcome, had been treated like pariahs. Many of them were scarred for life. She knew this intimately, because she'd married one of them. Danny had been broken inside. He'd left a piece of himself behind in the jungles of Vietnam, and he'd gone to his grave still missing that crucial piece.

And New York itself was different then. The West Village had been a little darker, a little edgier, in those days before gentrification took over, pushing out all but the wealthiest of residents—or those with rent-controlled apartments. Drugs, prostitution, and crime had been, if not rampant, at least more visible. She barely recognized the neighborhood these days, with its new restaurants and bars on every corner, its expanded green space, the older buildings that had been rehabbed.

Except, of course, for Freddy Wong's building. Freddy was a likable guy. Personable, always smiling. He was also colossally tightfisted. The kind of man her parents had always referred to as a skinflint. Freddy himself would undoubtedly call it being frugal, but in truth, he was a miser to his core, a man who'd never spent a penny he could find an excuse to hold onto.

Shabby was too kind a word for the building. It looked tired and depressed. The big red and yellow sign that hung over the restaurant entrance was cracked and faded, the plate-glass window at the front streaked and smeared with decades of city dirt and auto exhaust. The second-story windows still sat blank and expressionless, like a face with no eyebrows. She was certain the apartment was empty. And she knew Freddy still owned the place, because she'd looked up the number in the yellow pages, called it, and asked for him. She'd hung up before he answered, because what was she supposed to say to him over the phone? He might not even remember her. Much easier to show up in person. He'd always liked her. Chances were good that in person, she could sweet-talk him into giving her the key and letting her inside.

She stood there, uncertainty gluing her to the sidewalk, while in her stroller, Emma babbled contentedly. Her heart fluttered, and her pulse gave a little skip. Was she sure she was ready for this? It was a step she couldn't undo. Like a sight that couldn't be unseen, or words that couldn't be unspoken, taking a step back into her past couldn't be untaken.

Casey inhaled a deep breath to steady herself, steeled herself and, hands tightly gripping her daughter's stroller, she wrestled it off the curb and stepped into the street.

And her cell phone rang.

She stopped, pulled it from her purse and looked at it. Recognizing the number, she debated whether or not to answer. If she told him where she was, she would never hear the end of it. If she lied, he'd know. He always knew when she was lying.

The phone continue to ring. Muttering under her breath, she wrenched Emma's stroller back up onto the sidewalk and answered the phone. "Hey," she said, sounding a little breathless to her own ears.

"Hey. I'm sorry I sounded like I was in the middle of some top-secret CIA operation when you called. I had a couple of bigwig record execs here, checking on the progress of their wonder boy."

"And were they impressed with his progress?"

"Impressed enough to take him to lunch."

Mildly outraged, she said, "Without you? His producer?"

"I'm not somebody they have to wine and dine. He's the goose that laid the golden egg. I'm nothing more than hired help."

"They have expense accounts. And you're certainly more than hired help. You're the one responsible for his progress. I would be highly insulted if I were you."

"I don't care enough to be insulted. Besides, it means I have a couple hours free to have lunch with my gorgeous wife. And that trumps insulted any day."

Still holding the phone, she raised her eyes to the apartment across the street. Those blank windows, that browless face, seemed to mock her. A sudden gust of wind blew a strand of hair into her face, and she reached up and shoved it behind her ear. She'd already disappointed him once recently, when she'd taken the girls to Coney Island; she didn't have the heart to do it again. Not even if it meant her trip down memory lane would have to be postponed.

"Babe?" he said.

"Sorry. I got sidetracked. I'm a little out of the way right now, but Emmy and I can catch a cab and meet you somewhere."

"How about the Hard Rock Cafe? Paige has never been, and she's itching to check it out."

"A little touristy, and there'll probably be a wait, but I suppose there's a certain coolness factor involved for a teenager. She can go home and tell her friends she ate there."

"That's what I figured. You game?"

"I'm game. I'll flag down a cab, and we'll meet you there. Snag a table, because you'll almost certainly get there ahead of me."

She ended the call, took a last, long look at the apartment windows. This probably wasn't the right time, anyway. How was she supposed to maneuver the stroller up those stairs? If she left it on the street, somebody might steal it. And who knew how sanitary the building was? When she'd lived here, the place had been overrun with cockroaches. No matter how much she cleaned and sprayed, the roaches had considered themselves the tenants of note, while she and Rob and Danny had been nothing more than squatters. Once or twice a year, Freddy had paid for an exterminator. The rest of the time, she was on her own. If the place had been sitting empty for any length of time, she didn't want to think about what might be in there, and she didn't want to expose Emma to anything dirty or toxic. Better that she should come alone, another time, when Rob was at work and Paige could stay with Emma and nobody would question her whereabouts.

But she'd so wanted to get in today, had emotionally prepared herself for whatever demons she was about to face. Now, she'd have to prepare herself again. Although this had been a spur-of-the-moment decision, she'd known, somewhere inside her, that she would do this. She'd known it ever since she rounded that corner with Paige and saw that Wong's was still here, still in business.

And she'd been ready to do it now.

But there would be other chances, times that were more appropriate. Today, she would have lunch with her husband. Priorities were priorities, and Rob came first. Their relationship was a little rocky right now. She needed to find a way to mend it, needed to slap some good, strong mortar on the chinks between the bricks.

So she wheeled the stroller between two parked cars and flagged down a cab. As she settled herself and Emma into the back seat, she took a few calming breaths and arranged her face in a serene expression. There was no point in making Rob suspicious. This wasn't something she could talk about with him. He wouldn't understand, and she wasn't up to being badgered. She needed to face her demons alone. Later on down the road, when things were better between them, she would share it with him.

But not now. Not today. Today, she would wear her game face, interact with her husband, and tell herself that disappointment wasn't a heavy weight in her chest.

* * *

She made it through lunch without any bloodletting. The music was loud, the atmosphere playful and friendly, the food acceptable. Paige dropped her customary "Been there, done that" attitude long enough to enjoy the novelty, Emma gnawed happily on her sister's French fries, and Rob only studied her quizzically once or twice. When he asked where she'd been when he called, she flashed him a rueful smile and said, "We were headed to the World Trade Center. But we can always do it another day."

He arched his eyebrows, but didn't question her further. She wanted to exhale a sigh of relief, but knew it was far too soon to be relieved. Rob had this uncanny ability to see right through her, and if he suspected she was lying to him, he would never confront her in the presence of the girls. He'd wait until they were alone, and then, operating under the well-intentioned belief that it was for her own good, he'd badger her until she caved. It was the way he operated. She adored him, but had to admit that sometimes he was a little overprotective. He'd been that way with her for as long as she'd known him. A time or two, it had saved her from disaster. More often, it made her crazy. Normally, she had no trouble handling him. Underneath the tough-love exterior, the man was a marshmallow. There was a sweetness to him that shone through in his eyes, his smile. Yes, he had a temper, but it generally surfaced only when something, or someone, hurt somebody he loved. Or when she was doing something so incredibly stupid that she was in danger of hurting herself. How could you argue with a man like that?

Still, it was a relief when the meal was over and she was no longer under his eagle-eyed scrutiny. She kissed him goodbye, then killed a little time with the girls in the gift shop. Paige picked out a classic white Hard Rock Cafe New York tee, and Casey chose a tiny pink and white My First Hard Rock Cafe tee for Emma.

And they hit the street.

At midsummer, the height of tourist season, the streets swarmed with people carrying expensive cameras and gawking at the tall buildings. She hadn't seen this much polyester since the disco era. After leaving the air-conditioned coolness of the Hard Rock, she found the humidity stifling. It flattened her hair and left Emma fussy. She'd lived through heat waves in New York, and compared to some she remembered, this was pretty tame. But the humidity added to the discomfort she already felt in the midst of all these people. The locals, always in a hurry, shoved past without so much as an "excuse me," while tourists stood in colorful clusters and blocked the sidewalks.

Her grip firm on the stroller and Paige at her elbow, Casey moved steadily in the direction of Times Square. Her long-legged husband, who could cover twelve city blocks in the blink of an eye, was undoubtedly already back at work. While she, vertically challenged and pushing a heavy baby stroller, would take much longer to cover that kind of territory.

Her senses on hyper-alert, she moved with the crowd, gradually becoming aware of the child half a block ahead. Five years old. Hair the color of honey that fell in soft waves to her waist. Pink sneakers, pink shorts, a yellow tee shirt. A walk she would recognize anywhere, a chubby little hand that held tightly to the woman walking by her side.

Katie.

The buzzing began in her ears, spread to her extremities. It was impossible. The rational side of her knew that her daughter had been dead for eight years, that even if Katie were still alive, she would be a teenager now. But her heart refused to accept the truth, refuting the evidence she'd seen with her own eyes. *BELOVED DAUGHTER. Katie.*

Katie, Katie, Katie.

"Stay with Emma," she said to Paige, and took off down the sidewalk at a brisk pace, winding in and out between people, losing sight of the girl, searching frantically, finding her again. She knew the child wasn't Katie, couldn't be Katie, but still, she had to be sure. Had to see with her own eyes. She reached the end of the block. The light changed, and she raced across the intersection, brakes squawking and horns blaring as she danced in and out of traffic, breathing hard, her lungs aching from the thick, soupy air.

Mere feet away, she reached out a hand to grab the child by the shoulder. The little girl, perhaps sensing her presence, turned around and smiled at her.

Brown eyes. Narrow cheekbones. Pretty smile.

She looked nothing like Katie.

Casey stopped dead, hand still stretched out, grasping emptiness. The mother turned, met her eyes, and undoubtedly saw the crazy there, for she yanked her daughter's arm and herded her away from the lunatic who'd tried to snatch her away on a busy Manhattan sidewalk in the broad light of day. She turned back once, scowled, and disappeared into the crowd.

Her heart hammering, Casey stood, her chest aching from her mad dash, adrenalin racing through her veins as she slammed up against a hard wall of Truth: Katie wasn't coming back.

Ever.

The gaping hole inside her widened. Teetering at the edge of it, her arms crossed and her eyes filling with tears, she wondered, frantically, whether she was losing her mind.

Behind her, Paige said, "What in bloody hell was that about?"

"Shut up," she said, without turning around. Then added, "Please."

"Maybe you need to—"

She swiped furiously at a tear. Spun around to face her stepdaughter and said, "This never happened. Do you understand? Your father is not to hear about this."

"But I think—"

"I don't care what you think. Do you hear me, Paige? He can't know about this." Suddenly depleted, she stumbled to a nearby granite stoop, sank onto it, and buried her face in her hands.

While she struggled to regain control, her stepdaughter sat quietly beside her and awkwardly patted her back. In an attempt to slow her galloping pulse, Casey practiced the breathing exercises she'd been taught in Lamaze class. Gradually, she began to return to herself. Paige took Emma from the stroller, kissed the top of her fuzzy blond head, and placed her in her mother's arms. "This," she said, with a wisdom far beyond her years, "this is what matters. The only thing that matters."

A tear escaped from the corner of Casey's eye. She thumbed it away, nodded, and took a deep breath. Her baby daughter cradled to her chest, she rocked back and forth, her cheek resting against Emma's soft head. "You okay now, chief?" Paige said.

"Better. Not quite over it, but better." Over Emmy's duck-fuzz hair, she smiled at her stepdaughter. It was a wispy smile, but sincere. "Thank you," she said.

"We're family," Paige said. "Family takes care of family."

* * *

"So he said to me—" Rob's black-lacquered chopsticks hovered over her plate, and he took his time selecting the choicest bite of shrimp. "He told me, 'I suppose that back in your day, it was different. But nowadays, if it doesn't have a good dance beat, we don't call it music.'"

Merriment danced in his eyes. A swirl of evening breeze, disappearing as quickly as it had come, tossed a strand of dark hair into her face. She shook it back over her shoulder and propped her chin on her hand. "Cocky little SOB," she said.

"Oh, he's not so bad. He's actually starting to grow on me."

Above their heads, twinkle lights dangled from the wooden ribs of a huge red umbrella. "This is why I love New York," he said. "Try doing this at nine-thirty at night in Jackson Falls."

"Try doing anything at nine-thirty at night in Jackson Falls." She took a bite of his subgum rice and said, "I still don't understand why you put up with it. It's appalling, the way he treats you, like you're something he'd scrape off the bottom of his shoe."

He reached for another shrimp, and Casey pushed her plate across the table to him. "They're paying me *beaucoup* bucks to babysit," he said.

"And you care less about money than anyone else I know."

"But there's the entertainment value, and you can't put a price on that." He leaned back in his wrought-iron chair and rested a bony ankle on his knee. "He's desperate to one-up me. But, you see, I'm not desperate. There's a certain satisfaction in watching him flit around my head like an annoying little gnat. Sure, he's a pain in the ass. But he's not mature enough to understand that just by engaging in those behaviors, he's already lost the battle."

"If I live to be a hundred, MacKenzie, I don't think I'll ever completely understand you."

He waggled his eyebrows. "Gotta keep the mystery alive."

She coughed, picked up her napkin and covered her mouth while she choked on a mouthful of food.

"Fiore?" he said. "Please don't choke to death. I never did learn the Heimlich maneuver."

"I'm sure...somebody in this place...did."

He briefly surveyed the other diners and said, "This is New York. If you were sprawled out dead on the sidewalk, they'd just step over you."

She dabbed at her mouth, her eyes, and said, "You're probably right."

"I know I'm right." He reached into the pocket of his jacket, pulled out a small box wrapped in paper covered with bright red balloons and finished off with a sparkly red ribbon. "Happy anniversary," he said.

His face taut with anticipation, he watched her reach into her purse and pull out a starched white envelope. She set it on the table and said, "Happy anniversary."

Rob picked up his beer, took a long, slow sip. Set the bottle back down and said, "You first."

She took the box in her hands. Shook it, sniffed it, flipped it. A small box usually meant jewelry and, although she wasn't a woman who coveted baubles, Rob MacKenzie was a wizard at choosing pieces she found immensely appealing.

"Open it," he ordered, and she gave him a saucy smile before slowly, meticulously untying the bow. While he waited, feet dancing restlessly beneath the table, she set aside the ribbon and carefully unwrapped the package.

Inside the box she found another, smaller box. A jeweler's box. Casey glanced at him, and he nodded encouragement. She opened the hinged lid. Inside, on a bed of burgundy velvet, sat the most beautiful ring she'd ever seen. A single, oval-cut emerald, polished to a shine, nestled in a setting of delicate gold filigree. The gold wore the patina of age. "Oh, babe," she said, "it's beautiful. And an antique." New jewelry didn't wear the burnished dignity of this piece. "Where'd you get it?"

"It belonged to my great-grandmother. It's a family heirloom."

Her eyes questioned him. "I asked Mom for it when we got married," he said. "Take it as a token of her esteem, the fact that she'd be willing to part with it for you."

"I really shouldn't—"

"Of course you should. You're my wife. It's been passed down through the family, and you have every bit as much right to it as any other family member." He took her fingers in his. "I had it cleaned and sized. I originally intended to give it to you as a wedding present, but I decided to wait. So Mom's been holding it for me until I thought the moment was right. You planning to put it on, or just sit and look at it?"

He had a way about him, had always had a way about him, that could banish any dark clouds surrounding her and allow the sun to pour through. Casey took the ring from the box, slipped it on her right ring finger, held up her hand and admired it. "I wish I'd known your great-grandmother," she said.

He picked up his napkin, leaned over the table, and dabbed a tear away from the corner of her eye. "I don't remember much about her," he said. "She died when I was six. But if you believe the stories, she was quite the feisty old broad. I think you'd get along. You like?"

"I like. Your turn."

He picked up the envelope from the center of the table, ran a finger under the flap, tore open the seal. Pulled out the airline tickets and squinted as he read them. "Nassau," he said.

"A week. In February. By that time, we should be good and tired of winter."

He fingered the brochure that was tucked into the envelope with the tickets. "This is the same place—"

"You took me to back in '87. I made the reservations a couple of months ago."

They both understood, both pretended they didn't understand, the significance of that time frame. Two months ago. Before the miscarriage. Before she started losing her mind.

"First time I kissed you," he said, redirecting the conversation back to the topic at hand.

She picked up the ball and ran with it. "You did more than kiss me, MacKenzie. You were randy, impertinent, and wildly inappropriate."

"And you, my gorgeous sexy woman, loved every minute of it."

"I did. But the timing was terrible."

"It was. And yet, here we are."

"Yes," she said softly. She picked up his hand, brought it to her mouth, and kissed the knuckles. "Here we are."

They finished dinner. Before continuing with the plans he'd made for the rest of the evening, she insisted on finding a pay phone and calling the girls. Just to check in, to soothe her maternal anxiety.

"We're doing great," Paige told her. "We're just sitting around, getting stoned with my drug dealer while we watch *The Shining*. Since I didn't have any cash on me, Vito agreed to take Emmy into white slavery as payment for the drugs. He promises to take really good care of her."

"Not. Even. Remotely. Funny." Casey rolled her eyes and handed Rob the phone. "Here," she said. "You talk to her. If I ever had any question in my mind that Paige is your daughter, she just removed all doubt. She is clearly your kid."

Rob took the phone, raised his eyebrows. "Okay," he said into the receiver, "what did you say to my wife?" He listened, smirked, caught Casey's eye and quickly rearranged his face into an expression of extreme gravity. "Uh huh. Okay. Yeah, put her on...hey there, Miss Emmy Lou Who! Are you having fun with Sissy? You are? Love you, baby. Hold on, here's Mom."

She took the phone from him and said, "Hi, precious. Is Sissy taking good care of you?"

"Da."

"You be a good girl, now, okay? Mom will see you in the morning. Big kiss?" She and Emma both made kissing sounds. "Love you," she said, and then Paige was back. "Don't keep her up too late," Casey said. "It's already past nine-thirty. She'll be cranky tomorrow."

"Yeah, we're about to hit the sack. There's nothing decent to watch on TV anyway. Have fun. Don't do anything I wouldn't do."

Enveloped in light and color and sound, she and Rob walked the streets of Manhattan hand in hand. Times Square was an amusement park, a Disneyland for adults. Fingers linked with his, she squeezed between clots of people blocking the sidewalks:

groups of teenage girls talking trash; wide-eyed tourists carrying maps and pointing. Snippets of conversation, in a variety of languages, drifted on the night air. French, Italian, Japanese. They passed a record store that was blasting Springsteen's *Tenth Avenue Freeze-Out* onto the street. Above their heads, in a cornucopia of color and motion, lights twinkled and dazzled, touting products, promoting Broadway shows, scrolling the latest news headlines.

Rob was a calming presence, his touch keeping the anxiety at bay. That feeling of claustrophobia, that otherworldliness she'd been experiencing, subsided. Although it still lay simmering beneath the surface, as long as they maintained contact, she could survive Manhattan—even Times Square—with equanimity. Holding his hand, she felt somehow larger, more significant. Less likely to be trampled under harried, indifferent feet.

Hand in hand, they window-shopped. Unlike other men she knew, Rob MacKenzie enjoyed shopping. His tastes were eclectic and a little funky, and Casey was happy to be along for the ride. For the first time since they'd arrived in New York, she felt energized, instead of flattened. For a few hours, she could convince herself that nothing was amiss, that everything was normal, whatever normal meant. They joked about the blown-glass pipes in the window of a head shop, laughed at the antics of a trio of Welsh Corgi puppies in another. Paused in front of a hobby shop where an antique Lionel train set was on display. The train chugged along past a water tower, crossed a narrow bridge, and disappeared into a tunnel before reappearing at the other end, circling around, and repeating its journey.

"I always wanted a toy train," he said.

Was that wistfulness in his voice? Who knew? "You should have told me," she said. "I would've bought one for you years ago. Want to go inside?"

"Nah. Not tonight. Maybe another time."

"You're never too old for toys. Or to wonder what might show up under the Christmas tree."

He turned away from the window, flashed her one of those zillion-megawatt smiles, cupped her face in his hands, and kissed her, deeply and thoroughly, right there on the sidewalk. As a stream of pedestrians flowed around them, they might as well have been invisible. He broke the kiss, leaving her breathless. A frisson of excitement shot through her, the first she'd felt since before she lost the baby. She reached up and brushed soft fingertips across the bridge of his nose, down his jaw to his ear. "Hey," she said softly.

He tangled his fingers in the hair at the nape of her neck. "Hey," he said.

"You keep up that kissy-face stuff, we might not make it to the dance club."

"Don't try to weasel your way out of it, Fiore. We are definitely going dancing."

"Well, then."

"Well, then."

The dance club was unique, a high-energy place where the deejay played a wide variety of music that covered four decades. She wondered how he'd found it, then realized it was a stupid question. Rob MacKenzie had contacts everywhere in the New York music scene. No matter what he was looking for, somebody he knew could tell him where to find it.

Dancing was one of her greatest pleasures. Rob knew this, and had counted on it tonight. It was their thing. Wherever they found a dance floor, they took advantage of it. They danced at home, in the kitchen. In the bedroom. Both of them brimming with music and ready, at a moment's notice, to let it move them. But tonight, she hadn't been in the mood for dancing. She'd agreed to it, to this evening, only because her husband was the kind of guy who made a big deal out of special occasions—birthdays, anniversaries, holidays—and she didn't want to disappoint him. The dark mood she'd been in for weeks didn't lend itself to partying. But to her surprise, she found that the music and the physical activity helped to lift some of that darkness. When the music slowed, she stepped into his arms, inhaled the familiar scent that was his alone, and relaxed into his embrace.

"You okay, babe?" he asked.

"I'm fabulous." With a soft sigh, she laid her head against his shoulder, stopped thinking, and let herself just feel. His body felt delicious against hers. His lips, brushing a soft kiss to her temple, sent a shudder through her. Casey tilted her head back and gazed into those green eyes that looked back at her with love and longing. Lust, pure and undiluted, flowed through her. It had been far too long since she'd felt anything like this, far too long since they'd made love. While the incomparable Don Henley sang about letting somebody love you before it's too late, she clung to her husband, fervently hoping that tonight, they could fix whatever it was that had broken inside her.

She wasn't sure how long they stayed. An hour, two hours? Wrapped in his arms, she lost track of time. They danced fast to Bob Seger. Danced slow to a Bon Jovi power ballad, their bodies crammed so close it was difficult to tell where she ended and he began. Her brother Bill liked to refer to slow dancing as "priming the pump." That was exactly what it felt like, a form of foreplay, an entryway leading to what would come later.

When at last they left the club, fully primed for love, they hailed a taxi and spent the entire trip kissing with a passion she'd feared she would never feel again.

At their apartment building, Rob tossed a fifty at the cabbie and they walked hand in hand to the door. Rob greeted the doorman as they crossed the lobby to the elevator. Once inside, he backed himself against the wall and pulled her to him. Standing between his outspread legs, she leaned into him and, as the car began to rise, they shared a hot, open-mouthed kiss. Reveling in full-body contact and luscious anticipation, they sighed and trembled, breathed in each other's oxygen, and grinned like fools.

Upstairs, in the darkened living room, he took her face in his hands and kissed her again, slowly this time. Breathless and giddy, she ran a hand around the back of his neck, curled her fingers in his hair.

He broke the kiss. "Go on in," he whispered. "I'll be right behind you. I just want to check on the girls."

Another sweet, lingering kiss, and they separated. In the bedroom, she stepped out of her shoes, peeled off her dress, her bra, her panties, then stood in front of the mirror with her lips drawn in a narrow line, wondering what had happened to her body while she wasn't paying attention. The changes were subtle, probably not even noticeable when she was wearing clothes. But naked, in front of a full-length mirror, her flaws were clearly visible. And disheartening.

So this was what almost-forty looked like. This was irrefutable evidence of the relentless march of time. When had she developed that little pouch of a belly that she now gazed upon with such dismay? And what had happened to her breasts? While she was breastfeeding Emma, they'd grown plump and ripe and impressive. Now, shrunk back to their original size, they were guaranteed to impress nobody. Now, they were just the slightest bit saggy. She was certain there'd been no sag before Emma. And her hips, those perfect hips, had been left the size of a barn door by Emma's birth. She was as fat as an old cow. When had that happened? When had she become so uncomfortable in her own skin? Worse, when had the thought of her husband seeing her naked caused such shame and embarrassment?

All the eagerness, all the anticipation, fell like a soufflé as anxiety began to edge in. Casey ran her fingers through her hair, lifted and then dropped it, trying desperately to make it look sexy. But her hair was hopeless. It always had been. No matter what she did, it hung limp and lifeless, incapable of holding any style other than straight-and-parted-in-the-center-circa-1972. She took a final disparaging look in the mirror, turned out the light and crawled into bed. What the hell was wrong with her? She and Rob had always been open and free with each other. He knew, and had explored in excruciating detail, every inch of her body. Did she have unreasonable expectations of tonight? Expectations she knew were beyond the capabilities of her fat, fortyish body?

Rob came in, closed the door behind him, and undressed in the dark, letting his clothes fall haphazardly. A twinge of resentment niggled at her. He was a grown man, almost forty, and still he dropped his clothes and left them wherever they landed.

He slid beneath the covers, found her in the dark, ran a finger down her bare hip. In spite of her anxiety, doors began to open at his touch, a series of clicking locks releasing, one after the other, somewhere deep inside her. Rob MacKenzie had magic hands, and he knew how to use them, knew how to stoke her fires with a barely-there, whisper-soft touch of those calloused fingertips. It was all so very lovely, and she relaxed, allowed the anticipation and the heat to reignite as his fingertips traced delicate, delicious pathways along her sensitive skin. Down her hip to her knee. Up her ribcage to her breast. Along her collarbone, making her shudder. Oh, god, it had been so long. She buried her fingers in that sexy triangle of chest hair, wrapped a leg around his thigh, touched her tongue to the wonderful indentation where his breastbone met his ribcage.

"Hold on," he whispered. "Let me get something." With her leg still encircling his, he turned, raised himself, stretched to open the drawer in the nightstand, and took something out.

"What?" she said.

He closed the drawer, came back to her and said, "Protection."

In the silence, the sound of a foil packet being torn open was unmistakable, and everything inside her came to a screeching halt. "Wait," she said. "What are you talking about?"

"I bought a box of condoms yesterday. Why?"

"Behind my back?" That lovely, anticipatory high deflated like a balloon expelling a noisy rush of air. "You went out and bought condoms behind my back?"

"Jesus, Fiore, I thought you'd be glad. You haven't done anything about birth control yet. I didn't want to push you, so I took the responsibility into my own hands."

His betrayal was a hot poker in her chest. "I can't believe you'd so something like this."

"But we agreed to—"

"You agreed," she said. "You and Doctor Deb agreed. I never agreed to a damn thing."

"Oh, for the love of God."

"I am not going to do this, MacKenzie." Inside her chest, her heart felt as if it would explode. "I am not having sex with condoms. The issue is off the table."

"What, so you'd rather take a chance on dying? Because that's what lies ahead of you if you get pregnant again."

"Life is random and uncertain. Every day, we take risks, just getting out of bed. You could walk out of this hotel room and be hit by a bus, crossing the street."

"That's true, but my chances of being hit are a lot greater if I'm roaring drunk and spread-eagled in the middle of the street. Life may be a game of chance, but you can still stack the odds."

"I'm not stacking the odds."

"No? Well, I am. I'm not having sex *without* birth control. End of story. Because for some inexplicable reason, I'd like to keep you around for a few more decades." He flung back the covers, slam-dunked the unused condom packet into the wastebasket, and reached down for the clothes he'd left on the floor.

"Where are you going?"

"For a walk. It's pretty clear that nothing's happening here tonight." He zipped and buttoned his jeans, tugged his tee shirt over his head, then rose and stood over the bed. "I don't know what's wrong with you," he said, "but maybe it's time you got professional help. Because I think you're starting to lose your frigging mind."

He strode to the door, opened it, and stood silhouetted in the illumination from the street light outside the window. "Happy anniversary," he said.

And he slammed the door.

Rob

HE walked off his anger and frustration, block after block, with Leroy trotting along eagerly beside him. What the hell was he supposed to do with her? Over the years, he'd seen her through some rough times. When she lost Katie. When her marriage to Danny fell apart. When Danny died. He'd held her up, been her best friend and moral support, even during the times when she didn't want his help. Casey Fiore MacKenzie was a strong woman, the strongest woman he'd ever known, and she'd survived those stunning blows with her customary stoicism. When things had gotten dark or disjointed, the two of them had screamed and yelled the poison out of their systems, and then they'd moved on.

This was different. He didn't know why a miscarriage—okay, two miscarriages, as long as you were counting—should bring his strong, beautiful warrior woman to her knees. He wasn't some male chauvinist pig who thought a miscarriage was trivial and she should snap out of it. He was grieving the loss, too, and he understood that it was harder for a woman who had carried that child inside her body, who had bonded with that unborn baby from the moment she knew of its existence. He understood that her loss was so much greater than his. But that loss—and he didn't mean this to sound disrespectful—seemed so much smaller than the devastating losses she'd somehow plowed her way through in the past. So why was she falling apart now? What was it that made this so different? Why was it that the poison, instead of leaving her system, was lodging there, spreading through her veins, tainting her every breath?

Something inside her was broken, and it scared the hell out of him, because he didn't believe yelling and screaming would do either of them any good this time around. He'd tried patience, loving attention, a readily available sympathetic ear, and he'd made no headway whatsoever. Whatever was going on with her had finally sunk its sharp little teeth into the fabric of their relationship, and that was something they'd never allowed to happen before. The two of them, their marriage, had reached a corner he wasn't happy about turning, yet he felt helpless to prevent it. And there was little he hated more than feeling helpless.

Even at this time of night, the sidewalks were far from empty. Times Square was lit up like high noon. He passed an after-hours jazz club, paused to listen to the notes that climbed the stairwell and spilled out the open door. Looking down at the dog, he debated, then shrugged, made a *cluck-cluck* sound to Leroy, and they went through the doorway and down the stairs.

Inside, a three-piece jazz combo played to a packed house. Bass, piano, and drums oozed smooth, cool jazz. Fronting the combo, a slender, exotic-looking woman in a red-flowered sarong was scat singing, her voice climbing up and down the scale, improvised nonsense syllables tripping from ruby-red lips.

Nobody gave Leroy a second glance. Rob found a seat at the bar, ordered a beer, and sat nursing it while he absorbed the music. Of its own volition, his foot began tapping. He couldn't help it. He'd grown up on Motown and the Beatles, had never heard of scat singing until his freshman year at Berklee. There, he'd been introduced to jazz, and he'd fallen instantly in love with its complexity, its asymmetry, its unpredictability. With jazz, you never knew what was coming next. It wasn't a style of music that he wrote or played; for all his skill and experience, he still didn't consider himself a good enough musician to tackle jazz. But it had influenced his writing, strongly enough so that every so often, you could hear that influence in a chord progression or a series of notes that flew from his brain to his hand to the strings of his guitar.

He took a sip of beer, irritated by the itch the music spawned inside him. Why now, with Casey falling apart, his marriage in crisis, his life in limbo, were his insides suddenly screaming at him to get back up on the stage he thought he'd left behind forever?

It wasn't an option. Not even worth considering. Going back onstage meant going back on the road. He was a family man now, with a wife, two kids, a big house in a small town. He drove a frigging Ford Explorer, for the love of Mike. He hadn't bothered to replace the Porsche after Paige totaled it. What was the point, when he couldn't even fit his growing family in it? His days of cruising the freeways, stick shift in hand and wind threading fingers through his hair, were over. He was rapidly approaching forty, far too old to play rock star. Time and the world had moved on, had left him sitting on his ass in the dust. Nobody wanted to hear the kind of music he wrote; he and Casey were Edsels in a

Lexus world. It was the kids, the teenagers and the twenty-somethings, who bought record albums and concert tickets. Those kids wanted to hear songs about love, about sex. He was writing songs about growing older. While he'd been otherwise occupied with the business of living, his brand, his style, his music, had become obsolete.

The very idea of going back out there was ludicrous.

Besides, how would he raise the issue with his wife, who already had enough catastrophe happening in her life? *Guess what, honey, you'll never believe what happened the other day. I played an impromptu concert for thirty people. Did you know I have fans? Real, live fans who want to see me back in front of the footlights? And the weirdest thing is that for those few short minutes while I was playing, I was able to breathe again, for the first time in so long I can't remember when I last breathed.*

She would laugh at him. And if she didn't laugh at him, she would list all those reasons why it wasn't feasible: the house, the kids, the Ford Explorer. His Two Dreamers Records, the goddamn sheep ranch she was building in their back yard.

Then, there was the other piece of the pie he had to consider: this strange, dark place where his wife was living. The glass bubble she'd surrounded herself with, the one nobody could breach. Her poor, broken heart that even he couldn't mend. How could he come to her, confide in her about what amounted to little more than growing pains, when her own pain was so much bigger than his?

Sacrifice. Wasn't that what love and marriage were really about? Sacrificing your needs, subjugating your desires, in favor of the needs and desires of your loved one? That was the kind of man he was, the kind who would lay down his life for the woman he loved. Hell, that was the kind of woman she was, the kind a besotted man would gladly die for. And the road ran both ways, thanks to that damned invisible cord that connected them. Even before their long-time friendship had ripened into something more, she would have walked through fire for him.

So it wasn't like he had a choice. This woman who was so obsessed with the thought of having another baby, this woman who was so preoccupied with her pain that some days, she barely remembered he existed, was still the woman he'd married, the woman he couldn't breathe without. She might have been swallowed by grief, but Casey was still in there somewhere, locked inside that stranger who slept in his bed. Eventually, she would heal, and then she would come back to him fully. Even if she didn't, he would wait for her. It was the way he was made. He would always wait for her. He couldn't imagine doing anything else. He couldn't imagine his life without her.

In the meantime, he'd continue to do what he'd recommended to Luther: pull himself up by the bootstraps and keep on keeping on.

And rid himself, once and for all, of any asinine ideas about going back onstage.

* * *

When he got back, Casey was sitting on the couch in the dark, staring at the muted television. He closed the door quietly and bent to take off Leroy's harness. She looked up from the television and their eyes met, but neither of them spoke. Rob unclipped the harness, swept his hand down the dog's back, from his ears to the base of his tail, then clapped him gently on the rump. "Go on, buddy," he said. "Time for bed."

He cracked open the door to Paige and Emma's room, and Leroy squeezed through. Walking barefoot to the kitchen, he took a couple of beers from the fridge. He popped the caps, tossed them in the trash, then carried the bottles to the couch and eased down beside his wife. Silently handing her a bottle, he propped his feet on the coffee table. "So," he said, and took a long, cold swig of Heineken. "Are we talking about this, or what?"

The flickering light from the television screen lent a nightmarish cast to her face. With her free hand, she swiped furiously at a tear. "I'm sorry," she said.

He leaned his head back against the couch. On the silent TV screen, a black-and-white Lucy, her wayward curls done up in a checkered kerchief, was wailing, face scrunched up dramatically, while a monochromatic Ricky Ricardo rolled his eyes and muttered what was undoubtedly a string of incomprehensible Spanish.

"Seems to me," Rob said, running his thumb around the rim of the beer bottle, "that you've been spending an awful lot of time lately being sorry."

She studied him mutely. Then said, "This is not who I want to be."

"Who do you want to be?"

"Me," she said. "I want to be me! Whoever the hell that is."

He took another sip of beer. "I had high hopes for tonight."

"Yes. So did I."

"Every morning," he said, "I wake up and I can't wait to see your face. You're the reason I get out of bed every day. Even in sleep, you're the bright, shiny thing my world revolves around. The glue that holds me together. That holds this entire family together."

"I'm not holding much together right now. That's what you're saying."

"No," he said bluntly. "You're not. You're coming unglued. And the more you come unglued, the more our family falls apart. There's only so much I can do. I can try. I *am* trying. But I don't have the magic that's inside you. That's something only you have. I depend on that magic to always be there, and without it, I don't know what to do."

"Just love me, Flash. That's all I ask."

He slammed the beer bottle down on the coffee table. "Don't you ever, *ever* doubt my feelings for you! You have been the most significant person in my entire adult life. The other half of me. The goddamn air that I breathe!"

"Damn it, Rob, be quiet! You'll wake the girls."

"I don't understand," he said in a stage whisper. "I don't understand what happened here tonight. I don't get how something so right could go so wrong, so fast."

She set down her untouched beer, stood and crossed her arms. Walking to the window, she drew the curtain aside and gazed out at the lights of Manhattan. "I'm afraid," she said, her back to him. "I'm afraid all the time. I'm afraid when I wake up in the morning and I'm afraid when I fall asleep at night, and I'm afraid all of the time in between."

I Love Lucy segued into a commercial for the Clapper. *Clap on. Clap off.*

Casey turned around, slender arms still crossed over her chest. "I don't know what to do about it," she said. "I don't know where to put it. It's something new to me, this fear." She reached a hand up, scraped her hair back from her face. "No, that's not right," she said. "What's new to me isn't the fear. It's being controlled by the fear. No matter what happened to me in the past, no matter how scary life got, I always dealt with it." She paused, took a breath. "But I'm not dealing anymore. I can't tell you why. I don't know why. I just know that I'm clinging to what's solid and familiar to me. The things that I believe are good and right and true. Because all the rest of it is a dark and murky place, a drop-off-the-face-of-the-earth, there-lie-monsters kind of place."

He squared his jaw. "Great. So where does that leave us?"

"I'm trying to keep it from affecting us."

"Yeah? Well, you're not doing such a hot job of that."

"You don't understand."

"No," he said, "you're the one who doesn't understand." He got up from the couch, crossed the room, and took her face between his hands. "You think you're afraid?" His thumb gently rubbed at the soft skin of her cheek. "Try walking in my shoes. I waited sixteen years for you, and now that I finally have you, I can feel you pulling away from me, a little more each day. It scares the bejesus out of me. It would almost be better if you just ripped off the Band-Aid in one fell swoop. Because this step-by-step bullshit is making my head explode."

Disappointment clouded her eyes. "You have it all wrong, MacKenzie. As usual, you're completely and utterly missing the point."

"Oh?" he said. "And just how am I doing that?"

"You're missing the fact that you are the most solid and familiar thing in my universe."

"Look, I'm a patient man, but—"

"Patient? *Patient?* You're hot-headed, quick to jump to conclusions, jackass stubborn, and prone to tantrums when you don't get your way. I'm not sure how you equate any of that with patience. Even so, you're still my happy place."

"Yeah? Well, I'm not feeling very happy right now."

"Guess what, my friend? Neither am I."

Silence. He puffed out a hard breath through pursed lips. "So what do we do about it?"

"I have no idea. But I'm not backing down on the birth control issue. Having another baby is something I'm not willing to give up on. No matter what you say."

"Then we're at an impasse, because I don't intend to back down, either. Keeping you alive is something I'm not willing to give up on. No matter what you say."

"Damn it, Flash." A tear glimmered at the corner of her eye. "Why are you making this so difficult?"

"You just said it. I'm a jackass. I come from a long line of jackasses."

"And yet, I still love you. Why is that?"

"Believe me, babydoll, there are days when you're no picnic yourself. But I've loved you since the first time I set eyes on you. I couldn't change it now if I wanted to."

Fear widened her eyes before she shuttered them and the fear was replaced with defiance. "Are you saying you want to?"

"Don't put words in my mouth, Fiore." The tear rolled down her cheek, and he cursed himself for forgetting how vulnerable she was right now. "Look," he said, "it's late. We're not about to resolve a damn thing tonight. Let's dump out the beer and go to bed."

She nodded, wound her arms around his neck, and pressed her cheek to his chest. He brushed his lips against her hair. "So you're still my girl?" he said.

"Are you kidding, MacKenzie? Always. Always and forever. I may be a little crazy, but I'm not that crazy."

He let out a breath as the fear that had a tight grip on his insides eased a little. "Jesus," he said. "We are a mess, aren't we?"

* * *

Thus began the most miserable episode of enforced celibacy he'd ever lived through.

They'd experienced celibate periods in the past, but there was always a legitimate reason: the weeks before and after childbirth, the weeks that followed each miscarriage. The weeks he'd spent on tour with Chico Rodriguez, after Chico's lead guitarist had an unexpected medical emergency and he'd stepped into the breach. There'd been good, solid reasons for them to forego intimacy, reasons they'd both embraced, so it hadn't seemed a hardship. Those six weeks apart while he'd been on the road had been a challenge, but the homecoming had more than made up for the entire six weeks of deprivation.

This was different. This was deliberate, born out of conflicting desires and fears. A line had been drawn in the sand, and because neither of them had any intention of stepping over it, the situation created a tension between them that had never existed before. They'd become adversaries. If it hadn't been so serious, he might have found it comical. But this was a life-and-death issue, and Casey was determined to torpedo his well-meant intentions. Because they both knew there'd be no resolution until one or the other caved, every word, every glance, every touch was rife with implicit meaning. They'd always been able to hold a conversation without words. But now, the unvoiced conversations that coursed between them ran to silent accusations: *"You know, we wouldn't have to go through this if only you'd stop being such a jackass and see things my way."*

But of course, they were both jackasses, each of them unwilling and unable to see things from the other's perspective, so the gap between them widened, fueled by anger and hurt and resentment.

And, on his part at least, a growing fear.

* * *

Sweat, assisted by gravity, drizzled down his ribcage and along his spine, saturating his clothing and leaving him stewing in his own juices. The air conditioner had been on the fritz for the last three days. With the five-dollar part needed to fix it on back order, the atmosphere in this place could best be described as one step this side of hell. Somebody had brought in a fan, but all it did was move around stale air, and the damn thing was so noisy, he couldn't use it while he was recording anyway. New York City was clutched in the grip of a full-fledged heat wave, the kind of heat that accelerated the murder rate, left sidewalks steaming, and turned New Yorkers—not known for their courtesy under the best

of circumstances—into total assholes. All you had to do was turn
on the TV to the nightly news to see the effect the weather had on
normally sane and rational people. He'd lived through three New
York summers, and he'd grown up in Boston, so it wasn't as
though he didn't know the score. But he'd been spoiled by his
years in California, where this kind of mugginess, so thick you
could eat it with a fork, was rare.

One good thing had come of the weather: the notable absence
of Phoenix's posse. Even Luther, who was built like a linebacker,
had succumbed to the brutal heat. The gentle giant had spent half
of yesterday mopping sweat from his face with a snow-white
handkerchief before giving in and returning to his hotel.

Work wasn't going well. The heat, the time squeeze, the
pressure to perform, were all getting to Phoenix. He'd been snippy
all morning and into the afternoon. Cold pizza and tepid Coke
hadn't done anything to sweeten the kid's mood, and when Rob
asked him, for a fifth time, to dig deeper into his emotional
repertoire to mellow out a line that sounded too harsh, the kid
slammed his headphones to the floor and said, "It's only flippin'
pop music! What in bloody hell is *wrong* with you?"

Sighing, Rob made a mental note about covering the cost of
the headphones from his rapidly-dwindling budget. Into the mic,
he said, "It's only your flipping career. What in bloody hell is
wrong with *you?*"

"Bugger off," the kid said.

Rob glanced over at Kyle, whose balding pate gleamed with
perspiration, and made an executive decision. "We're quitting for
the day," he said. "Kyle, go home and spend a few hours with your
wife, before she forgets what you look like. Phoenix, front and
center."

"Man, you don't have to say it twice," Kyle said. "I'm outta
here."

"See you tomorrow, buddy."

The kid dragged into the control room, a sneer on his pretty
face. "What?"

"You're coming with me."

"And where might we be going?"

"For a walk."

"In New York." The kid raised a single dark eyebrow. "In this heat."

"That's the way it plays out."

"You're fuckin' serious."

"Jesus, Phoenix, lighten up a little. You're seventeen. Life's supposed to be fun at seventeen."

"No thanks to you. Bleeding sadist." But he followed Rob down the corridor, past the reception desk, where Sheila sat, fanning herself with the sports section of the *New York Times*, and out the front door.

Outside, heat rose in waves from the pavement. Traffic was at a standstill, all those combustion engines adding a heady cocktail of heat and gasoline fumes to the sultry atmosphere. An elderly couple with cameras conferred over an open map, while a statuesque blonde wearing too much eye shadow and a black leather miniskirt—in this heat—clicked down the sidewalk on silver stiletto heels. "Stop staring," Rob said to the kid, who was standing on point like a bird dog. "She's way out of your league."

Half a block away, a vendor sold hot dogs from a pushcart. Rob bought two with the works, one for him and one for the kid. "You're welcome," he said, handing a hot dog and a bottled water to Phoenix.

The kid eyed him through those mirrored sunglasses, which did nothing to camouflage his identity. Not that it mattered. In these temps, any girl who recognized him would be too weak from heat exhaustion to do anything about it. "Thank you," Phoenix said fussily, and bit into his hot dog.

They ate, and walked, in silence. Eventually, his hot dog gone, Phoenix said, "I don't suppose you've a destination in mind?"

"Right over here." Rob veered across the densely crowded sidewalk to a sporting goods store that featured a wide array of athletic shoes in its window display. "Ever play basketball?" he said.

"Are you barking mad?"

"I take it that means no."

"It means yes. But not in this bloody heat."

"Oh, come on, Russell. Where's your sense of adventure?"

"I left it back in London. And don't call me Russell. That's not my name any more."

He clapped the kid on the shoulder and steered him through the entryway. "Live a little," he said.

After some deliberation, which took longer than it should have because the store was so nicely air conditioned, he bought a regulation basketball. While the sales clerk rang it up, he picked out two white terrycloth sweatbands. He paid, and they headed back out into the brutal heat in search of the small public court he vaguely remembered from his New York days.

He took a couple of wrong turns before he found it, tucked in between brick buildings on a narrow cross street. Nobody else was crazy enough to be out here, so they had the place to themselves. Rob dropped his water bottle on a bench, peeled off his tee shirt, and donned the sweatband. Lazily tossing the ball from hand to hand, he said, "Okay, kid. Let's see what you've got."

"You're a musician," Phoenix said, shucking his own shirt and dropping it beside his water bottle on the bench. "I'm not picturing you as an athlete."

Rob bounced the ball on the pavement. "I was six feet tall at fourteen. It was pretty much a foregone conclusion that I'd play. I was on my high school team for a couple of years. I liked it well enough, but my heart was elsewhere. You?"

"Played a little at school. But I can probably beat the likes of an old sod like you."

"Think so? You're on."

In spite of the heat, they played with an intensity and a determination that mirrored the complex rivalry of their off-court relationship. Rob dove in, snagged the ball, took a jump shot, and missed.

Phoenix snickered. "What a Nancy," he muttered as he captured the ball. "I'll show you how a real man does it."

"Hah. Good luck with that."

They fought for control of the ball. Phoenix won, dribbled it to the end of the court, jumped and made the shot.

"Not bad, kid." Breathing heavily, Rob snatched the ball out of Phoenix's hands, dribbled it a couple of times, raised his arms and shot. The ball hit the backboard, circled the rim of the basket—while they both stood silent with anticipation—then dropped into the net. "Score! So tell me, Hightower. Best band ever."

"The Stones." The kid grabbed the ball, said, "Yours?"

"The Beatles. Followed closely by Steely Dan. Favorite Stones song?"

"*Beast of Burden.*" He dribbled the ball, aimed, and shot. It went cleanly into the basket. "Favorite Beatles song?"

"*Let It Be.*"

Phoenix shot again, missed the basket this time. "I don't know Steely Dan."

"Well, then, sonny, you've missed a crucial piece of your musical education. I'll have to play them for you. Walter Becker and Donald Fagen. Nothing short of gods."

They lasted forty minutes before the heat got to them and they collapsed side by side on the bench. Rob peeled off the sweatband, swiped his arm across his forehead, picked up his bottle of water and took a long sip. Then he upended it over his head, letting the coolness refresh his overheated body.

With his tee shirt, he wiped his face, his hair, then pulled it back on over his head. "Jesus," he said, stretching aching muscles he'd forgotten he owned. "I haven't had a workout like this in years."

Beside him, Phoenix pulled his own shirt back on. "Tell me, mate. You don't talk like a New Yorker. So where are you from?"

"Boston. Wheah we nevah learned to pronounce ouah ahs."

The kid blinked twice before he got it. "And where's Boston?"

"Couple hundred miles northeast of here. But Casey and I live in Maine, another hundred-fifty miles beyond that. Middle of nowhere. God's country. Sometimes, it's so quiet, you can hear your own heart beating."

"And you like that kind of thing?"

The kid sounded so horrified, he had to laugh. "I take it you don't spend much time away from the city?"

"Not deliberately."

"It does take some getting used to, if you're a city boy. But you know what? It's home to me now. It grows on you after a while. Besides, it's where Casey is. And wherever Casey is—" He paused, let out a breath. "—that's home."

"A tad besotted, are we?"

He shrugged good-naturedly. Said, "I'm worried about her." A cloud passed over the sun, providing temporary and much-needed relief from its brutal onslaught.

"Why?"

"She hasn't been herself at all. Ever since she lost the baby. She's hurting, and withdrawn. Grieving beyond what I'd call healthy. And I can't get through to her. It's like we're two strangers, sitting at opposite ends of a mile-long dinner table, with all that empty space between us."

"You can't put a time limit on grief," the kid said, playing with the cap to his water bottle. "When my Uncle Bert died, it took my Aunt Annette a couple of years before she started smiling again."

Rob considered the kid's words, eyed him with deliberation, suddenly seeing him anew. First the Stones, and now this. Who would have guessed that underneath the snotty teenager, there lived a real human being? "Hey, Phoenix?" he said.

The kid replaced his sunglasses. Warily, he said, "What?"

"Do you love what you do?"

"Not sure I'm following you."

"The music. Is it a passion for you? Is it something you'd do even if you didn't get paid? Are you one hundred percent certain you're on the right path in life? Or are you only doing it for the money?"

"This is a trick question, isn't it?"

"Not at all. I'm serious. I've just been giving it some thought lately."

"You've been thinking about my right path in life."

He fought a twitch at the corner of his mouth. "More like my right path in life."

"Ah. I see. You're finding out that life isn't quite what you expected."

"I love every minute of my life. Until you have kids, you don't realize what life is all about. There's just…something missing."

"The performing?"

"I thought I was ready to quit that side of the business. I was tired of the road. I wanted to be with Casey. And I didn't want to be a long-distance dad. I wanted to be there with my kids, raising them with my wife, being there for all those once-in-a-lifetime milestones. I thought I'd be happy as a producer."

"And you're not?"

"It's a necessary part of the process. I'm good at it. As one piece of the jigsaw puzzle, I like it fine. As the only piece? Not so much."

"Well, for the love of God, man, stop whining to me and do something about it. I don't need to listen to this. You're boring me."

"Ah, hell, it'll probably pass." He stretched out his legs, leaned back against the bench. Closed his eyes, raised his face to the sun, and said, "It's probably just working with you that's done this to me, anyway."

"Sod off, MacKenzie."

This time, he didn't bother to hide his grin. The insufferable teenager was back. But he'd managed to crack the façade and uncover, if only briefly, the decent kid beneath the outer brat. If he kept chipping away at it, maybe eventually he could destroy the smokescreen and set that kid free.

"Come on," he said, sitting back upright and clapping Phoenix playfully between the shoulder blades. "If Luther comes back and discovers you've vanished without a trace, they'll be calling out the SWAT team. I should probably get you back to your hotel before that happens."

* * *

He'd finally made contact with Kitty Callahan. She had flown into town this morning and given him ten solid hours of hard work. Four hours ago, Phoenix had gone back to his hotel, trailed by Luther and the ubiquitous posse. After that, the work went much more quickly. It was a relief to work with somebody like Kitty, who didn't waste time, didn't argue, didn't pout or throw tantrums. She took her place in the sound booth, listened to what he said, then did what she had to do.

It was past eleven when they wound up the recording session. Rob swept his personal items—scribbled notes, his Papermate pen, his stash of Hershey's Kisses—into his briefcase and slung the strap over his shoulder. He clasped hands with Kyle. Said, "See you tomorrow, buddy," and walked out the door with Kitty.

They paused on the sidewalk outside the studio. Even this late, the streets were filled with people. With a huge yawn, he locked his hands behind his neck and stretched until his joints cracked. "You cannot know," he said, lowering his arms, "how grateful I am that you could make it here today."

"Glad I could help out. Want to get a beer? There's a little bar just down the street. One of those places the cool kids haven't found yet."

"I don't know. It's pretty late."

She raised an elegant, blond eyebrow. "This is New York, my friend. Shank of the evening."

"Good point." And his wife was probably sound asleep, oblivious to the fact that he wasn't home yet. "Sure," he said. "As long as it's just one."

Like every other bar on the planet, this one was loud and smoky. They found a booth on the back wall, ordered draft beers, and he drew in the scent of tobacco smoke, surprised to realize that after all these years, he was still tempted.

She saw it in his eyes. "Once a smoker, always a smoker," she said.

"I'm that obvious?"

"Been there, done that."

"I worked so hard to quit. It probably added years to my life. There's no rational reason why, after seven years, I should get a whiff of my old nemesis and want it so bad, I could scream."

Kitty tucked a strand of blond hair behind her ear. Leaned over the table and said, "I'm the same way. I'd never touch it again. My voice, you know? But that doesn't take away the utter longing to draw that lovely smoke into my lungs one more time."

"And die young."

She shrugged. "Live hard and fast, my friend. Live hard and fast."

A shiver raced down his spine. "Don't even say it. That's what Danny used to say. And we all know how that turned out."

"Ouch."

Their beers arrived, in clunky, frosty mugs. Kitty took a long drink, licked the foam from her upper lip, and said, "So. How are things with the inimitable Mr. MacKenzie?"

It was his turn to shrug. He took a sip of beer and said, "Things are okay."

"Really? Then why do you seem so not okay?"

Kitty knew him too well. Like Casey, she possessed that laser vision that saw right through his skull to what was going on inside. Rob gripped his mug in both hands and said, "I'm starting to think I'm not cut out for producing."

"Of course you're not," Kitty said. "You're a musician. You make music. You thrive on performing. Why did you think you'd be happy quitting the business and burying yourself in some recording studio? Was it Casey's idea?"

"No. Not at all. Matter of fact, she questioned my decision. But I was tired of the road. Ready to settle down and start raising a family. And I always believed—" He paused, took a long swig of beer as he tried to corral the thoughts that ran rampant inside his head. "I think," he said, the words coming slowly, "I always believed that as long as she and I were together, everything else would fall into place. If I had her, I'd be happy."

"And you're not happy?"

It was a good question, one he'd been afraid to ask himself for fear of what the answer might be. What it might tell him about himself. He loved his wife, adored his daughters. He loved being home with them. Loved being a family man. Loved being there for Emmy's first word, her first step, for that heart-shattering smile every time he walked through the door. He liked the slow, comfortable rhythm of life in a small town. Yet there was something unsettled inside him, some dissatisfaction that had begun as a small irritation and was gradually building up, layer by layer, into full-blown resentment. A need for something more. Not a replacement for his current life, but something *in addition to.*

But did he really want to go back to performing? He'd had enough of life on the road. Hadn't he?

Kitty arched an eyebrow. "Have you talked to Casey about this?"

"Hell, no."

"Why not?"

"I can't." At her quizzical look, he explained. "Ever since that last miscarriage, Casey's been…not herself. She runs hot and cold, and she's all over the place. Some days, she seems perfectly normal. Other times, she's a basket case. She's determined to have another baby, even after the doctor made it clear to both of us that it could kill her. Since she refuses to use birth control, and I'm dead-set against killing her, we're not even having sex. Even the girls can sense how strained things are between us. Paige doesn't say a word. She's seventeen years old, and she doesn't want to get caught in the middle. But Emma's just a baby. Not even two yet, and she doesn't understand. But she picks up on those negative vibes, and acts accordingly."

"Wow. Ask what you think is a simple question, and open up the gates to hell. I'm sorry."

He lifted his mug, avoided her eyes by burying his face in it. The beer was cold, and wonderful. He drained it, flagged down the waitress, lifted two fingers.

"Maybe," Kitty said tentatively, "once you're finished with the Hightower project, things will go back to normal."

"Maybe." He recognized, belatedly, the inappropriateness of discussing his sex life—or the lack thereof—with Kitty, a woman with whom he had a history. "I'm sorry," he said. "I didn't mean to run off at the mouth. Casey would have a cow if she knew I was discussing our sex life with anyone. Especially with you."

"Casey doesn't like me?"

"She likes you just fine. As long as you're nowhere near me."

"So she knows we slept together."

"I've told her it wasn't a big deal. She just doesn't choose to believe it."

"Don't feel bad, hon." She rested her hand on his. "You're among friends here. You can say anything you want to me."

He acknowledged that truth with a nod. "It's just that I'm so damn frustrated. I feel helpless, and I don't like feeling helpless."

The waitress brought their second round of beers, and he picked up his and drank half of it in one long swallow. "I love that woman," he said, studying Kitty over the rim of his mug. "I probably love her too much. I can't change that. It is what it is. But there's always been balance in our relationship. Even when she was married to Danny, we had this reciprocal thing going on. It wasn't even on a conscious level. She had my back, and I had hers. In a way, the connection we had was more of a marriage than her real-life marriage to Danny."

He drank more beer while Kitty waited for him to continue. "But I don't know who she is anymore. I don't know where my wife has disappeared to. She's lost somewhere inside herself, and I'm trying like crazy to find her and pull her out of the quicksand before it swallows her up completely. Except that I can't seem to find her, and it scares the hell out of me. Because if I lose her, I'll lose myself right along with her. I don't remember how to be me without her. I haven't been without her, in one way or another, since I was twenty."

Kitty picked up her beer, took a sip. Then a breath. "All right," she said. "Since you're being brutally honest, I'm going to do the same thing. Maybe it's time you learned how to be without her."

Not sure where this was leading, he sucked in a breath and waited for her to continue.

"You look like death, Rob. Your eyes are bloodshot, your hair is a mess, and I'd be willing to bet you haven't had a decent night's sleep in weeks. You're on a rollercoaster ride to nowhere. That woman is tearing you apart, and it kills me to see you go through this." Again, she placed her hand on his. This time, she left it there, her heat radiating outward and into his flesh.

"Maybe," she said, "it's time to extricate yourself from this mess you've found yourself in. And consider your alternatives."

For an instant, he didn't understand what she meant. And then he did.

He wasn't a stupid man. He'd never been a stupid man. But he hadn't seen this coming. How could he have known that for all these years, she'd been carrying a torch, while he hadn't given her a second thought? Stunned, he studied her face. Kitty never seemed to age. She was still as breathtakingly beautiful as she'd been at eighteen. But she was more than just a pretty face. Kitty Callahan was a warm, vital woman with a big heart. She was smart, talented, a great listener. Comforting, when a man needed comfort. Good in bed, when what he needed was sex. Their off-and-on relationship, if that was what you wanted to call it, had lasted for a decade. But never once had he kidded himself that it was anything more than superficial. Never once had he envisioned himself settling down with Kitty. The chemistry simply wasn't there.

He'd stupidly assumed she felt the same way.

"Jesus, Kitty," he said, floundering, "I'm flattered, but—"

"Never mind. Don't bother to say it." Ever the lady, she removed her hand. His wedding band, where she'd touched it, felt hot. Electrified. "I just thought, if things were really falling apart between you and Casey, it was worth one last try."

"I think the world of you," he said. "I always have. I like you. I respect you. But—"

"You don't love me. I get it."

"I'm sorry. I never meant to lead you on."

"You didn't. This is not your fault."

"I love Casey. I've always loved Casey."

"I know. Even when we were together, I knew."

And there was the basic difference between them. He'd never thought of them as together. Had never considered them to be a couple. But he couldn't tell her that. He wasn't that callous. So he focused on the rest of her sentence instead.

"That's pretty funny," he said, "because I didn't know I loved her."

"It's that Y chromosome, hon. Men have blinders because of it. Here I was, pining over you, while you were pining over her, and you didn't even realize any of this pining was going on. And after all this time, nothing's changed. Even when the ship is sinking, she's still your lifeline."

"I don't intend to let the ship go down."

"Of course you don't."

"You're an amazing woman, Kitty. If things were different…Jesus, I'm so sorry."

"Don't be. We'll just chalk this up to exhaustion and too much booze. Then we'll forget we ever had this conversation, and nobody else will ever have to know." Her eyes widened and she said, in a small, disappointed voice, "Oh."

"Oh?"

"You're planning to tell Casey, aren't you?"

He scraped a hand through his hair and said, "I tell Casey everything."

"I suppose she'll be all smug and self-righteous, knowing that she was right all along."

"Casey's not like that."

"Well, then. Aren't you the lucky one?" She gathered up her purse and rose from her seat. "I have to leave. I'm flying to L.A. first thing in the morning. I haven't been home in three months."

"Don't be mad."

"I'm not mad. A little sad, maybe. But it's not as though things weren't over between us a long time ago. I've lived this long without you. I'll keep on living without you."

"At least let me get you a cab."

Outside the bar, he flagged down a taxi, and they stood at the curb, neither of them knowing what to say. "I hope your wife knows what she has in you," Kitty said.

"We have each other. It's a two-way street."

"And what happens if she doesn't come out of this funk? What if she doesn't come back to you fully?"

"It doesn't matter. I'm not going anywhere."

"You're such a Galahad, it makes me a little nauseated. On anybody else, it would be ludicrous. On you, for some crazy reason, it seems to fit. I suppose you realize this means that if you go back on tour, I won't be going with you."

It hurt a little, deep inside his chest, to realize that this meant they'd never work together again. "I'm sorry," he said for what felt like the twelfth time.

"Don't be. I'm tough as nails. I've been in the entertainment business for the past two decades. Toughness goes with the territory. But I won't forget you. Ever." Kitty stood on tiptoe and pressed a soft kiss to his cheek. She smelled wonderful, ripe and womanly and fragrant, and he felt the tiniest twinge of regret.

Then she gave him a cheeky grin. Said, "See you around, kid," slid into the taxi, and was gone.

Feeling like a fool, he stood on the sidewalk and watched until the taxi was out of sight. His stomach clenched, and for a few seconds, he thought he might vomit. Somehow, he'd let them both down. Kitty and his wife. Mystified as to how he could have accomplished this without any action on his part, he shoved his hands in his pockets and began striding toward home. He shouldn't feel this guilty, damn it. There was nothing for him to feel guilty about. He'd done nothing wrong. The only thing he could be found guilty of was stupidity, and even that wasn't his fault. As Kitty had pointed out, that kind of stupidity was imprinted on the Y chromosome. He couldn't be held responsible for something his dad had passed on to him.

So he would tell her. When he got home, probably still feeling as guilty as though he'd taken Kitty up on the ridiculous offer she'd blindsided him with, he would tell his wife what had gone down tonight. Casey wouldn't say a word. She'd just give him that look, the one that had probably been perfected by Eve and passed down to every female since then, the look that said, *Really? You're really that stupid?*

Maybe he should bring her flowers. Some kind of peace offering. Even though she knew him well enough to understand that he'd never, in this lifetime or the next, touch another woman, it still didn't hurt to have insurance. Something a little extra to boost his groveling to the next level.

He'd already taken five steps past the entrance to the tattoo parlor before it clicked. Rob stopped to consider his options. A tattoo was forever. A permanent external symbol of his internal feelings for her. It would buy him brownie points. Of that much, he was certain. What woman wouldn't be immensely flattered to have her name permanently engraved on the body of the man who'd promised to love her for eternity? Even Casey couldn't be immune to that kind of grand gesture.

Besides, there was something appealing about the idea of marking himself as her property. Something hopelessly romantic, maybe even a little sexy. He'd never considered it before, mostly because he hadn't thought it necessary. He wore a gold ring. That should be enough to keep predatory women at bay. Or so he'd thought. Tonight's fiasco with Kitty had proven him wrong.

He thought about it for a full thirty seconds. And then, swallowing back the bile that was gathering somewhere in the vicinity of his tonsils, he turned, retraced those five steps, and walked through the door of the tattoo parlor.

Casey

OUTSIDE the open bedroom window, birds joyfully greeted the dawn that crept through the blinds. Half-asleep, she shifted position, plumped her pillow, rolled over, and her fist accidentally connected with her husband's arm.

"Ow! Jesus Christ on a fucking pogo stick!" Clutching his arm, he rolled away from her and into a sitting position, uttering a string of obscenities that was shocking, even for him.

"What?" she said. "What's wrong?"

He just shook his head and rocked back and forth. "Flash?" she said.

"Gimme a minute."

"I'm sorry. But good God, I didn't hit you that hard."

"Not your fault," he said through clenched teeth.

"Then what—" She caught sight of his upper arm, and her eyebrows rose almost to her hairline. "What the hell is that, MacKenzie?"

"What the hell does it look like, Fiore?"

"I would say it looks remarkably like a tattoo. What have you done?"

"I got a tattoo. And you just about sent me into the next millennium when you slugged it."

"Are you crazy?"

"That's not quite the response I was hoping for."

"I don't suppose you'd care to enlighten me?"

"I had this wild notion that the word 'charming' might come tripping from your lips."

"Char—oh, for the love of God. Let me see."

"You can see. You can't touch."

"Babe?"

"Fine. But don't say I didn't warn you. If you touch it, I refuse to be held responsible for my actions." He let go of his arm, turned gingerly so she could see. Looking red and inflamed, possibly infected, undoubtedly painful, was her name, spelled out in fancy Celtic lettering.

He'd had her name tattooed on his arm? "I guess this explains why you came in so late last night."

"I didn't think you knew what time I got home."

"Clearly. Why is it so red and puffy? It's not infected, is it? Do I need to take you to the hospital for an antibiotic? And possibly a lobotomy while we're there?"

"It's normal. The guy said it'll look like this for a few days before it settles down. It should take a couple of weeks to fully heal."

"It must've hurt like crazy."

"It did. Bled like a son of a bitch."

"What were you thinking? What on earth would make you do something like this?"

"I thought you'd be impressed."

"You do realize that this is permanent?"

"No kidding."

"I suppose this means I have to keep you."

"Hah."

"I don't understand why you'd do something like this, out of the blue, without even discussing it with me ahead of time. You've lived almost forty years without any body art whatsoever. Why now? Unless—" The wheels started turning inside her head. She narrowed her eyes. "What did you do?"

"What do you mean, what did I do? I got a tattoo."

"Before the tattoo. What did you do that was so awful you felt it necessary to disfigure your body to take the attention away from the real issue?"

"Jesus, Mary and Joseph."

"Answer the damn question, MacKenzie."

"What is it with women? What is this psychic ability you all have? I was working my way around to telling you anyway. You can retire the interrogation lamp and the nightstick. I had a few drinks with Kitty."

"So you were drinking when you got this thing."

"Not that much. Just a couple of beers. Maybe three."

"With Kitty."

"She wasn't with me when I got the tattoo. I did that after I put her in the cab to her hotel. She's flying to L.A. this morning."

"How nice. What happened with Kitty?"

"Nothing happened. Not a damn thing."

"You are the worst liar I've ever known. You get all shifty-eyed and you start sweating. What went on between you and Kitty?"

He let out a massive sigh. "We went for a drink. She asked me the customary, 'So how have you been?' and I made the mistake of telling her."

"About?"

"About you. About us. About our current state of—" He glanced up, saw the look in her eyes. Closed his eyes, cleared his throat, and said, "Sexlessness."

"You discussed our sex life with an old girlfriend."

"Right now," he said, "we don't exactly have a sex life."

"And you just had to let her know that, didn't you? Keep it up, and you won't have one ever again. Let me guess. She offered to comfort you in your time of need."

"Better than that. She suggested that I might want to dump you. For her."

Around the buzzing in her head, she wet her lips and smiled. "And your response was?"

"You're looking at it, babydoll."

"Let me make sure I have this right. You broke her poor, black little heart by declaring your undying love for me. You then walked into a tattoo parlor and got my name engraved on your upper arm to reinforce that declaration. Then you came home and climbed into bed with me."

"That pretty much covers it."

"You're an idiot. You do realize that?"

"I've been told that a time or two."

"But you're my idiot." Softening, she checked out the tattoo a second time. The lettering was elegant, the work top-notch. "So," she said, "I guess this means that the next time some woman has the audacity to make such an impertinent suggestion, you'll have a ready-made answer for her."

He reached out a finger, touched her shoulder, trailed it down to the swell of her breast. "If it would make you feel any better," he said, "I could have a heart drawn around it."

She removed his hand from her breast. "That would be extremely tacky, MacKenzie. I think my name should be sufficient to keep the predators at bay."

"If not, that little derringer you carry should do the trick."

"Funny. There's always a joker in every crowd."

"And lucky you. You married him. Are you mad?"

"Because I married The Joker?"

"Because of the tattoo. And everything that preceded it."

"As much as I'd like to be, as you so clearly pointed out, it's my bed you slept in last night."

"It's your bed I intend to sleep in every night for the next fifty-seven years."

"And after that?"

"After that, we renegotiate. I might be ready for a new wife by then."

"Brat." But he'd made her laugh, for the first time in ages. She studied the tattoo a final time. "I suppose," she said softly, "I should be flattered that you think enough of me to deface your body in my honor."

"Stop fishing for compliments, Fiore. You know damn well I think enough of you to take a bullet for you if I had to."

She raised an eyebrow. "Only if you had to?"

"Well, I'm not going out looking for one, just to prove it to you, if that's what you mean. But if I should happen across one, by accident…"

"That's sweet. I think I'll keep you. Tattoo and all."

"Good to know."

"Don't look so relieved. Did you really think I was going to toss you out on your incredibly sexy little tush?"

"Not really." His expression, and his voice, grew suddenly serious. "But you've been a little unpredictable lately."

It was true, and she deeply regretted that this darkness hanging over her had wrought such havoc in his life. It shouldn't have affected him this way, but they'd always been so connected that everything she did, everything she said, everything she felt, affected him. Sometimes to the point where she wondered if they were too dependent on each other. If, God forbid, anything should happen to either of them, how would the other carry on? She'd survived Danny's death because she had Rob. If anything ever happened to Rob, she couldn't imagine surviving. He was her life, her breath. How would she ever breathe again without him?

"I love you," she said.

"I know you do."

"That's it? That's all you have to say?"

He waggled his eyebrows and said, "I love you, too."

"Much better. And I wasn't planning to say this, MacKenzie, but since you're being such a twit, I'll say it anyway: I was right."

"When have you ever not been right?"

"There was that one time, around 1982."

"I must've missed the occasion."

"Maybe we could reenact it. I so hate it when you miss something important."

"Shut up and come over here. Maybe we can grab a couple more hours of sleep before Emma wakes up. But first, we need to swap sides until this thing stops hurting. Unless you like hearing a grown man cry."

Rob

ARIEL Records held Phoenix Hightower's eighteenth birthday bash in the ballroom at an upscale Midtown hotel. A high-level private security firm guarded the door, and nobody got in unless they were on the invite list. It didn't matter if your name was Ringo Starr; if you weren't on the list, you didn't get into the party.

Hand in hand, Rob and Casey stood just inside the doorway to the ballroom, taking it all in. At one end of the room, a live band played bouncy pop music. Overhead, hundreds of black balloons with purple strings hugged the ceiling. A broad, sparkly HAPPY BIRTHDAY banner hung from the ceiling above the band. The place was crawling with celebrities, all of them invited because the record company wanted Phoenix to rub elbows with the entertainment industry's elite. Sequined dresses and plastic smiles ran rampant. Most of them were here not because they gave a tinker's damn about Phoenix Hightower, but because it was one more opportunity for a photo op or a little networking.

"I hate this shit," he muttered.

"Just smile and nod a lot," she said. "That's how you get through these things. You'll come home at the end of the evening with a sore face from smiling too hard and vertigo from nodding too much, but any photos that show up in the tabloids tomorrow will make it look as though you had a wonderful time."

His wife should know. She was a veteran of these idiotic see-and-be-seen events. As one of the entertainment industry's elite, Danny Fiore had been obligated to attend. As his wife, Casey had been expected to be by his side, smiling right along with him. Rob, who'd spent most of his career flying under the radar, had managed to avoid all but the most crucial of these celebrity shindigs.

"I don't know why they wanted me here tonight," he said.

"It's all politics. You know that. You're in the middle of making an album together. How would it look to the rest of the world if you skipped out on the kid's birthday party?"

"I don't give a damn how it looks to anyone."

"But the record company does. They've invested big bucks in both of you, so whether you like it or not, you dance to their tune.

Play the game, make everyone happy, then go home, take off the suit coat, and forget the whole thing ever happened."

"I'd like to forget the whole thing ever happened." He wasn't good at playing games. Or at wearing formal attire. He'd refused to wear a tie, or to waste money on a pair of dress shoes that would sit in his closet for the next ten years. With the dress shirt and the linen jacket, he wore jeans and Adidas. That was as formal as he intended to get tonight.

"Stop sulking. And I meant the event, not the album."

A waiter in a white shirt and black vest, bearing a tray of glass flutes filled with bubbly liquid, stopped before them. "Champagne?" he said.

Casey took a flute from him and said, "Thank you."

Rob shrugged. Whatever it took to get him through the night. The waiter handed him a slender, stemmed glass. He tilted his head in acknowledgment and took a sip. It was good champagne; no twelve-dollar-a-bottle supermarket crap for Ariel Records. They clearly intended to go all the way with this ridiculous celebration of a spoiled kid's eighteenth birthday.

He surveyed the crowd, glanced over at his wife. "You okay with this?" he said.

"So far, so good."

Her eyes were clear tonight, her face relaxed. She'd seemed more like herself the last couple of days. Was it possible that the worst of the dark days had passed, and she was on the way to recovery? She flashed him a cheeky smile, and he returned it. "We march forward?" he said.

"We march forward."

Champagne in hand, his fingers resting on the small of her back, they wound their way through the crowd, exchanging nods and greetings as they went, while the band played a surprisingly decent rendition of Bon Jovi's *Bed of Roses*.

"There you are!" A cheerful Drew Lawrence, president of Ariel Records, greeted Casey with a kiss. "Casey, you look more beautiful than ever." He shook Rob's hand and said, "Glad you two could make it."

"We wouldn't miss it," Casey said. "Where's the birthday boy?"

"Somewhere over there," Drew said, waving vaguely. "Taking photos by the cake. You should see it. Really retro. It brings back memories. There's this little bakery out in Queens…" He paused, apparently realized he was rambling. "So." He cleared his throat and said to Rob, "You and Phoenix have worked out your differences?"

"There was really nothing to work out. He called in sick, I got the day off. Win-win."

"Right." Drew nodded to a passing couple, then said cautiously, "It hasn't happened again, has it?"

"No."

"I hear things are coming along nicely." The statement almost sounded like a question that Drew was afraid to pose.

"Probably another week, and we should be done recording. Then I'll take the masters home with me and do the mixing there."

A crease appeared in Drew's otherwise smooth, collagened forehead. "Did we know you planned to do that? Is Two Dreamers even set up for that?"

Rob slugged down the rest of his champagne and said, "We have a fully functioning studio out in the williwacks. Casey and I dropped a fortune on it when we had the new house built. If anything we've recorded needs to be cleaned up, we can bring the essential people to Jackson Falls to finish the work. But I don't think that'll be necessary. For the most part, the sessions have gone well."

"Good, good." Drew looked immensely relieved, and Rob suspected that he'd been less than confident about this album. "Listen," the record executive said, "can I steal your wife for a few minutes? There's somebody I'd like to introduce her to."

He glanced at Casey, read the acquiescence in her eyes, leaned and kissed her temple. "If you need me—" he said, for her ears only.

"I'm fine." She patted his cheek, then turned and bestowed Drew with a beatific smile. "Mr. Lawrence," she said, linking her arm with his, "let's go adventuring."

He watched them go. Then, alone, he wandered the room, his attention divided between the party and his awareness, at all times, of Casey's location. Familiar faces came at him out of the crowd, faces of people he knew, other faces that were familiar only because he'd seen them splashed across the pages of *People* or *Rolling Stone.*

A burst of well-oiled laughter led him to the bar, where he traded his empty champagne glass for a Heineken. Leaning against a support beam with his ankles crossed, he nursed the beer and, his finely-honed radar focused on his wife, watched the band perform.

The singer, a zaftig young woman in her late twenties, had a strong, distinctive voice and an engaging style. The lead guitarist was an adequate player, and the drummer was really good. Add in bass, rhythm, and piano, and they had a pretty good thing going. Not bad, for a cover band. Not that there was anything wrong with cover bands—that was how he and Danny had started out—but if they expected to get anywhere, they needed to be writing and performing original material, not regurgitating music already made popular by other artists. He wondered idly whether they were signed, then realized that if they were playing an Ariel party, they must be. No record company would hold a private party of this size with a band they'd hired from some talent agency. They had to be new Ariel artists that Drew and his minions wanted to showcase.

Unlike the man of the hour, who was nowhere to be seen. Rob surveyed the room, but there was no sign of Phoenix. Through an opening in the crowd, he caught sight of Casey. His wife wore a form-fitting dress of cobalt blue that left her shoulders bare and showed just a modest amount of cleavage. The hem, on the other hand, was slit up to her thigh, displaying a significant length of slender, shapely leg. He wasn't sure how she could walk on the five-inch heels, but right now, standing with crossed arms and one shoe peeking out from the hem of the dress, she looked as though she'd been born wearing them. She said something, and the middle-aged couple beside her smiled. Drew Lawrence responded to her words, and she threw back her head and laughed.

There was nobody in this world whose laugh sounded like Casey's, and he'd heard far too little of it lately. Tonight, in that dress, in this setting, it was impossible to tell that she'd had more than her share of dark days in the past few weeks. Watching her, he could almost believe that this beautiful woman whose laughter floated on the air wasn't a doppelgänger, that she was his strong, capable, lovely wife.

But appearances were known to deceive. Tonight, she had deliberately put on what she referred to as her company face, which would easily mislead anybody who didn't know her well. It seemed to be working. Her companions appeared delighted with her company, and he suspected he was the only person in the room who knew that beneath that warm and charming persona was a woman who had crying spells for no reason, nightmares that kept her awake at night, and random bouts of grief so strong they would have flattened a lesser woman. She tried to keep it all hidden, and thought he didn't know about most of it, but he knew her too well. When she hurt, he hurt, and lately, he'd been hurting most of the time.

Somebody hip-bumped him. He turned to see who it was, and found Phoenix standing there, holding his own bottle of beer. "I had serious doubts," the kid said, "that you'd actually show up tonight."

"It was a struggle." He eyed the bottle of Rolling Rock. "And by the way, Phee, you're not old enough to drink."

"Too late for that. I've been doing it since I was twelve. No reason to quit now. And stop calling me Phee."

Maybe there was no reason to quit now, but that didn't mean the record company should be supplying it gratis. The kid should at least have to work for it. Nobody was doing him any favors, handing everything to him on a silver platter. He needed to learn the meaning of good, honest work. That was what built character, and right now, the kid could use some character building. He was hovering on the cusp of something, and it could go either way. If he fell on the right side of the fence, his future would be bright. If he fell the wrong way, he might be doomed.

And, damn it, it wasn't up to Rob MacKenzie to save the kid from himself. He had enough problems of his own. His wife, his daughters, his marriage, his career. He didn't need to add any more responsibility to an already heavy load. "Happy birthday," he said glumly, and upended his beer.

"Where's the lovely Mrs. MacKenzie?"

"Drew spirited her away. Looks like I'm on my own. Where's Luther?"

"I told him to mingle. This is a highly secure private party. His services aren't really necessary tonight. Come check out my cake."

He gestured with his beer bottle. "You're certainly old enough to appreciate it."

The kid wound his way through the room, stopping every so often to converse with his fawning subjects. Rob followed, alternately amused and irritated by the fawning. This bouncy pop crap that Phoenix was singing would not stand the test of time. Where would all these people be in five years, when there was a new kid in town, and Phoenix was just a faint memory?

They stopped in front of the cake. Ariel Records had really gone all out. The gargantuan cake was a wonder fashioned of sugar and flour and white icing in the shape of an old-fashioned portable record player, the kind that opened and closed like a suitcase. The cover was up, and on the turntable was a 45 record with the Ariel logo and the title of Phoenix's first hit single. The words HAPPY BIRTHDAY PHOENIX were written in red lettering on the cover of the record player. The damn thing must have cost a fortune. "Nice," he said.

"You don't like it."

"I didn't say that."

"You didn't have to say it. What, are you jealous because nobody ever did anything like this for you?"

Stung, he said, "You know what, Phee? One of these days, you'll learn to think before you open your mouth." And he turned and stalked away.

"Hey!" Phoenix's voice floated behind him. "I was just needling you. Don't be so bleedin' touchy!"

Ignoring him, Rob shoved his way through the crowd, marched up to the singer, who had just put to bed Laura Nyro's *Sweet Blindness*, and handed her one of the Two Dreamers business cards he always carried in his wallet. "Great pipes," he said. "If Ariel Records doesn't treat you the way they should, give me a call."

He left her standing there, card in hand and mouth sagging open, and went in search of his wife. "Excuse me," he said to her companions, catching her by the arm and dragging her away from their conversation. "I need my wife."

When they were far enough away for some semblance of privacy, she said, "That was very rude, Flash."

"I don't care. We're cutting out. I've had enough of this."

"What happened?"

"Nothing happened. I just don't want to be here anymore."

"Rob—"

He turned to respond, and the singer said into her mic, "We have a special treat for you tonight. The birthday boy is going to sing us a couple of songs."

Applause. Some of it enthusiastic, most of it merely polite. "Come on," he said, more gently, and began moving her toward the door.

Behind them, Phoenix took the mic. "Thank you," he said. "I promised the record company that I'd do this tonight…under one condition. That my producer perform with me. So where are you, Rob MacKenzie?"

Six steps from the doorway, Rob turned and glared. "That little bastard," he said.

"Over here," some woman shouted, waving a hand in the air and pointing to Rob. "He's over here."

Expectant faces turned in his direction. "Shit," he muttered, as the spotlight that had been focused on the band suddenly illuminated him with bright, white light. "Now what do I do?"

"You smile and nod, and you get up on the stage and perform."

"Great," he said through the fake smile that he'd plastered on his face.

"What's wrong, babe? It's not rocket science. You've been performing since you were nine years old. You love performing."

Still smiling, he said, "Not with that little piss-ant."

"Then you have two options. Bite the bullet and get it over with, or walk out and make a scene. I'm behind you, one hundred percent. No matter which door you choose."

It was too late for door number two. Everybody in the room was looking in his direction. There was no way he could gracefully bow out now. There was no way he could bow out at all, not without making a fool of himself. His eyes met hers, communicated a silent message. She took his hand, and together, they moved in the direction of the stage. The party guests, their enthusiasm level pumped up a notch, parted like the Red Sea as he and Casey made their way to where Phoenix waited, microphone in hand. "What took you so long?" Phoenix said, and everybody laughed.

Rob glared at him, peeled off the linen jacket and handed it to his wife, unbuttoned his cuffs and rolled them up, and hopped up onto the stage. The singer he'd just given his card to beamed, and the guitarist lifted his guitar strap over his head and handed Rob the guitar.

Compared to what he was accustomed to, it was a small audience, probably three hundred people. Still, it had been a while since he'd performed in front of an audience any larger than the thirty people who'd gathered in the music store to hear him play. He lifted the strap over his head, adjusted it against his shoulder, ran his fingertips over the strings to check the tuning. His ear told him it was right, so he leaned toward the kid and said, loud enough for the audience to hear, "What are we playing?"

"Funny you should ask," Phoenix said. "Since you're so fond of the Beatles, how about *Twist and Shout*? That is, if you even know it."

There was scattered applause. Rob glanced over his shoulder, the drummer nodded, and he leaned toward Phoenix again, this time speaking quietly, for the kid's ears only. "Bite me," he said.

And launched into the achingly familiar riff that started the song.

Casey

THERE was something significant about this moment, something
life-altering, although she couldn't pinpoint what it was. The song
was one that everybody knew, and with its irresistible rhythm,
there wasn't a body in the house that wasn't moving to the music.
Early Beatles, from the days when their music was fun and light-
hearted and could be understood without an interpreter. Rob let
Phoenix take the lead, although he could certainly have carried it
himself.

For inexplicable reasons, Rob MacKenzie had never
considered himself a decent vocalist. Was it because he'd always
played second banana to Danny? Was he still harboring some
ridiculous feeling of inferiority? If so, it was time for her to kick
his sexy butt from here to Kingdom Come. Measuring his voice
against Danny's was crazy, because a voice like Danny Fiore's
didn't come along every day. *Nobody* could sing like her late
husband.

But that didn't mean Rob couldn't sing. His voice was clear
and true and strong. Tonight, he'd chosen to harmonize and let the
birthday boy carry the melody. Phoenix was, after all, the reason
they were all gathered here tonight. It was an amazing experience,
hearing the two of them blend their voices in a harmony so sweet it
was impossible to believe they hadn't been singing together for
years.

Something happened to Rob MacKenzie when he stepped
onstage. He wasn't like Danny, who'd changed personalities the
instant he stepped into the spotlight. Larger than life, Danny Fiore
had possessed an enormous talent and an ego to match. He'd been
the consummate showman, and that in-your-face personality had
been as responsible for his popularity as his amazing voice or his
staggering good looks.

Rob's talent was quieter. There was no ego involved. Where
for Danny, it had been about the fame, about making a name for
himself and proving his worth, for Rob, it was about the music.
Period. Onstage or off, he possessed an incredible ability to lose
himself in the music, to forget any audience even existed. That was
part of what drew people to him. His lack of pretension was rare in
the entertainment business, where everybody and his second

cousin wanted to be the center of attention. Rob didn't give two hoots about the attention. He just wanted to play his music.

There was a reason they called it playing. That's what it was. Creative play, the kind that fed your soul and gave you wings. He'd been so lucky—they'd both been so lucky—to make a life and a career built around the music they loved. Rob came to life on stage, not because he had an inflated ego, not because he wanted to be the center of attention, but because music was how he communicated with the world around him.

It was Phoenix who brought surprises to the table. The *enfant terrible*, he of the canned, pre-fab pop music, could actually sing. And it was no wonder that every teenage girl on the planet was gaga over him. In spite of any possible personality flaws, the kid was heart-stoppingly handsome: long and lean, with gorgeous blue eyes, a beautifully sculpted face, and that perfect dark hair that fell in soft waves to his shoulders. And so young, with little more than peach fuzz on his upper lip. At eighteen, he had a long way to go before he'd reach manhood.

That wasn't the last surprise. Rob, who was never one to grumble, had been grousing about Phoenix Hightower almost from day one. The kid was a thorn in his side, and he'd clearly been mad at Phoenix when he'd grabbed her by the arm and dragged her to the door, intent on making his escape from this lovely event.

Yet their onstage chemistry was unparalleled. They struck sparks off each other in a way she'd seen only once before: when he'd worked with Danny.

While she pondered the possible significance of this development, they finished the song, to roaring applause and shouts of "Encore! Encore!" Rob looked up, sought her eyes, and gave her one of those amazing, heart-stopping grins.

And it struck her, hard, that he'd made a monumental mistake when he'd stopped performing. Music was Rob MacKenzie's religion, the spiritual connection that brought him closer to whatever he perceived as God than sitting in any church ever could. If she hadn't been so consumed with her own problems, she would have noticed that he was getting restless.

Their Two Dreamers record label kept him busy. They'd started small and stayed small, with just two new artists signed to the label so far. Writing, producing, recording, and promoting two debut albums took up most of his time. Although the business end of it had been a tangle, her sister had helped with that.

But he'd stopped playing. Not completely, of course. But for most of his adult life, Rob had spent at least an hour every day— most days more than that—playing his guitar. He didn't do it anymore. She couldn't remember the last time she'd seen him pick up a guitar and play it. Not unless he was sitting in on a recording session. He'd been too busy making other musicians successful to devote any time to his own music. And it was a dreadful mistake.

He'd taken on the side job of producing Phoenix's album only because Drew had begged. He hadn't done it for the money, but out of loyalty to the man who'd been responsible for getting their music heard by more than just a local audience. Drew could be a pill at times, but if he hadn't heard Danny Fiore singing in a Manhattan club fifteen years ago and recognized that he was looking at a future superstar, none of this would have happened. He'd taken the three of them on as a package deal, and their careers had skyrocketed to a place light years beyond their youthful dreams.

So whenever Drew called, Rob always answered. Even when he didn't want to. Drew Lawrence had launched a very successful career for Rob MacKenzie. And Rob's philosophy was, and always had been: *Never forget where you come from.*

Her husband was, without question, the most talented man she'd ever met. He breathed music the way other people breathed oxygen. He was smart, enthusiastic, intuitive, playful, and his instincts were spot-on. Rob excelled at everything he did: songwriting, arranging, producing, even the scut work of promoting.

But none of those things defined Rob MacKenzie. He was, first and always, a musician. A musician needed to be heard, and where Rob excelled the most was in front of an audience. Because as good as he was at all those other things, his heart belonged, had always belonged, to performing.

Onstage, their heads close together, he and Phoenix conferred, too quietly for the mic to pick up what they were saying. Rob raised his eyebrows, and Phoenix began talking again in a low voice. Rob shrugged, and Phoenix nodded to the rest of the band.

And the piano player started out.

Three notes in, she recognized the song. She knew it because Rob had written it, had recorded it on his second—and last—solo album. How Phoenix had known, she had no idea. But clearly, for some reason she had yet to determine, the kid had planned this "impromptu" performance in advance.

This time, it was Phoenix who stepped back and let Rob take the lead. *Lady, My Lady* was a love song, a bluesy, tender ode to hunger and thirst and longing for a woman the singer couldn't have. He put every ounce of his emotion, every ounce of his soul into the song.

And she realized, with a shock, that he'd written it about her.

Danny had still been alive when Rob penned this song. She'd still been married to him, newly reconciled after a year-long separation, and she and Rob were just beginning to recognize the impossible feelings they had for each other. She'd been so deep into denial that she'd refused to even entertain the possibility that she was in love with him. And Rob had been hurting. She hadn't realized it at the time; she'd been too busy struggling to glue her broken marriage back together, too confused by her own weighty and conflicted emotions to be able to deal with his. And he'd deliberately avoided her; Rob had come to Maine only once during those last months she and Danny were together.

But he'd written this song, and he'd recorded it, the only song on that second album that he'd written without her. It had been his lone acknowledgment, until long after Danny was dead, of his feelings for her, of what had happened between them on that white-sand beach in the Bahamas. And she'd been so buried in her own denial, it had taken her until now to recognize the truth.

His eyes met and held hers. Goosebumps sprang to life on her arms, her legs, her breasts, and she had the oddest feeling that she was seeing him, really seeing him, for the first time. Gazes locked together, they might have been the only two people in the room. She was vaguely aware of Phoenix, the pop sensation, the birthday boy, singing harmony on this song she would have expected he'd never even heard of. But it was Rob MacKenzie, the perennial also-ran, who stole the show with a stunning interpretation of lyrics he'd written when he was in the kind of pain that no man could understand until he found himself in love, deeply and irrevocably, with his best friend's wife.

Pain. Yearning. Restrained passion.

And an unvoiced yet implied determination to wait as long as it took for her to open her eyes and see him standing there, his heart in his hand. That heart, and this song, the only gifts of love he had to give.

Tears filled her eyes and trickled down her face. Ever cognizant of her every emotion, he raised an eyebrow, and through her tears, she beamed a warm, loving smile. Understanding lit those green eyes of his, and he smiled back. Then he looked at Phoenix, nodded, and together, with voices blended in perfect harmony, they launched into the final verse of the song.

As time goes moving on,
I don't care what people say
I'm just gonna stay right here
and love you anyway

As the last note faded away, there was enthusiastic applause from the crowd. Phoenix gestured in Rob's direction and said into his mic, "Ladies and gentlemen, Mr. Rob MacKenzie."

Rob nodded at his audience, said, "Thank you," and handed the guitar back to its owner. He stepped down off the stage and moved directly to where she stood waiting.

He didn't say a word, just swiped at her tears with his thumb. "Why didn't you tell me?" she said. "Why didn't you tell me you wrote it for me?"

"How was I supposed to do that? It wouldn't have changed anything."

"Maybe it would have."

"We've had this conversation before, babe. You and I can't change the past. It is what it is. There's only one direction we can go, and it's not backwards."

"I don't say this as often as I should. And things have been so crazy since I lost the baby. *I've* been so crazy. But I love you, as much as any woman could ever love a man."

"And if I were a praying man, I'd get down on my knees every morning and give thanks for that. I love you, too." He leaned down and gave her a sweet, tender kiss. Studied her face and said, "You might want to find a powder room and fix your face."

"Raccoon eyes?"

"Just a little. Go on. I'll wait for you here."

In the elegant powder room, she did her best to fix the damage the tears had done to her face. When she rejoined Rob, somebody had brought the gargantuan birthday cake out in front of the band, and one of Drew's lackeys was busy lighting the candles. Rob was engaged in conversation with a guy she recognized as the lead singer for one of the hottest rock bands to ever sign with the Ariel label. Drew had clearly brought them all here tonight to impress the birthday boy with his own importance. *See? Even Troy Duncan showed up for my birthday party. That must mean I've arrived. I'm Somebody.*

Rob put an arm around her and cradled her loosely against his side. Troy Duncan's cool blue eyes took her measure, and Rob introduced them. "My wife, Casey," he said. "Troy Duncan."

Duncan pumped her hand with enthusiasm and said, "Casey Fiore MacKenzie. It's so great to meet you. I was just telling your husband how impressed I am with your work."

"Thank you."

"When you think of legendary songwriting teams, who comes to mind? Goffin and King. Lieber and Stoller. Lennon and McCartney. Fiore and MacKenzie."

"Wow. I'm flattered."

"Don't be. You've earned the recognition."

The candle-lighting completed, the singer said into her mic, "Let's all sing the birthday song to Phoenix!" She started, in a rich, deep contralto, and the assembled multitude joined in, a fair number of them actually singing in tune. Rob rolled his eyes, but Casey joined in. When the song was over, the singer said, "Happy birthday, Phoenix Hightower! Now, make a wish and blow out all those candles!"

"All those candles," Rob muttered. "The kid's only eighteen. She makes it sound like he's Methuselah."

"Oh, stop being a curmudgeon. It doesn't become you."

Troy Duncan grinned—clearly as enthused about this birthday bash as Rob—and Phoenix, flanked by Drew and a smiling record company exec, made a big deal out of blowing out those eighteen candles. Flashbulbs popped, and a cheer went up around the room as the kid managed somehow to get them all blown out. Drew shook his hand, the minion did the same, and then a banquet waitress, who'd been standing by with a rolling cart of plates and napkins and silver, began carving up the cake that somebody had put so much effort into creating.

"I think that's our exit sign," Rob said. "Unless you want cake?"

"I'm not interested in cake. Although it might be nice to bring a piece home to Paige."

Rob headed off in search of cake, Duncan drifted away, and she was alone. Time to give her felicitations to the birthday boy. She crossed the room with determination, stood on the fringes of the group of hangers-on who were jockeying for position at the kid's side. Phoenix looked up, saw her, said something, and the hangers-on all dropped back. "Mrs. MacKenzie," he said, moving toward her with his hand out. "Thank you for coming."

His handshake was brisk and confident. Not too long, not too short. She said, "Happy birthday, Phoenix. And congratulations. Eighteen is a true milestone. You're now officially an adult. With your talent, you can hold the world in your hand, as long as you make good choices."

"I thank you. Although that last part sounds remarkably like something your husband would say."

"Really? I'm not surprised. We've been together for so long that we're starting to look alike."

"I would have to disagree with that. You're far prettier than he is."

Was this eighteen-year-old kid flirting with her? The idea was so absurd that she laughed. "You should listen to him," she said. "He's a smart man."

"He's also, without a doubt, one of the most maddening people I've ever met. Yet, for some reason, he seems to have grown on me."

"That's funny, because he says the same thing about you."

The kid raised a single, dark brow, and a brief smile lit his lips. "Really?" he said.

"Really. But don't let him know I told you that, or I'll never hear the end of it."

"Too late, I'm afraid." Phoenix nodded over her shoulder. "He's standing directly behind you."

Rob

I COME bearing cake," he said as she turned. "And your wrap."

She gave him one of those Mona Lisa smiles that always turned him inside out and said, "Busted."

He handed her two small bags of sliced cake and draped the white silk wrap around her shoulders, freeing her hair and running a thumb along her collarbone. "Good-night, Phee," he said. "Stay sober. I need you at the studio by eight-thirty in the morning."

Phoenix raised his beer bottle in acknowledgment, and Rob guided his wife through the crowd, out of the ballroom, and outside into the summer evening. He nodded to the doorman, who leaned against the building, twenty feet from the door, taking advantage of a quiet moment to court lung cancer.

"Finally," he said. "I thought we'd never get out of there."

"I don't know why you find Phoenix so annoying," she said. "I think he's quite charming."

"Ah, geez. He got to you, didn't he?"

"He was a tad bit flirty. And he is pretty cute."

"He's obnoxious, and stubborn, and—*cute*?"

She gave him a cheeky grin. "It's all right, sweetheart. I think you're cute, too."

"I'm forty years old," he said irritably, "and nobody's called me cute since kindergarten."

"You're thirty-nine," she said. "And it's a beautiful night. Let's walk."

The curb beside them was empty. This was Manhattan, and they were standing in front of a luxury hotel. Where the hell were all the taxis that should have been lined up at the curb? Looking skeptically at her feet, he said, "Are you up to walking? In those shoes?"

She glanced down and said, "Well, I wouldn't want to walk from here to New Jersey in them, but I can handle a few blocks."

For some reason, the idea of walking made him uneasy. "It's late."

She raised elegant, dark brows. "Since when has late bothered you?"

He shrugged. She was right. They'd been walking the streets of New York at night since forever. There was no valid reason for his unease. So he caved. "I guess there's no reason why we can't walk."

"There," she said, falling into step with him and looping her arm through his. "Isn't this nice?"

"Beats hell out of that party we just left." He slid his gaze toward her, took note of the lack of tension in her body. She'd just survived a birthday party with three hundred guests, had made nice with more than a few of them, but he saw no signs of anxiety in her. "I'll probably end up regretting that I even brought this up," he said, "but you seem to be doing better the last few days."

"I am," she said, sounding surprised. "I'm feeling a little better."

He wasn't crazy enough to think this meant that whatever was wrong with her had suddenly and miraculously been cured. But this had to mean she was on the road to recovery. Didn't it?

They turned a corner onto a side street where sodium arc lights spilled pools of illumination that alternated with areas of darkness. He felt a prickle at the back of his neck, stared hard into the velvety darkness ahead, but saw nothing. "Look," he said, "can we talk about this?"

Her arm, looped with his, tensed. To her credit, she didn't pretend to not know what he was talking about. "Please don't ruin the evening," she said. "I don't want to fight."

"Neither do I." He squared his jaw. "And I don't want you to construe this as begging. I've never had to beg a woman for sex, and I'm not about to start now. Not even with you. I have a little too much pride for that."

"Point taken."

"But don't you think we should try to find a compromise? The way we're living—it's just not natural."

Silence. And then she said, in a quiet voice, "I know."

"So why the hell are we putting ourselves through this?"

"Because," she said. "Because you don't understand—or apparently care—how important this is to me! Sometimes, I feel small and insignificant, because you simply won't listen to me. I don't understand your attitude, Rob. We've always had such great communication. But on this topic, you've gone completely deaf and blind."

"Small and insignificant? Be serious! I've bent over backwards to keep you happy. To accommodate your every wish. But what's the point, if you're still not happy?"

"Don't you dare to put words in my mouth! I *am* happy!"

"Then let's stop the battling." He came to a halt, took her hands in his, and looked into her eyes. "Let's set our differences aside for tonight. It doesn't mean we stop talking about it. It doesn't mean we're making any permanent decisions. It's not forever. It's just one night out of our lives."

She bit her lower lip. She always did that when she was torn, uncertain of how to proceed. "I don't know."

"One night, babe. One night when we can be together, the way it used to be, before the miscarriage, before all this craziness started." He rubbed her knuckles with the pad of his thumb. "I love you so much," he said. "I just want to be with you."

"I want to be with you, too. But why is it that I have to be the one who's expected to sell out?"

"It's not selling out. But we have to use birth control. We're looking at a life-or-death scenario. We can't take any chances."

"Right. So, in other words, I sell out."

"Jesus, Mary and Joseph! I'm not saying that what I want is more important than what you want. But any way you look at it, my need to keep you alive trumps your need to have another kid. If we do it your way, you could die. Don't you think we owe it to ourselves to think the situation through with clear heads and work out a solution we can both live with before we make some monumental mistake? I don't want to lose you, and if you get pregnant, there's no going back. I'm just asking for a temporary compromise. That's all."

"Evening, folks."

Both their heads swiveled around in surprise. In a pool of light at the edge of darkness stood a young man. Muscular and fit, with brown hair and pale eyes, possibly blue, possibly green, indistinguishable in the dark, he was probably no older than twenty-five. Holding out a drawstring bag, he said, in a native New York accent, "Valuables, please."

"Oh, for the love of—" Rob bit off his words as the man's eyes hardened. Beside him, Casey remained silent, showing no outward sign of fear. This was his fault. He should have trusted his gut. It never failed him. They should have waited for a cab instead of walking. And what kind of idiots stood arguing on a dark New York City sidewalk at midnight?

"Come on, people, you think I got all night? Move it! Jewelry, wallets, cell phones. In the bag."

The guy was a few inches shorter than him, and probably about the same weight. If he wasn't carrying a weapon, Rob could probably take him.

Casey's eyes narrowed, and she gave a barely perceptible shake of her head. She'd clearly read his mind. So had the mugger. There came the distinct snick of a switchblade being released, and light glinted off shiny steel. "If you want your pretty lady's face to stay pretty," the guy said, "you'll make this quick."

Rob exhaled a hard breath. As Casey calmly removed her diamond earrings, he reached into his pocket and pulled out his wallet. Glaring at the mugger, he dropped the wallet into the bag with her earrings. "Keep going," the guy said, gesturing with the blade. "Rings, watches."

Clearly aghast, Casey said, "You can't possibly want my wedding ring!"

"Give it to him," Rob said. "Don't argue with the asshole."

"Smart man," the mugger said. "Your watch, too. And your cell phone. You stupid rich people always carry cell phones."

He took out his phone, heaved it into the bag, pried off the wedding ring that hadn't left his finger since the day Casey placed it there. "You don't want my watch," he said. "It's a friggin' Timex. Worth about thirty bucks."

"A penny saved is a penny earned. Give it to me anyway. Lady? Your purse?"

She opened her jeweled clutch and showed him. "There's nothing of any value. Just lipstick and mascara."

"Fine. You can keep that." The guy began backing away. Said, "A pleasure doing business with you."

And he disappeared into the shadows, his rapid footsteps echoing off brick and brownstone.

* * *

"Thank you, officers." Rob closed and locked the door behind the pair of New York's finest who'd taken the robbery report. He'd already cancelled his cell phone service and his credit cards, had made those calls while they waited for the police. Because he'd only been carrying a couple hundred in cash, losing the wallet was more of an inconvenience than anything. Getting a new driver's license and a new Social Security card would be a pain in the ass, but a minor annoyance compared to the loss of their wedding rings. They could buy replacements, but the sentimental value was irreplaceable. Those rings had held deep meaning. Now they were gone, and the chances of getting them back were somewhere on the wrong side of zero. According to the police, they'd probably already been fenced. The situation had left him steaming. His wife, who'd lost her engagement ring, her wedding band, and the earrings he'd bought her on their honeymoon, was devastated.

She sat on the couch, legs tucked beneath her, wearing sweatpants and a tee shirt and holding the cup of tea he'd made for her while they waited for the cops. "You okay, kid?" he said, flopping down beside her.

"I'll live. But I can't believe this. While it was happening, it felt like a lifetime, but when it was over, I realized it couldn't have taken more than thirty seconds."

"It's my fault. I knew better than to walk home that late. And I sure as hell knew better than to stand on the sidewalk and argue, on a side street in Manhattan, at midnight. I put both our lives in jeopardy because I was thinking with the little head instead of the big one."

"That almost sounds sweet, until I really think about it. And I share equally in the blame. Walking was my idea. I'm not an idiot. I spent enough years living in the city to know the dangers. It's a little ironic, don't you think? The entire time we've been in New York, I've imagined danger lurking on every street corner. Yet when danger was really there—"

He slung an arm around her shoulders. She leaned into him, and he pressed a soft kiss to her temple. "And our rings," she said. "Our beautiful wedding rings."

"We'll get new ones. They're just things. They can be replaced."

"They're not just things. Their significance can't be replaced. Or the memories. You put that ring on my finger on our wedding day. We can't redo that."

"We could if we wanted to." He kicked off his shoes and buried his nose in her hair. She smelled like fresh-picked strawberries. "We could renew our vows."

"After just three years? People would think we were crazy. And I don't need that. We'll get replacements and move on. But I'm heartsick that the bastard took them."

"It could've been a lot worse. When I think of what might've happened, that's when I feel sick."

"Don't. We're both fine. Shaken, furious, violated. But we're fine."

He lifted his feet and rested them, ankles crossed, on the coffee table. "You're a tough old broad."

"Not so tough these last few weeks."

"That's why you have me. I'm your backup. In spite of what you seem to think, everything I do is for you. You and the girls. And you're stuck with me. I promised you sixty years with a negotiable renewal, and that's what you're getting."

"Then what was with the death wish tonight? I knew exactly what was going through that twisted little brain of yours. How could you even consider taking him on?"

"You know, sometimes it gets really annoying, the way you read my mind. You know me too damn well."

"That doesn't answer the question."

"It was a momentary aberration. Besides—" He lifted her teacup and took a sip. Handed it back to her and settled back against the couch. "I could've taken him."

"Are you serious, MacKenzie? He was fifteen years younger than you, solid muscle, and carrying a switchblade. When was the last time you got in a fight? An actual physical altercation?"

"Oh, probably about…middle school?"

"I rest my case."

"And I plead the Fifth." He closed his eyes and smiled to himself. "But if he hadn't been carrying the switchblade, I could've taken him."

Casey

THE morning sun's rays crept through slotted blinds and fell in alternating patterns of light and shadow on the bed where they lay. Beside her, Rob slept still and hard, the way he always did. She envied him that ability. Even after something as stressful as a mugging, he was able to fall asleep—and stay asleep—while she lay awake, pondering the mysteries of the universe and stewing about things that were unlikely to ever happen.

It was simply the way they were wired. Three years of marriage had taught her a few things she hadn't known about the man who'd been her best friend for two decades. Living together, sleeping together, had highlighted their differences. He hated to be hot; she hated to be cold. Driving anywhere together was a running battle between the heater and the air conditioner. She carried a sweater everywhere, even during the hot summer months. Rob, on the other hand, spent most of those same months stripped to a level just this side of indecent. They fell asleep at night in each other's arms, but by morning, her husband was hugging the edge of the mattress in order to escape her body heat.

It all averaged out. They might have differences, but they both loved Led Zeppelin's *Stairway to Heaven*, and he'd introduced her, decades ago, to the music of Billie Holiday. That common ground trumped all differences.

She loved to watch him sleep. Naked, he lay face down, arms folded beneath his head, his covers long since discarded, the faint zebra striping from the blinds giving him an exotic look. He needed a haircut. Although he'd had the wild tangle of curls sheared off before Emma was born, he hadn't really tamed them. Now that he was wearing his hair short, it always looked good for a week or two after each cut before reverting back to its natural state of wild abandon.

Rob MacKenzie was a good-looking man. She knew he didn't believe that, but then he seemed incapable of seeing himself the way she saw him. He wasn't handsome in the way Danny had been, with his summer-sky eyes and smoldering good looks. Rob's face was open and friendly and painted with a depth of character that had been missing in her first husband. Every line, every imperfection, told a story. His green eyes were warm and inviting and honest. He expected the best out of people, and he usually got it.

And women fell at his feet.

She moved closer in order to study his tattoo. The redness and the swelling had disappeared, and although she hadn't yet tested her theory, it appeared as though most of the pain had left with them. She touched her lips, gentle as a feather, to the letters printed on his bicep. Her name. He didn't react. Feeling bold, she took a gentle nibble from his arm, a couple of inches below the tattoo.

"Mmm," he said.

She took another bite, this time from his side. He growled low in his throat, but she couldn't translate it. Was it a growl of pleasure, or of irritation?

More boldly, she threw a leg over him and slithered on top of him, straddling that cute, round little ass. She ran the fingers of both hands up the center of his spine to his shoulders, then began working the muscles with her fingertips. "Mmn," he said again. "Is that you, Esmerelda?"

She gave him a hard little smack and continued kneading.

"Hortense?" he said. "Raquel? Rapunzel?"

"Funny boy."

He turned his head to one side, smacked his lips, stretched his arms. "Morning, wife."

She stopped kneading and said, "Good morning, my gorgeous, sexy man."

"Don't stop. It feels good."

"That's the general idea."

"Right there. Knotted muscle. You have magic hands. So what did I do to deserve this?"

"I've been thinking. About what you said last night, before we were so rudely interrupted by our larcenous new friend."

Outside the window, a pair of birds called brightly back and forth. "And?"

"I've decided that you're right. The way we're living isn't working for us. We've both been holding out on general principles, to prove the validity of our respective points. But the truth is that we're only punishing ourselves. And that's a sad, stupid thing. So I'm going to consent—" She ran the heel of her hand up the smooth, warm flesh of his back. "—to using condoms while we work this situation out. But I refuse to use anything more permanent than that, and we'll have to continue discussions until we reach a reasonable solution we both can agree to."

"Anybody ever tell you that you'd make a good lawyer?"

"What?"

"Nothing. Keep going."

"What else do you want me to say?"

"Not the mouth. The hands."

"Oh." Hiding a brief smile, she continued her ministrations, digging deep into knotted muscle, eventually drawing her palms down his back in long, smooth strokes. He shifted beneath her, dislodged her, and rolled onto his back. On hands and knees above him, she leaned down, her dark hair a curtain that surrounded them, and kissed him. He deepened the kiss, swept a hand down her bare back to her tailbone, and pulled her down on top of him.

And everything inside her went liquid. It had been so long, too long, since they'd been together like this. Still kissing, they rolled, slow and hot and languid. He reached out an arm and blindly punched buttons on the clock radio beside the bed until soft music filled the room. Foreigner's *I Want to Know What Love Is*. Sound insulation. His body a heavy weight that pinned her down, he explored her with his mouth, his hands. She nipped his shoulder, his Adam's apple, and he cupped her breast, drew it into his mouth, and suckled gently on the sensitive peak.

She wrapped a leg around him, rolled his hips as he gave the same delightful attention to her other breast. "Hot mama," he said, and she laughed and dragged his mouth back to hers.

Their kisses were hot and wet and unhurried. "I know what love is," he said, his words a warm gust of breath against her neck.

"Must you? Do I really have to put up with the song lyric thing again?"

"Humor me, Fiore. Just humor me."

"Fine," she said. "So tell me, great oracle. What is love?"

He cradled her head in his hands, locked his gaze with hers, and planted a gentle kiss at the corner of her mouth. "Love is better at forty," he said, and plunged hot and slick inside her, "than it was at twenty."

"Oh, baby," she said. "You are so right."

* * *

"I can't believe it," he said. "I can't believe I forgot the frigging condom."

"It was my irresistible charm that sidetracked you."

"You did it on purpose. You manipulated me. I hope you're happy."

They lay together in a slick, sweaty tangle, his leg wrapped around hers, her cheek pressed against his chest, his heartbeat strong beneath her ear. She pursed her lips and blew a gentle stream of air down the center of his chest, stirring the inexplicably dark vee of hair that grew there. "Shut up," she said. "You're distracting me."

Lazily, he said, "From?"

"From basking in the afterglow. Right now, I'm purring like a fat, satisfied cat."

He ran a hand down her side, knuckles stroking her bare thigh. Pausing mid-stroke, he said, "So this little, um…pussycat…got exactly what she wanted?"

"Oh, stop. You're being crude. I hate it when you're crude."

"Liar. You love it when I'm crude. Especially when I'm a-rockin' and a-rollin' you."

"Circumstances, my friend." She pressed a kiss to his damp skin. "Circumstances."

"So in other words, the minute the rockin' and rollin' is over, you go back to being Miss Priss."

"Behave," she said, nuzzling that wonderful, springy chest hair, "or I'll take a chunk out of your flesh."

"Giving all new meaning to the term *bite me.*"

"I'd forgotten what it felt like. Can you believe that? It's been so long that I'd actually forgotten."

"You forgot what sex felt like?"

"Not sex, fool. But the way you make me feel when we do it. I'd forgotten your amazing and inspiring ability to rock my world. As a matter of fact, my memory seems to be getting hazy again. I might need another reminder."

"As much as it pains me to say this, I'll have to take a rain check. I nccd to be at the studio by eight-thirty, and before I leave for work, I want to call the DMV and ask them to issue me a new driver's license. It would be really nice if they could put a rush on it."

She'd almost forgotten. His words were a solemn reminder of that empty spot on her left-hand ring finger. She closed her eyes, let out a sigh, and just floated. In spite of his words, neither of them made a move to get up. "We have to talk about it," he said. "At some point, we have to talk about it."

"About what happened last night?"

"About what we just did. Without protection. It was a stupid move on both our parts."

"Don't spoil this. Please don't spoil it. We can talk about it tonight. Right now, I just want to lie here a little longer and hold you."

"Couple of minutes. Then I really have to get up."

"I'll make you breakfast while you shower."

"Emma's still sleeping. You should stay in bed. We were up late."

"And early."

She felt, rather than heard, his soft laugh. "And early. So that means you should stay in bed and sleep a little longer. Once Emma's up, all bets are off."

"I'll have plenty of time for sleeping in my old age. I'd rather cook breakfast for you."

"A man can't argue with that." He tangled his fingers in the hair at the back of her neck and tilted her head so he could see her eyes. "Are you okay after last night? Really?"

"I am. Really. It felt so surreal, and it happened so quickly, I didn't have time to be frightened. I was outraged, more than anything. How dare he take everything from us that wasn't nailed down?"

"Like I said last night, you're a tough old broad."

"Thank you. I think."

They shared a long, sweet kiss, and then he ran his hand down her body, gave her a sound smack on her bare rump, and said, "Up and at 'em, wench. This boy needs breakfast."

* * *

By the time he came into the kitchen, cradling the cordless phone between ear and shoulder while rolling up his shirt sleeves, she had eggs, bacon and toast waiting. He moved directly to the cupboard, took out a cup, and poured coffee into it. Stirring milk and sugar into the cup, he rolled his eyes. "On hold," he mouthed. Then he straightened up, suddenly alert. "Yeah," he said into the phone, "this is Rob MacKenzie. I live in Jackson Falls, I'm in New York right now, and last night, my wallet was stolen. I need you to mail me a new driver's license. No, that won't work. I need you to mail it here. To New York. We're living here temporari—yeah, okay. I'll hold."

"Sit," she said, and put his plate on the table.

He carried his coffee cup to the table, sat, dumped salt, pepper and ketchup over his eggs. "You eating?" he said.

"Later. The baby will be up any minute. Do you think Phoenix will be on time this morning?"

"Hard to say. The kid likes to party, and he doesn't like to listen to me." Rob tucked into his eggs like a man who hadn't eaten in a month.

"The two of you last night," she said, "you sounded wonderful."

"You know, that's something I've been meaning to—yeah, hi." He set down his fork, listened to the person at the other end of the phone. A matched set of grooves sprang to life on either side of his mouth. "I understand that," he said, "but I'm in a bind here. I'm out of town, I'm here with my wife's car, and I really don't want to—uh huh. Right. I absolutely understand your point of view. But I can't drive without a license, I'm four states away from home, and—fine."

Scowling, he told Casey, "They put me on hold again. Goddamn bureaucratic red tape. They can't mail it to New York. It has to go to the address that's printed on it."

"You told Drew last night that we'd only be here a few more days."

"How the hell am I supposed to drive in the meantime?"

"How many times have we taken the car out since we got here?"

"I don't like feeling trapped. I—yes. Hi. How can you help me? Funny you should ask. I need a new driver's license, that's how you can help me." He paused, listened. "That would be just peachy, y'know, but I'm three hundred miles away. Uh huh. Photo I.D.? I don't have a freaking photo I.D. I already explained this to the first woman I talked to. My wallet was stolen last night. My wife and I were mugged. We're in New York City. The only photo I.D. I had was my license, and—" He stopped abruptly and rubbed at his temple. "You know what? I don't have time for this right now. I have to be at work in twenty minutes. I'll take care of this in person, when I get home next week. In the meantime, don't hold me responsible for driving without a license. Because that's exactly what I'm planning to do!"

He pushed the button to end the call, said, "Remember the days, not so long ago, when you could slam down the phone to make a point? I really miss those days."

"You could still do it, but it wouldn't have the same effect."

"No kidding." He stood, took a slug of coffee, and snagged a single bacon slice from his plate. "Gotta run. Have I mentioned that you look really hot this morning, wife of mine?"

"You're deranged. I haven't combed my hair or brushed my teeth, and this robe looks like something my grandmother would've worn."

"Hot, sexy woman," he said, backing her up against the kitchen counter. She snaked her arms around him and they shared a steamy, passionate kiss. "You look," he said, "like a woman who was just thoroughly ravished. And was utterly—" He kissed her again. "And completely—" Again. "—Satisfied."

"Jesus Christ," Paige said from the doorway. "Do you think the two of you could get a room or something?"

They glanced up and into each other's eyes, and Rob shot her a wink. Behind him, his daughter, looking rumpled and sleepy in men's flannel pajamas, carried her baby sister propped on her hip. Emma, wearing the same barely-awake look, rubbed at one eye with her fist.

"We already have a room," he said. "And a word of advice. When the bed's rocking, don't come knocking."

"Ew, Dad. That is gross."

"Not from where I'm standing." Leaning over, he kissed the top of Casey's head, said, "Later," and popped the bacon into his mouth.

* * *

While she fed the girls and cleaned the kitchen and bathed Emma, she thought it over. Today, while she was feeling strong and decisive, still high on this morning's amazing sex and bearing a steely determination to put the situation to bed, she would exorcise her demons. She'd made it through last night's birthday party without a shred of anxiety, and then she'd faced a street hoodlum and survived that as well. Granted, Rob had been there by her side last night, radiating love and strength. But even in his absence, fortified by his love, she was certain she could cross rivers by just raising her wings and flying to the other side.

She hadn't realized how fractured, how incomplete, she'd felt without the intimacy that had been such a huge part of their relationship. How fraught with tension their marriage had been as they both stubbornly refused to back down from their opposing positions. This morning had reminded her of what she'd been missing and had left her believing she could scale mountains. Things still were far from perfect between the two of them. They still couldn't agree about the life-altering decision of whether or not to attempt another pregnancy. She understood his reluctance, even if he didn't understand her determination. But her world seemed, finally, to have begun righting itself. While she was still riding the crest of that wave, she needed to try to find the Casey who'd disappeared after the miscarriage. If she could survive the events of the past twenty-four hours without falling apart, then she clearly possessed the strength of will to search out the missing pieces, and face the ghosts who lived in that empty apartment over Wong's Tea House.

A niggling guilt gnawed at her. She ignored it. Rob would pitch a fit if he knew where she was going. At the very least, he'd insist on going with her. As much as she loved him, this was something she had to face alone. This was her battle to fight, her past she was confronting. Not his, even if he had been a huge part of that past. If she continued to let him carry her, she would never heal, would never overcome the darkness, would never get past this thing, with its dark and sharpened teeth, that she couldn't even give a name to.

But the guilt was still there. Rob MacKenzie was a good man, a trusting man, and she owed him the truth. He wouldn't be pleased to know that she'd withheld something like this from him, even though she was withholding it in the interests of self-preservation. He'd figure it out anyway. Rob always did. He had this uncanny ability to read her mind. It was sometimes amusing, often disconcerting, and nearly always maddening.

She waited until early afternoon, Emma's nap time, when Paige could babysit her sister without expending much effort, while sitting in front of the TV, engrossed in the soap operas she'd gotten hooked on this summer. It was also far enough past the lunch hour so Casey should be able to catch Freddy when he had a few minutes of free time.

For some inexplicable reason, it was important that she look her best. Maybe for when they carted her off to the psych ward at Bellevue? Or maybe she was hoping that Freddy would be so distracted by her stunning good looks that he wouldn't notice the craziness in her eyes. Frowning at her mirrored reflection, she took note of every wrinkle, every line, the spiderweb of cracks spreading outward from the corners of her eyes. On her husband, those eye crinkles and laugh lines looked good. They added character to his face. On her, they just said *old*.

She brushed her hair, pulled it back in a loose braid, then carefully painted on her face. When she was done, her wrinkles hidden, she looked a decade younger than her real age. Still critical of her appearance, she nevertheless pronounced herself presentable. Sharply feeling the loss of her wedding and engagement rings, she took the jeweler's box from her lingerie drawer and slid the emerald onto her ring finger.

It wasn't the same. The weight, the heft, were all wrong. After three years of wearing the rings he'd given her as a promise and a symbol of their love, she'd become accustomed to their feel, and the antique ring felt foreign on her finger. But it was exquisite, was a family heirloom, and Rob had given it to her. If she had to wear a substitute for the lost rings, there could be none better than this. She felt like she was taking a piece of him with her. Extra ammunition in case she needed to borrow a little of his strength if this venture turned bad. She wasn't concerned about losing the ring. For one thing, it was broad daylight, and muggers were primarily nocturnal creatures. Beyond that, lightning seldom struck twice. If she lost another ring to a thief, she would consider it an act of God, a sign that the universe was telling her to leave her jewelry at home.

She told Paige she had an errand to run, and the girl accepted her explanation at face value. "I'll probably be gone for a couple of hours," she told her stepdaughter, bending to give Emma a big, smooshy kiss. "If there's an emergency, call my cell. If for some reason you don't get me, call your father at the studio."

"Emmy and I will be fine," Paige said. "As soon as you're gone, we're ordering pepperoni and anchovy pizza, and we're spending the afternoon stuffing our faces. Right, Em?"

"You can't give her pepperoni. She could choke."

"I'm kidding," Paige said. "Geez, sometimes you're so gullible."

"And sometimes, I don't know how to take you."

The train was crowded, and too warm, its air conditioning feeble and struggling. Across the aisle, an elderly Asian man read a newspaper in Chinese. A gaggle of teenage boys pushed and shoved each other playfully, while a stern-looking woman in sensible shoes gave them a disapproving look. To her left, a young woman fanned herself with a copy of *Ulysses*. On her right, a Hispanic girl with a stroller, looking far too young to be a mother, cooed softly to her baby. Breaking the standard subway protocol of avoiding eye contact, Casey smiled at the girl and then said, "How old is she?"

"Eight months."

"Mine's fifteen months. Emma. There's nothing like it, is there?"

The girl's smile lit up her pretty face. "My parents blew a gasket when they found out I was pregnant. They said I was too young, that I'd regret it." She gazed with adoration at her babbling, dark-eyed little girl. "But I don't regret it. I wouldn't trade Rosa for the world. She's the best thing that ever happened to me."

And, mother to mother, they shared an intimate smile that spoke volumes.

When she got off the train, the subway platform was stifling. As she fought her way through the crowd, she could feel her makeup melting. Out on the street, it was better, with a nice breeze that cooled her face. She set off at a brisk pace in the direction of Wong's, with no idea of what would happen when she got there. Maybe Freddy wouldn't be there; maybe he wouldn't remember her. Maybe he wouldn't let her into the apartment.

Or maybe he would.

Her composure was perplexing. Shouldn't she be nervous? Instead, she seemed to have developed nerves of steel. It wasn't until she turned the corner and saw Wong's, halfway down the block, that her throat tightened and her heart rate kicked up a notch. There was something fated about this, too. She could feel it in her marrow. Butterflies, unbidden, sprang to life in her belly. Was she really going through with this? Across the street from the restaurant, she stood on the sidewalk and studied the building, stared at those blank windows as though willing them to give her some kind of sign. *Stop. Go. Proceed with caution.* Which color were the lights? Which options did fate want her to take?

But the windows remained blank and expressionless, offering nothing. No wisdom, no recognition. She was on her own, then. There'd be no help from anyone or anything. That was the way she wanted it, the way it had to be. Wasn't it?

She took a deep breath to still the nerves that had proven they weren't really made of steel. Then she stepped off the curb and crossed the street.

A bell over the door tinkled when she stepped inside. Wonderful smells, delicious and exotic, assailed her from every direction. Ginger and cooking grease and strong black tea. The Asian woman behind the hostess podium picked up a menu, smiled, and said, in heavily accented English, "Table for one?"

She wet her lips. "Actually," she said, "I'm here to see Freddy. Is he available?"

Rob

IT bothered him for hours, this morning's massive screw-up. How could he have forgotten to use a condom, when the birth control battle they'd been waging for weeks could become a matter of life and death for his wife? It was pathetic, the way he sniffed around her like a randy dog, gratified by any scraps she deigned to toss his way. He should exercise a little more self-control, exhibit a little more self-esteem, act a little less like a drooling Rottweiler in the presence of a thick strip of sirloin. But sex fogged his brain and clouded his judgment. It had always done that. If anybody needed proof of that, he had only to point to the insanity of his marriage to Monique. She'd led him around by his dick until one day when, in the middle of one of their legendary battles, he'd looked at her, really looked at this woman he'd married.

And he'd realized that things were not going to change, that this was not where he wanted to spend the rest of his life.

He'd walked out the door without a backward glance, while Monique wailed and shrieked and tossed half the contents of her kitchen at his retreating back. But he'd walked with his self-esteem intact, and that was more important than any concern about courting physical assault with a heavy steel frying pan. He'd managed to escape the marriage mostly unscathed, and he thought he'd learned a lesson about thinking with his brain instead of his libido.

Now, he wasn't so sure he'd learned a damn thing.

Not that Casey was anything like Monique. And their marriage was nothing like that brief, ill-fated one. He loved her with all his heart. She wasn't just his hot little *mamacita*, she was his best friend, the voice inside his head that reminded him of the difference between right and wrong, the one person on this planet who made him want to be a better man. But sometimes, he still felt like that lost and scattered twenty-something he'd once been, still being led around by his dick. He supposed good sex had a way of doing that to any man, and this morning's sex had been earth-shattering. He wasn't sure whether it was because he'd been celibate for nearly two months, or because, for him at least, being in love made the sex better. Not that sex was ever bad, but with

Casey, it was stupendous, hot and sweaty and noisy, steamy enough to destroy a man's brain cells.

Which didn't really explain why the whole birth control thing had flown like a little swallow from his brain prior to the act. They'd been right in the middle of the action, going at it hot and heavy, when he remembered that tiny detail he'd been so willing to take a stand for just minutes earlier. How could he have forgotten? By then, of course, it was too late. He wasn't about to stop for anything. The house could have been on fire and he wouldn't have stopped. Okay, maybe in the event of fire or profuse bleeding, he might have at least considered it. But he wouldn't have been happy about it.

They really needed to have that talk. Not an argument, but a calm, logical discussion between two reasonably sane adults. They needed to have it while she was strong and anxiety-free, and while they were both fully clothed. Because once the clothes came off, nobody in this relationship was capable of thinking clearly.

Which was why he decided to cut out early and head home in the hopes of having that talk. Phoenix had finished his day's work by lunchtime and flown the coop. This afternoon was devoted to listening to the morning's work and doing a little mixing. Kyle could take care of that. Tomorrow, they would confer about his choices, but it was a near guarantee that Rob would agree with them. He trusted Kyle implicitly. As a matter of fact, he'd already approached the guy about coming to Jackson Falls to finish the album at Two Dreamers. They worked together so well, they could almost read each other's mind. That was what he was looking for in a sound engineer, somebody who knew him well enough to anticipate his decisions before they were made. And to agree with them. Or, if he didn't, to speak up and explain his reasons for disagreeing. Kyle Barton was all of those things and more.

When he unlocked the door to the apartment, the television was playing. Paige was watching one of those "daytime dramas" that she'd become so enamored of. He referred to them as How to Rot Your Brain 101. His mother watched soaps, and he'd never understood the attraction, especially when you could stop watching for three months and still pick up where you left off, because they dragged out every storyline and nothing significant ever happened. It was like watching paint dry.

But it kept his daughter off the street, which in New York was a good thing, and gave her something to think about that wasn't Mikey. Besides, if he'd dared to intervene, Casey would have been there to reward his paternal concern with the Death Glare, so he kept his mouth shut. In parenting, as in life, you had to pick your battles, and this one, while annoying, wasn't important enough in the greater scheme of things to be worth battling over.

"Hey," he said to the nearly comatose teenager curled up on the couch.

"Hey."

He looked right, then left. Said, "Where is everybody?"

Eyes still glued to the television, she said, "Emma's napping. Casey went out to run an errand."

"She say where she was going?"

"No."

"What time did she leave?"

Paige glanced at the clock. "An hour ago."

"Did she say how long she'd be gone?"

"A couple hours. She didn't get any more specific than that."

He went to the kitchen, got himself a beer, then returned to the living room and sat on the couch beside her. On the television, an attractive blonde was talking to some guy named Lance. The name conjured up all kinds of images he could have lived without. He picked up the cordless phone and dialed Casey's cell. It rang a half-dozen times before bouncing to voice mail. "Hey," he said, "it's me. Wondering where you are. Call me when you get this."

He nursed the beer while he watched *Days of Our Hospital's Turns*, or whatever the hell it was called. Fifteen minutes passed, and he tried her cell again. Again, it bounced to voice mail. Uneasy, he said to his daughter, "Was everything okay when she left? You now how strange she's been lately. Was there any, um…weirdness?"

The first show had now segued into a second, *The Slow and the Stupid*, or something along that line. "Not today," Paige said.

"What's that mean?"

His daughter picked up the remote and turned off the soap opera. "Something happened," she said. "That day we had lunch at the Hard Rock Cafe. I promised I wouldn't tell you. She made me promise. She didn't want you to find out. If I break that promise, she'll never trust me again."

The sinking feeling began in his gut and settled into his diaphragm, making it hard to breathe. "Break it," he said. "I'll take the heat. What happened?"

"Something weird. Well, only if you consider it weird to chase after some kid on the street because you think she's your dead daughter."

Casey

WORN smooth by generations of feet, the stair treads sagged in the center. Graffiti covered the walls. *Brenda loves Joey. Legalize marijuana! There once was a woman from France/who went to a dance without pants.* The single light bulb hung bare from the ceiling, just as it had fifteen years ago, so dusty it barely illuminated the narrow stairwell. The higher she climbed, the greater her trepidation. There was no way of knowing what manner of ills she would release by opening that door and scattering them, to be carried away on the winds like the silk from a split milkweed pod. Her breath tightened in her chest as she approached the second-floor landing, where the stairs turned and continued on up to the third floor. Casey paused before the door, raised her hand and slid the key into the lock. There was a single sharp click, and the knob turned in her hand. With a squeal of rusty hinges, the door swung open.

She pushed it wider. Inhaled a deep breath to still her trembling.

And stepped into her past.

The apartment had been empty for a long time. A musty smell hovered on the air, and a layer of dust, thick enough to write her name in, covered every surface. Heat, dense and humid, made it difficult to breathe. The sound of her footsteps on ancient hardwood ricocheted off bare plaster walls as Casey crossed the room and wrestled open a grimy window. A breeze rolled in, gusty and wonderful, carrying on it pungent odors from the restaurant downstairs. She'd forgotten that the smell of cooking food drifted up here. Had forgotten what it felt like to be young and hungry and tortured by those smells, by the piquant Asian delicacies Freddy's chef prepared.

She opened a second window, reveling in the feel of the wind cooling her overheated skin, took a hard breath, and turned to face her fate.

Had the living room really been this small? She remembered it being bigger. But time had a way of warping memories, of shaping them into what you wanted them to be, instead of what they really were. The room was maybe ten feet by twelve. Big enough for a couch, a chair, a coffee table. On the long wall, under the windows, Rob had slept on the ancient couch she'd picked up somewhere—she couldn't remember where—because there was only one bedroom. He'd spent his nights sprawled like an octopus, all outflung arms and legs. One pillow over his head and one under it, bony knees poking out from beneath his old blanket. A second blanket folded under his hips to protect the family jewels from the broken spring that delighted in terrorizing him. He'd never complained. Rob wasn't one to complain. He just took life as it came, and when it threw him a curveball, he dealt with it.

The kitchen was the same as she remembered. The old slate sink, the window that leaked when it rained, the old-fashioned black-and-white floor tiles where she'd sat and watched the blood pouring from between her legs when she lost that first baby. This kitchen had been the bane of her existence, overrun with cockroaches, no matter what she did. She'd tried Raid. Mothballs. She kept all her perishables sealed in Tupperware, never left dirty dishes in the sink, obsessively kept the counters wiped down with dish soap and Clorox. None of those things had made one iota of difference. Once or twice a year, after extensive prodding, Freddy would pay for an exterminator, and they'd have a month or two free of the damn things. But that didn't last, either. Eventually, they learned to peacefully coexist with the creatures. It was either that, or move, and moving involved things they couldn't afford, like security deposits and moving vans.

Now that the place was empty, she found no evidence that the roaches had ever been here. Maybe because there was no tenant, and therefore no food to draw them. Undoubtedly, they found plenty of that downstairs. Holding her breath, she gingerly opened the cupboard door below the sink. But nothing scattered and ran. The cupboard was empty, except for the open container of Comet the last tenant had left behind.

The stove was new-ish. Knowing Freddy, he'd either bought it at a scratch-and-dent sale, or it had conveniently fallen off the back of a truck somewhere in Jersey. The refrigerator, one of those old round-shouldered things with a latch handle you pulled to open, sat silent. When she lived here, it had hummed and buzzed and sometimes clacked and hammered. Circa 1940, it had a minuscule, boxy freezer compartment tucked in the upper-right corner. She'd kept it stocked with fudge ripple ice cream, store brand, the only luxury she was willing to pay for. Late at night, while her husband and the rest of the world slept, she and Rob would sit at her old wooden kitchen table, eating ice cream and playing around with chords on his guitar.

She touched the refrigerator's shiny chrome handle. It was smooth and cool. Hard to believe it was still here, after all these years. *They made them to last in those days.* The thought came unbidden. Like her, the refrigerator had weathered a multitude of seasons and survived them.

The bedroom was more difficult, for she had no idea what would be waiting behind that door. She pushed it, and it opened with a squawk of protest. The room was dark, its lone window on the back side of the building, oblivious to the afternoon sun. There was barely enough room for a full-size bed in here. She and Danny hadn't minded. They'd been young and in love, and despite his six-foot-four, 190-pound frame, they'd never felt confined or cramped. This was where she'd slept with him, where they'd conceived a baby that had never drawn breath, where he'd admitted to sleeping with another woman.

She knew all these things intellectually, but couldn't connect to them emotionally. She'd expected to find pieces of her heart shattered all over the floor. But this was just another empty, dusty room with holes in the painted plaster and a closet door with a broken hinge.

How was she supposed to feel about that? There should have been a flood of emotion, painful memories assaulting her. Resentment, fury. Instead, there was nothing. It was as though the events that had shaped her life had happened to somebody else. Watching them unfold in her mind, like images on a television screen, she could feel empathy for that hapless young woman who'd lost her baby, whose husband had cheated on her.

But she couldn't feel her pain.

Numbly, she moved on to the bathroom. Nothing had changed here. The same cracked mirror over the sink, the same tired blue floor tiles, the same stained porcelain fixtures. Behind the toilet, almost hidden in a nest of dust bunnies, lay the corpse of a cockroach. Dry, long dead, a lone reminder of the past, a welcome home of sorts. She fought back hysteria, unsure whether to laugh or cry; after everything that had happened to her here, it was the damn cockroach that got to her.

That and the sunlight filtering through the maple tree outside the kitchen window. It spilled through the dirty windowpane and lay in dappled patterns on the counter. She'd always loved the way the afternoon light illuminated her kitchen. In summer, filtered by greenery, it was soft and golden-green and comforting. In winter, it poured in between bare branches like a river of lava, setting fire to the kitchen and raising the temperature of the room, for just a while, above its customary fifty degrees.

As she stood in the kitchen, a long-forgotten memory drifted past. A hot summer night, the Fourth of July. The two of them, she and Rob, sitting on the back fire escape, drinking warm beer, as heat lightning flashed in the distant sky and firecrackers went off all around the city. There'd been magic in the air that night, and she struggled to remember why Danny hadn't been with them. Had he been working? Sleeping? She had no idea. Odd, that the clearest, the warmest, the most vivid memories she had of this place all included Rob. And almost none of them included Danny.

The first tear spilled and rolled, landing with a plop on those black-and-white kitchen tiles. What now? She'd been so certain, so sure that coming back here, where she'd lost that first baby, where her cheating husband had stolen away her trust and her innocence, would bring the answers she so badly needed. But it hadn't. It was clear that the ghosts she'd hoped to find didn't exist. The answers she'd sought would not be found here.

Devastated, she slumped to the dusty floor and, knees bent and back braced against the wall, she wept. Not for the young woman she'd been, the one who'd suffered so many losses. Not for the lost babies, although she'd loved them, every one.

Instead, she wept for the strong and confident woman who'd lost her strength and her way, the woman who, like Little Bo Peep with her sheep, didn't know where to find them. Rocking like a child, she sobbed for the woman she was meant to be, and for the woman she'd accidentally turned into. Sobbed and shuddered because she couldn't find a way to meld the two together and become whole again.

Heedless of her pain, time continued on. The sun's position changed, and the afternoon light marched across dirty floor tiles.

Eventually, inevitably, the crying ended. She stood on wobbly legs, brushed the dirt from her pants, and went into the bathroom to check the damage.

It was bad. Really bad. Her eyes were red and puffy, and mascara streamed down her cheeks in matching rivers of black. Casey propped her purse on the edge of the bathroom sink, took out a fistful of tissues, and turned on the water. It ran rusty at first, then cleared. She wet the tissues and cleaned up the mess she'd made of her face. Rob would take one look at her and demand to know why she'd been crying. As if he thought she could explain her own madness.

Shuddering, she checked the mirror a final time. This was as good as it was going to get. At least the black streaks were gone. She tossed the ruined tissues in the toilet and flushed them. Gathering her dignity around her like a warm, comforting cloak, she went back to the living room and closed the windows. Picked up the key she'd left on the kitchen counter. Took a last look at the place she'd once called home.

Then went back downstairs to return the key to Freddy.

* * *

When she opened the door to their apartment, Rob was pacing the living room, his hair a mess, as though he'd been running his fingers through it, over and over and over. He stopped, wheeled on her, and said, "Where the hell have you been all afternoon?"

"What?"

"I've been calling and calling, and you didn't answer your phone!"

"My—" Baffled, she opened her purse and took out the cell phone, noted its blank screen. She pushed a button, then another, but there was no response. "The battery must have died. Why? What's wrong?" Panic shot through her. "Is Emma—"

"Emma's fine. And I don't know what's wrong. Maybe you'd like to tell me!"

"I don't understand what you're talking about."

"I know," he said. "About what happened the other day. With the little girl."

She turned and stared at Paige, betrayal a hard pain in her chest. "You told him?"

"I'm sorry," Paige said. "You scared me. I love you. I was worried about you."

"Don't blame her. I bullied it out of her. Why would you hide something like that from me?"

She turned her attention back to her husband. "Maybe because I knew you'd react the way you're reacting!"

"Where were you this afternoon?"

Casey straightened her spine and raised her chin. "If you really have to know, I was at the apartment."

He narrowed his eyes. "Apartment?" he said. "What apartment?"

"Freddy's goddamn apartment!"

"Freddy's—Freddy *Wong*?"

"Do you know any other Freddy?"

"You went back there? I don't understand. Why on God's green earth would you go back there?"

"Because! Because I was looking for something. I thought maybe I'd find it there!" She paused, took a hard, sharp breath. Said softly, "I didn't."

And all the anger drained out of him. She could actually see it dissolving, flowing away from him like a red river of pain. "Shit," he said, and took two giant steps across the room and folded her into his arms. "What the hell were you thinking?"

She clung to him, shook her head, unable to articulate her jumbled emotions. Pain, anger, disappointment. Crushing disappointment. "Just hold me," she said.

"We have to talk about this, babe. We have to talk about a lot of things."

"Later. I can't do it now."

His hand came up to stroke her hair. "Fine. But not much later, okay?"

She nodded, raised her head, saw the clock on the wall and realized what time it was. "Why are you home so early?"

"I came home to talk to you." Catching a loose strand of hair that had broken free from her braid, he tucked it behind her ear. "But it looks like we have bigger fish to fry than the little minnows I was planning on."

"I'm sorry."

"Don't be sorry." He caught her chin in his hand and studied her face. His beautiful green eyes were pained, and it broke her heart to know that she was the one who'd put that pain there. "We're in this together," he said. "We'll fix this together."

Her eyes welled with tears, and a single teardrop broke free and spilled from the corner of her eye. "I don't think we can," she said. "I don't think we can fix it."

Rob

HE hung his toothbrush in its holder and studied his reflection in the bathroom mirror. The ravages of age were beginning to march across his face. He still wondered, every time he looked into a mirror, what Casey could possibly see in him. He'd never been much to look at, but with age, it was getting worse. All those wrinkles. These days, when he looked into the mirror, it was his father who stared back at him. The first time it had happened, he'd thought he was hallucinating. Until it happened again. And yet again. Now, he just accepted it. Just as he accepted the growing understanding that life didn't go on forever. Time was a fickle mistress who ravaged your body and your mind, lied through her teeth, then left a trail of laughter behind her when she moved on.

In the end, what did any of it mean? What was the significance of all those moments that made up this thing called a life? Lying in the dark with his wife, naked skin pressed to naked skin, giving love, receiving it in return; the innocence of his children's laughter, filling his heart with joy; the immeasurable sweetness of his fingers drawing magic, against all odds, from the strings of his guitar. What did all of these things mean? How did they fit together? Were they jigsaw pieces with smooth, perfect edges? Or were they a tangle of misfitted fragments that only peripherally touched each other's boundaries?

He'd never given much thought to any of this. Rob MacKenzie had always been a simple man, not given to introspection. But lately, these questions, and others like them, circled his head like vultures circling a carcass. And he had a growing suspicion that it was his carcass they were circling. He wasn't sure how he'd arrived at this particular time and place. Wasn't sure if the emotions that left him choking at random moments were more lies from that fickle bitch, Time, or if he'd really taken a wrong turn somewhere.

And if he had taken a wrong turn, was it too late to backtrack and change course?

He switched off the light, went barefoot to the bedroom, peeled off his clothes and got into bed. In the darkness, he found her, and drew her into his arms. They adjusted their fit for maximum body contact, sinking into each other's warmth. "Hey," he said.

"Hey."

They lay in silence, broken only by the sound of breathing. This was home, in a way nothing else had ever been or would ever be. He'd had two great loves in his life. One was his music, the love that had chosen him at the age of nine. The other was this woman, the woman he'd fallen in love with while she was still married to his best friend, the woman who was slowly becoming unwound as he watched helplessly from the sidelines.

"You want to talk about it?" he said.

"No. But I probably should."

"We're all alone now. Just you and me. You can tell me anything."

"I know." In the darkness, her voice was very small.

"What happened? With the little girl?"

"I don't know. She was just there, walking along in front of us, part of the crowd. At first, I didn't pay any attention to her. But gradually, I realized that she had hair like Katie's. All those curls, that beautiful blond bounce that Katie's hair had. And she was the same age, even wore the same brand of clothes I used to put Katie in. She was even built like Katie—those little tanned arms and legs—and something happened inside me. I can't explain it. I knew better. I'm not crazy, damn it! I knew she wasn't my daughter. Katie's been dead for eight years. And I knew that even if Katie wasn't dead, she'd be thirteen years old now. She wouldn't look anything like that little girl. But my heart started pumping, and—I don't know. It was like there was this crazy person inside me that had to see her just one more time before she went away forever. For a couple of minutes, some part of me really believed that she'd have Katie's face. And—I'm so ashamed of this—I left Emma with Paige and chased after her. Just ran blindly after her, right through an intersection, with cars squealing all around me like some crazy cops-and-robbers movie. I could have been killed. And for what? When I caught up to her, she turned around and looked at me, and—" Her voice broke, and she cleared her throat. "I'm not crazy, Rob. I'm not! But the way her mother glared at me, she clearly thought I was unhinged."

"You're not unhinged." He no longer knew whether or not those words were true, but she needed to hear them, and he'd spent his entire adult life putting her needs ahead of his own. It was an ingrained habit, one that wasn't likely to change anytime between now and death.

"But what if I am? What if I really am losing my mind? What I did…that's not normal behavior. No matter how you look at it, there's nothing normal about chasing after a strange kid on the street because she looks just like your dead daughter. The daughter, I might add, who's been dead for eight years."

"You know what Phoenix said to me? You can't put a time limit on grief. That kid's smarter than he looks."

"And you like him a lot more than you let on."

"He's growing on me." He drew her closer, gave her cheek a tender kiss and found it damp. His heart sank. "What about today?" he said. "The apartment? I thought you were doing better. The last couple of days, you've been more like yourself. And this morning…" He trailed off, not sure that asking wouldn't make things worse.

"I know. I thought so, too. And this morning was lovely. But—"

"But sex is never the answer."

"Sometimes it is. Just not this time. But I can't think of a pleasanter way to search."

In spite of the gravity of the situation, he laughed. "I love you," he said. "I've loved you since the first time I saw you, and I'll love you until I draw my last breath. And I don't care if you're crazy. I hope you realize that I wouldn't love you any less if you were."

"Thank you."

"I just thought it needed to be said. So tell me why you thought you'd find some kind of an answer in that hellhole."

She let out a soft sigh. "Everything that I am today," she said slowly, choosing her words carefully, "is filtered through the lens of what happened to me there. It was an odd, turbulent time in my life. It's where I lost that first baby. It's where…other things happened. I understand exactly how Dorothy felt after she came back from Oz. Some of it was scary and terrible, but some of it was beautiful. I just thought that, since living there marked me so deeply, going back might help to open up some of those closed doors inside me. It was probably a stupid idea."

"It wasn't stupid. But—" He wasn't sure how to broach the subject. He'd brought it up before, but that was in anger. This time, he was serious. "I think you need to see someone."

"A shrink."

"Some kind of therapist, yes."

"But I'm not crazy. Damn it, Rob, do you really think I'm that crazy?"

"Of course not. And you know as well as I do that seeing a therapist doesn't mean you're crazy. It did us a world of good when we went with Paige."

"That was different. We were learning how to parent a teenager with behavioral problems."

"And she was grieving the loss of her mother."

"I'm not ready. Not yet. I still think I can find the answer myself. It's out there somewhere. I just haven't looked in the right place yet."

"You're playing Russian roulette with your life. Is staying an independent cuss who refuses to accept help worth the possibility of losing yourself forever? I don't want to lose you."

"You won't. I'm not going anywhere."

"Maybe not physically."

"See. You do think I've gone around the bend."

"I think you have some serious issues that need to be addressed by a mental health professional. Because it's in your best interest. And because I wouldn't survive losing you."

"I won't live my life making decisions based on fear. I can't do that."

"I don't want you to."

"Then stop pushing me. If the time comes when I think I need help, you'll be the first to know. In the meantime, let me try to work this out on my own."

It wasn't the answer he wanted. But it was the only one he was going to get until she was ready to admit that she needed help. If they were both lucky, he'd manage to survive her temporary insanity without falling off the edge of the earth himself.

* * *

He spent the morning waffling. It wasn't like him; generally, he made a decision and then took action, and he wasn't shy about acting on his impulses. But this wasn't about him; this was about Casey, and making this call felt a lot like tattling. If he did this, and she found out, she'd probably fillet him and serve him for dinner. But there was also the little matter of love, and in Rob MacKenzie's book, love trumped fear of retribution every time. He was deeply in love with his wife, and he was losing her in little bits and pieces. The combination of those two truths was terrifying, far more terrifying than his fear of Casey's anger. He'd faced that before and survived. If he had to, he could face it again.

He waited until midday, hoping the doc would be on a lunch break, and not with a patient. While Phoenix and the studio crew were eating pizza, he borrowed Luther's cell phone, went outside, and leaned against the side of the building. He needed privacy to make this call; there was no need to spread Casey's personal business around the studio. He dialed the number, cupped his hand around the phone to muffle traffic noise, and waited.

At the other end, the phone was picked up, and a perky, feminine voice said, "River Valley OB/GYN. How can I direct your call?"

"Hi," he said. "I'd like to talk to Deb Levasseur."

"I'm not sure if Dr. Levasseur's available. I'll have to check. Who's calling, please?"

"Rob MacKenzie. It's about my wife. It's important."

"Hold, please."

He pressed himself against the building, crossed his ankles, and watched a giggling, boisterous trio of teenage girls pass. They eyed him briefly, dismissed him as a person of no importance— undoubtedly someone's dad—and continued on, chattering like a flock of blue jays.

"Rob? Deb Levasseur. How can I help you?"

"Thanks for taking my call. I'm sorry if I interrupted anything—"

"Are you kidding? I'm sitting at my desk, eating a ham sandwich and dictating patient records for my receptionist to type. Your call is a welcome interruption. Is everything okay with Casey?"

"I guess that depends on your definition of okay. Physically, she's fine. Mentally, not so much."

"What's going on?"

So he told her, pacing back and forth in front of the studio while he talked. Deb listened without interrupting until he was done. Then she said, "I knew something was wrong when I saw her. She was too complacent, too evasive. That's not like her."

"I'm scared," he said. "I think she's having a nervous breakdown."

"It's probably not that serious," she said. "It's also not unusual."

"Not unusual? She's never done anything like this before!"

"Let me clarify. Although it's not typical behavior for Casey, it's not unusual behavior for a woman who's experienced a miscarriage. Or, in her case, two miscarriages within a short time. And her determination to get pregnant again isn't surprising, either. She's nearing forty. Her biological clock is telling her that time is getting short. It's not impossible, of course. Not yet. But it is more difficult and less likely with every year that passes."

"I don't know what to do. I've told her she needs professional help, but she refuses. She says she can find the answers herself. So far, she's not having much luck. She's so goddamn stubborn."

"You said she's refused to use birth control...is there any chance she may be pregnant again?"

"Hell, no. She refused to use birth control, so I refused to touch her. Until yesterday, we hadn't been intimate since before the miscarriage. She thinks I'm not being supportive. I think that keeping her alive is about as supportive as it gets." He rubbed his temple, slowly. "She doesn't see it that way."

"What happened yesterday?"

"She caved. She decided we were both being ridiculous, and she told me she'd be willing to use birth control as long as we didn't give up on negotiating another pregnancy."

"That sounds like progress."

"It would be progress, for sure, if I hadn't been the idiot who got carried away and forgot the damn condom."

"Oh, my. Not the news I wanted to hear."

"That makes two of us."

"So you're still in New York?"

"We are. My job here will be done in a few more days, and then we're coming home as soon as I can get us out of this place. By Labor Day at the latest. I thought bringing her to New York with me was the right thing to do. I didn't want to leave her alone after the miscarriage, and I figured that here, I could keep an eye on her. I was more worried about her physical health than her mental health. She seemed sort of brittle when she left the hospital, a little bitter and fragile, but I didn't see anything really off about her. I thought it was natural for her to feel that way after losing another baby. And I thought New York would get her away from the scene of the crime, so to speak, and she'd be so busy here that it would distract her from thinking about what she'd been through. But it hasn't worked that way, and the things she's done behind my back scare the hell out of me. Running through traffic, chasing ghosts, taking trips down memory lane. God knows what else. I'm spending most of my time in the studio. She has too much alone time. I don't think it's good for her. It gives her too much time for thinking."

"Thinking isn't necessarily a bad thing. It sounds as though she has a lot to work out in her mind. And your older daughter is there, too?"

"Yeah. Thank God. Otherwise, I never would've heard about the episode with the little girl. Casey would never have told me about that if Paige hadn't spilled it to me. So now I have Paige watching her. I don't like to do that. It feels a little too much like betrayal. But this thing is snowballing out of control. Just thinking about her ducking cars in the middle of Manhattan makes me sick to my stomach."

"I can certainly understand that."

"I don't want to see this get any worse. I don't know if she needs meds, or counseling, or—I don't know. Maybe a support group. They must have support groups for women who've miscarried."

"They do. I'm not sure what we can scare up around here, but if she'd be willing to travel to Lewiston or Portland, there would be options. Look, Rob, I can't tell you what to do, but I admire your husbandly concern. Not a lot of men would be as understanding as you."

"I just want my wife back. That amazing, smart, talented, confident woman I married. I know she's in there somewhere. I keep seeing glimpses of her, but then she disappears again."

"We'll find her. I'll give her a call, ask her to come in for a follow-up. While she's here, I'll talk to her about counseling."

"It might be better if you didn't mention my name when you do that. Or if you do, give me a call, so I can lock up all the knives before she gets home."

"Depending on how forthcoming she is, I may have to tell her. But I'll try to avoid mentioning you until she's sitting in my office."

"I'll be on the lookout for the mushroom cloud. Dr. Levasseur—thank you."

"It's Deb. And you're welcome. Thank *you*. If you hadn't called, I would never have known what was going on."

* * *

On a bright and cloudless morning at the beginning of September, they wrapped up the recording. He could finally kiss this place goodbye. Kyle would come up to Maine, they'd finish the mixing at Two Dreamers, and the album would be completed.

And he'd never again have to deal with Phoenix Hightower.

So why was it that on this, his last day in the studio, his stomach was tied up in knots? What the hell was that all about? He didn't like Phoenix Hightower. Didn't like his massive ego, his arrogance, his flippant attitude. He absolutely was not, repeat, *not*, going to foster any warm and fuzzy paternal feelings for the little hood rat. Theirs was a business relationship, nothing more. They were not friends. Matter of fact, they barely tolerated each other. Their belief systems were polar opposites. They came from two different schools of thought, each of them with both feet firmly planted in his own camp. Rob was concerned with making the music the best it could possibly be. Phoenix was concerned with…Phoenix.

He was not going to allow that snot-nosed little turd to burrow under his skin. Except that he had a sneaking suspicion it was already too late. Somehow, this bratty, obnoxious, fatherless, possibly motherless kid had managed to do just that. And he couldn't figure out how or when it had happened.

The kid reminded him of somebody. It had been eating at him since the first time he walked into the studio and they shook hands. He hadn't been able to figure it out. Not until the night they sang together onstage, and then he couldn't imagine how it had taken him so long to see it.

The kid was a carbon copy of Danny Fiore.

It wasn't his looks, although Phoenix had the perfect hair and the soulful blue eyes that drew in teenage girls like flies to flypaper. It wasn't his arrogance, although he and Danny shared the same colossal ego. And it wasn't his attitude, because that was where he and Fiore totally diverged. Danny had been a white-hot arrow, aiming himself directly toward the stars, with no time for side trips along the way. Phoenix, on the other hand, didn't much care about his career. He was in it for the girls, the money, the partying. His career, his future, the music itself, were of little import. *Live for today, to hell with tomorrow.* That was Phoenix Hightower's philosophy. And while on the surface, Danny's oft-repeated philosophy, *Live hard and fast, and die young enough to leave a good-looking corpse,* looked similar, it was only a superficial resemblance. Danny's definition of living hard and fast was working himself to death with single-minded determination to reach out and catch that brass ring.

It was some other place where Danny and Phoenix ran on parallel tracks. Something else that Rob had subconsciously reacted to: they were both broken.

Like Danny Fiore decades earlier, Phoenix was misshapen, twisted. Somewhere in his development, something dark and painful had shaped him into a broken creature who needed to be glued back together.

But was it really up to Rob MacKenzie to play savior to every broken musician who crossed his path? Even if it was his responsibility, was that because he really gave a damn about Phoenix, or did he simply want to assuage his own guilt because he hadn't tried hard enough to save Danny? He'd stood there and watched his best friend falter, and he hadn't even bothered to try to prevent his fall. Because in some part of him, he knew that if Danny fell far enough, his marriage, which already existed on a fault line, would split apart at the seams. And when it did, guess who would be waiting to console Danny's wife?

He'd never really believed that life was about weights and balances. But if it was, his Karmic scale was seriously tilted in the wrong direction. For purely selfish reasons, he hadn't done enough to help Danny. Maybe he could redeem himself, tilt those scales in the other direction, if he helped Phoenix.

It was a crazy idea. But did it really matter which side of the fence his intentions fell on? If he could teach the kid to ground himself so he wouldn't crash and burn, did it really matter why he was doing it?

Jesus Christ on a Popsicle stick. Why was he always stuck with these moral dilemmas?

* * *

With what was left of his little studio family gathered around, wearing solemn faces, he said, "So. It looks like we've come to the end of the road. I guess it's up to me to say a few words before we go our separate ways. It's been great working with you. All of you. Except maybe you, Luther." They all laughed. "We've worked really hard here, we've suffered—and survived—a New York heat wave, as well as Phoenix's, um…moodiness." Smiles all around. "I've even survived a mugging. But the important thing is that we survived. And I think we've put together a terrific record. I can't wait to finish the mixing, so we can all hear the final result."

Glances were exchanged all around, but nobody spoke. He looked from face to face, then said, "Okay, then, folks. You're dismissed. Kyle, I'll give you a call in a few days. Phee, I need to talk to you."

"Blimey, old man," the kid groused, "I've told you eleventy-hundred times that my name isn't Phee."

"And I'll probably call you that until the day I die. Luther, give yourself a couple of well-deserved hours off, compliments of yours truly. I'm taking our friend here to lunch."

"You," the kid scoffed, "want to take me to lunch."

"I don't want you to think I'm an ogre all the time."

"I don't know, mate. Will it be a step up from a bleedin' sidewalk hot dog and a bottle of water?"

"Better be careful, or I'll rescind the offer." He held out a hand to Luther, shook it, and clapped him on the shoulder. "Go," he said. "I may end up regretting this, but I'll take responsibility for the kid."

"I'm an adult," Phoenix said. "I don't need a babysitter."

"Truth," he said.

They took a cab because it was too far to walk, and if he took Phoenix Hightower on the subway, there would be pandemonium. They'd both be lucky to come out of it in one piece. While the taxi driver spent the entire trip talking into his cell phone in some foreign language, Phoenix stared out the window at the unfamiliar surroundings. When they crossed the bridge, the kid said, "Where in bloody hell are we going for lunch? Saturn?"

"It's called Brooklyn."

"Brooklyn? Sounds like the punch line to a joke."

"You say that now, but wait until you taste the food in this place. You'll be singing a different tune." A thought occurred to him, and he peered at the kid closely. "You're not allergic to shellfish, are you?"

"Can't say that I've ever eaten shellfish."

"You've never had lobster?" The kid shrugged. "Clams?" Again, that shrug.

Rob leaned back against the seat and said, "We'll make sure they have an oxygen mask and an epi-pen on standby, then. Just in case."

Phoenix just scowled.

The restaurant was exactly as he remembered it, small and sunny, with Formica-topped tables and vinyl-upholstered chairs that dated back to 1963. Two blue-haired elderly ladies sat at one table, a lobster in front of each of them. Another table held a couple in their fifties, sharing a massive King crab. The middle-aged hostess, who doubled as their waitress, led them to a table at the back of the room and handed them menus. "You can take off your hat and glasses," Rob told the kid. "You don't have to worry about being seen here. Trust me, nobody here has a clue who you are."

To the waitress, he said, "We'll have a pot of steamers for the table, and we'll each have the lazy lobster. I'll take whatever you have on draft, and the kid here will have—"

"I'll have the same."

"Nice try, but no dice. He'll have a Coke," he told the waitress, and handed the menus back to her. "Thank you."

When she was gone, Phoenix said, "Has anybody ever told you that you're a humorless dick?"

"Loudly and often. You'll have to stand in line."

The kid glanced around and the corner of his mouth drooped. "This looks like the type of place where old people go to eat."

"I'm surprised you haven't heard. That's where you find the best food."

"Yes, well, that remains to be seen."

"Jesus, Phee, do you have to try so hard to win the Miss Congeniality prize?"

The kid snorted, and Rob fought back a smile. The waitress returned with their drinks, and he took a long slug of beer. "Really hits the spot," he said.

"Sadist."

"Allow yourself to be a kid, Phee. The older you get, the quicker life moves, and the thing is, when you're older, you'll wish you'd appreciated it more, being young. Because I have to tell you, buddy, you can't go backwards."

"I'm not a kid. As we've already clearly established, I'm eighteen years old. An adult."

"There's not a person in this restaurant who wouldn't laugh if they heard you say that."

"Yes, well, what else can you expect? They're all positively geriatric."

"Has anybody ever told you that you're a negative Nellie?"

"Clever retort."

"I thought so. Tell me about the upcoming tour."

The kid slithered back on his tailbone and crossed his arms over his puny chest. "November first, we open in New York. Madison Square Garden. After that, two dozen other places I'm not familiar with. This country of yours is incredibly spread out."

"Compared to that teeny-tiny island you're from, yes, it is."

The kid raised a dark eyebrow. "Is this one of those 'mine's bigger than yours' pissing contests?"

"Make of it what you will. I'm just making idle chit-chat to pass the time while we're waiting for our lunch." He took a sip of beer and said, "How much longer are you contracted with Ariel?"

"Two more albums. Why?"

"Just curious. You're a talented kid, and Ariel's a one-trick pony. If you want to keep on making bouncy pop records for twelve-year-olds, Ariel's your label. But if you ever want to start making serious music—" He took out his wallet and pulled out a business card. Handing it to Phoenix, he said, "Give me a call and we'll see what Two Dreamers can do for you."

The kid studied the card, then look up with a smirk. "So this is what lunch was about? A solicitation? I should have suspected you had an ulterior motive."

"No ulterior motive. Just an offer. So you'll know you have options. That's what it's all about, Phee. Choices. As long as you have choices, you'll never find yourself trapped, with no way out."

"Thank you for the charming little homespun life lesson."

"Stop being such a little shit and tell me about yourself."

"Why in bloody hell would I want to do that?"

"Because that's what civilized people do, Phee. They talk to each other."

All he got in response was a sullen grunt.

"Okay, I'll start. Feel free to jump in at any point if you feel the need to express yourself. I grew up in South Boston, in a family of nine kids. My twin sister and I were number six and seven, respectively. She's eight minutes older than me and has never let me forget that. Growing up, we didn't have much money. My dad worked for the MBTA. That's the public transit system. He drove a city bus. My mom worked part-time, cleaning houses for women with a lot more money than we had. You can imagine how tough it was, raising nine kids on a limited amount of money. But my parents were frugal. Even in those tough times, even with nine kids, they still managed to buy their own house. Matter of fact, they're still living in it, although their standard of living has improved immensely since I started supporting them. We all graduated from high school, every one of us. Several of us went to college. Maeve is a lawyer. Rose is a social worker. Mom and Dad are damn proud, because neither one of them ever graduated. They both had to quit school and go to work when they were teenagers."

"Is there a point to this story?"

"I'm in the mood for sharing. It's a beautiful day, neither one of us has to be anywhere, and I have a captive audience."

Their food arrived, and Phoenix looked at his boiled lobster with mild horror. "I'm supposed to eat this thing? It looks like a giant insect."

"Best insect you've ever eaten. I guarantee it."

Phoenix picked up the plastic bib the waitress had left, looked at it curiously, and said, "Dare I ask what this is?"

"It's a bib. Eating lobster can get messy, although I had them cut it open because I thought the horror of trying to break open a hard-shell lobster might be too much for you to take your first time. The bib's to protect your clothes."

"You're not wearing yours."

"I'm not wearing it because only wussy tourists from Duluth wear plastic bibs when they eat lobster. Look around. You don't see any wussy tourists from Duluth, do you?"

"Definitely not. Although I have to confess that I haven't a clue where Duluth might be. How am I supposed to approach this creature?"

"Since they so kindly sliced it down the middle for you, just pull the meat out with your fingers and dip it in your butter. Start with the claws. And prepare yourself to be blown away."

Gingerly, the kid pulled out a piece of claw meat, dipped it in the butter, and took a bite. "Not bad," he said.

"The tail meat's better. And you have butter all over your chin." Rob handed him a napkin. "Take a few of these steamers, too. Second-best thing you ever ate."

The kid reached into the bucket and scooped out a few steamers. "Interesting," he said, picking one up and studying it.

"Open it like this and pull it free from the shell." Rob demonstrated. "Then you peel off this little black thing and throw it out. Now, clams can be gritty sometimes. They live in sand. So your best bet is to swish it around in your bowl of water to clean it. Then dip it in the butter. Don't nibble at it. Just pop the whole thing in your mouth and eat it."

Phoenix did as instructed. Studying his face, Rob said, "Is that fantastic, or what?"

Through a mouthful of clam, Phoenix said, "Fairly tasty."

"Fairly? Jesus, man. That's like saying Freddy Mercury was an okay singer."

They ate for a time in silence. Then Rob said, "Your turn."

"My turn?" The kid looked puzzled.

"I told you about my life. Now it's your turn to tell me about yours."

"I don't talk about my life."

"I know the official bio. Born in London, raised in a working-class neighborhood. Mother was a secretary, father worked in retail. You were discovered singing at a school talent show by some record exec who was there to watch his own kid perform. Yadda, yadda, yadda. So how much of that is true, and how much is bullshit?"

"It's all true. Every word of it."

"I don't believe you. It's too pat. It's standard record company press release bullshit. So, spill, Phee. What's the real truth?"

"The real truth? I'm eighteen years old, I'm from London, and when I get up on stage and shake my hips, twelve-year-old girls fall into a dead faint. That's all anybody needs to know."

"My dad. The bus driver? He's an alcoholic. He hasn't had a drink in twenty-three years."

"I'm sure you're proud of him."

"My oldest sister, Cathleen, had a double mastectomy last year. She's only forty-nine years old."

The kid continued to eat, ignoring him. "Damn it, Phee," Rob said, "I'm trying to establish some kind of genuine communication here."

"I told you, I don't talk about my life."

"How old were you when your old man died? And what's the story with your mother?"

The kid looked up. "My mother?"

"Luther implied there was something about your mother."

"There is nothing about my mother," the kid said hotly, "and if you insist on continuing this line of conversation, I will be forced to get up and leave."

"Good luck finding your way back from Brooklyn, Russell."

Fire flickered to life in the kid's eyes. Fire, and something else Rob couldn't identify. "My name," he said, "is not Russell. It's Phoenix. And this conversation is over!"

"Jesus Christ, you're a hard nut to crack. Listen, I don't know what your deal is. But I'd like to help. I'd like to be your friend."

"Why? Why in bloody hell would you want to be my friend?"

"Because! Because I think you're needy. Because there's something in your past that's screwed you up, and you won't talk about it. Because you're headed down a self-destructive road. Because I don't think you're so far down that road that you can't turn your life around and make it into something meaningful."

"Meaningful?" The kid said the word as though he'd never heard it before.

Rob leaned over the table. "This isn't what it's about, Phee. The parties, the girls. The booze, the sex. Blowing money just because you can. There's so much more to life, and you're missing it all because you're wearing blinders. You have talent, but you're squandering it. This career of yours? It'll disappear, faster than you can say Jack Shit. Because this music you're making won't last. It's a fad, and in a year or two or five, a new fad's gonna come along, and you'll be yesterday's news. And then what? Your money will be gone, your fans will all be lusting after the new flavor of the month, and when you walk down the street, people will say, 'There goes Phoenix what's-his-name. Didn't he used to be famous?'"

"Are we through with today's morality lesson?"

"You know what? I give up. I tried, but you're obviously not ready to hear it." He picked up his napkin and wiped his hands, scraped back his chair, and stood. Pulled out his wallet and tossed a couple of bills on the table. "That should be enough to cover lunch and your cab fare back to Manhattan. Go get 'em, Tiger. Just remember, if the time ever comes when you decide I was right, you know where to find me."

And he turned and stalked out of the restaurant.

He walked two blocks, then stopped at a pay phone and dialed Luther's number. "I just thought you should know," he said, "that I just left our friend sitting in a little seafood restaurant on a street corner in Brooklyn."

"Outstanding. I suppose now I have to go and fetch him."

"I don't mean to make your job more difficult. But, you know what? He's a big boy. As he pointed out to me twice within a half-hour, he's eighteen years old. An adult. Old enough to figure out his own way home. I left him money for cab fare. He may be a pain in the ass, but he's not stupid."

"And I have a responsibility."

"Which is why I called you. Look, I said some hard things to him. He needs to think those things over and come to his own conclusions. There's only so much you or I can do. If he keeps being pampered and coddled and babied, he'll never grow up. And he's in desperate need of growing up."

There was silence at the other end of the phone. Finally, Luther said, "I could lose my job."

"I'm the one who left him. I'll take the heat. You had no way of knowing. This phone call never happened."

Again, silence. "Listen," Rob said, "I've spent a lot of time with that kid over the last three months. I've watched, and I've listened, and I've held my tongue. But what that boy needs, more than anything, is tough love. He needs to stop being mollycoddled, and he needs to learn to take responsibility for his own life. I just offered him the first step." He took a hard, sharp breath. "The rest?" he said. "It's up to him."

Casey

HOME at last. Nothing had ever felt quite so wonderful as her own house. Or quite so stuffy, since the place had been closed up for all those weeks. While Rob and Paige carried in the luggage, Casey ran around the house, flinging open windows to let in some badly-needed fresh air. Her house plants had survived and thrived, quite miraculously, considering that it was her sister who was tending them. Colleen had good intentions, but no green thumb, and Casey suspected she may have had a little assistance from Harley or his teenage daughter, Annabel.

Labor Day traffic, driving up from New York, had been a nightmare. All those tourists headed to Maine for the final summer holiday of the season: trucks hauling trailers, SUVs loaded with kids and dogs, compact cars carrying canoes and kayaks. Their drivers were tired, cranky, and in a hurry. State troopers dotted the landscape. Rob had insisted on doing the driving, despite the fact that he had no license to show, should he be pulled over. In spite of her concern, she bit her tongue and kept her opinion to herself. His license was still valid, but if he was stopped somewhere out of state, driving without it, he could still wind up with a ticket and a tangle of bureaucratic red tape.

But they made it without a hitch, pulling into the driveway midway through Saturday afternoon. The summer heat they'd left behind in Manhattan was little more than a memory here in the foothills of Western Maine. Already, even though it was only the first weekend of September, patches of red foliage were visible here and there, and the onset of fall was evident in the air. Some of those campers, especially the ones in tents, were going to get the surprise of their life when evening fell. September nights in Maine could be chilly.

Even Leroy was thrilled to be home. He raced from one room to the next, skidding on her hardwood floors, and she made a mental note to take him to the groomer to have his nails clipped. When he was done cavorting, he began sniffing quiet corners and secret spots, all the places where Igor used to sleep. They'd unexpectedly lost Rob's geriatric but feisty Siamese cat back in May. Igor had been in good health in spite of his age, and his unexpected death had upset the entire family. Even though the cat had never fully warmed to Casey—the little hypocrite had liked her well enough when she had an open can of tuna in her hand— she'd still considered him a beloved family member. Cats and dogs, they said, weren't supposed to get along. But Igor and Leroy had bonded. It had been nearly four months since Igor had died in his sleep, and Leroy was still searching everywhere for his old friend.

The construction was completed, and after she unpacked her clothes and hung them in the closet, she and Rob took a quick tour of the facility. The contractor—the same one who'd built their house—had done an amazing job. As well he should have, considering how much money they'd poured into the project. In a few weeks, when she'd settled back into the rhythm of her everyday life, she and Colleen would head over to Four Winds Farm and pick out their first herd of livestock.

When they came back into the house, the phone was ringing. It was Trish, calling to invite them to a family barbecue she'd planned for tonight. Rob, who answered, turned down the invitation.

"We're wiped out," he said into the phone. "I think we need a little down time tonight. We'll probably see you sometime tomorrow."

He hung up the phone, saw the look on Casey's face, and said, "What?"

"I think that's the first time you've ever said no to anyone in this family."

"Yeah? Well, I suspect there'll be more of that in the future. You're not very good at saying no. I, on the other hand, am not the least bit shy about turning down invitations." He studied her face. "You look tired. Maybe you should take a nap."

"I don't want a nap. It's a beautiful day, I don't want to sleep away what's left of it."

"Then a nice, long soak in the Jacuzzi. Turn on the bubbles." He waggled his eyebrows. "If you play your cards right, maybe you'll even have company."

It sounded wonderful. "I think I'll take you up on that."

So she headed upstairs to the Jacuzzi, threw open the bathroom window to let in fresh air, filled the tub with steaming water, and settled in. The bubbles were relaxing. Casey leaned back until the water reached her chin, and just let go. So much had happened in the last few weeks, all of it pretty intense, and she could feel the tension in her body. She took a couple of deep, cleansing breaths, then practiced the relaxation technique she'd learned in Lamaze, deliberately releasing the tension from one set of muscles at a time.

She'd reached a stage of deep relaxation when Rob came into the bedroom. She heard him undressing, the clink of his belt buckle as he peeled off his jeans. Naked, he walked into the bathroom, gave her one of those smiles that shot straight to her pelvis, and climbed into the tub.

They adjusted arms and legs and bodies, until he was sitting behind her and she was leaning back against him. He wrapped an arm around her, kissed her neck, and said, "Hi."

"Hi. Where's Emma?"

"Asleep. Paige is downstairs, talking to one of her friends on the kitchen phone. Which means that you and I are all alone."

"Mmn. I like alone."

"Me, too. You feel pretty good in your birthday suit, Mrs. MacKenzie."

"Likewise, Mr. MacKenzie."

"Oh, man." He let out a huge sigh. "I am so glad to be home."

She turned her head, pressed a kiss to his wet bicep, the one with her name printed on it. "You haven't had five minutes of down time in the last few weeks."

"Don't remind me."

She closed her eyes and drifted. Said lazily, "What's your time frame for finishing the album?"

"I told Kyle I'd give him a call in a day or two to make plans. If we don't run into any problems, I think we can do it in…oh, probably three weeks. He can stay in the apartment over the studio. I already told him he can bring his wife if he wants."

"And is he bringing her?"

"I don't know. I guess it depends on how much he likes her."

"Oh, stop. You're awful."

"Why am I awful? I'd take you with me if I had an opportunity like that. But not every guy is as fond of his wife as I am."

"In spite of the fact that she's a shrew."

"You don't have a shrewish bone in your body." He kissed the back of head. Then said, "Well, maybe one or two little ones."

"That was mean."

"It was. But you love me anyway."

"I do. That just confirms my madness."

"Oh, no, Miss Muffet. No negativity allowed. You know the Jacuzzi rules. No bubble bath, no bathing suits, and no talking about problems. Just lots of happy, happy, happy."

"Which just confirms our mutual madness."

"How about we stop talking and just soak until the water gets cold?"

"And cop a feel or two along the way?"

"I wouldn't argue against that."

"And when the water's cold? What then?"

"I could think of a thing or two we could do to pass the time, but knowing our luck, Emma will probably be awake by then. And you'll get up and leave me, and I'll be stuck doing those things all by myself."

"Yikes! Nowhere near as much fun."

"Amen, sister."

"Good thing I'm not your sister. Or this would be a really awkward conversation."

"Babe?"

"What?"

He tightened his arms around her, cupped his hand around her breast, and said, "Shut the hell up."

* * *

She spent Labor Day lying low. A big, late breakfast with Rob and the girls. An hour spent sitting on the porch steps in the sun, reading a book, while Emma played at her feet and Rob washed the New York City grime off the car. Casey pulled her skirt up past her knees to bare her legs to the afternoon sun. Its heat was pleasant, but she wore a sweater over her shoulders because in spite of the sun's warmth, the air carried the bite of fall.

They had a quiet dinner with Trish and Bill, and Casey spent a half-hour on the phone with her sister-in-law Rose before she went to bed. Tuesday morning, the big yellow school bus picked up

Paige for the first day of her senior year. The girl grumbled a bit about having to ride the bus, now that her cousin Luke had graduated and started a job, but Casey could tell she was excited to be heading back to school.

After Paige left, she and Rob drove to the DMV in Lewiston so he could get a replacement for his stolen driver's license. That took most of the morning, so they had lunch at a local Chinese place, then hit the mall to pick up new sneakers for Emma before they headed home.

They spent the rest of the day puttering. It was so nice to be back where the pace was slow, and the sounds outside her window were those of nature, instead of honking horns and squealing tires. While she washed windows, Rob mowed the lawn. Although he'd paid a local kid to take care of the grass while they were gone, it was long overdue for a trim. And they had a huge lawn, so it kept him busy for hours. She loved the sound of the mower that floated in her open windows, loved the smell of fresh-cut grass. When she was a kid, as often as not, it had been her job to mow the yard around their house, and it had always been one of her favorite chores.

Mid-afternoon, she enjoyed a cup of tea and some conversation with her sister, who filled her in on the progress of their incorporation paperwork. After much deliberation, they'd chosen a simple name for their company: Sisters Woolen Yarns. Not too cutesy, not too long, but straightforward and to the point.

"I can't believe we're really doing this," Colleen said.

"What you really mean is you can't believe I dragged you into this venture."

"I was going for subtle, but if you want to use the sledgehammer approach, that's fine with me."

"You are so going to love this."

"Just as long as you remember that I take care of the business end. You're the one who'll be wading through sheep shit."

"Odd words coming from a woman who grew up on a dairy farm."

"Not really. In case you forgot, I'm the one who avoided the barn as much as possible. You're the one who was always out there, wallowing in manure."

"What are you talking about? You raised a prize-winning heifer for 4-H, just like I did."

"Not exactly the high point of my seventh-grade career. So tell me. Where'd you get that beautiful emerald, and why aren't you wearing your wedding ring?"

"Long story."

"There's not a damn thing going on in the studio today. I have the whole afternoon free."

"In that case—" She stood and held out her hand. "I'd better refill our cups. This could take a while."

* * *

It was late afternoon when she remembered her cell phone. She hadn't used it since it died on her during that ill-fated trip into her past. Casey dug the dead phone out of her purse, found the charger, and plugged it in. She wasn't sure she'd even use it, now that she was home; Rob was the one who liked to play with gadgets. But he might be able to make some use of it until he got around to replacing his.

He'd been quiet since they got home two days ago. Not moody, but contemplative. Something was off with him. He was distracted, clearly working something out in his head, but she had no idea what it might be. Maybe he was simply thinking about the album, and the three weeks of work he still had ahead of him before it was finally finished. Rob got this way every so often, and she knew from experience that all she could do was wait it out. Badgering him to share his feelings would be pointless. He'd share them with her if and when he was ready.

That night, as they were preparing for bed, he said, "Can I ask you a serious question?"

In the middle of taking her robe from the closet, she paused, hanger in hand. "Of course," she said, and placed the hanger back on the wooden rod. "Ask away."

"Do you think I threw Danny under the bus?"

"What?" It was the last thing she'd expected to hear. These days, they hardly ever even brought up Danny's name. "What on earth are you talking about?"

"Because I think I did. I've been thinking it for a long time."

Standing there in just her underwear, she gaped at him and said, "I don't understand."

Her husband tucked his hands into the pockets of his jeans and started pacing. "The guy had serious issues, but I never bothered to find out what they were. He was my best friend, and what did I do? I bailed on him after Katie died. I didn't care enough to stick around and try to help him through it."

"That wasn't your responsibility."

"It damn well was! He was my best friend! He'd lost his daughter, and his wife had just left him. I should've stuck around. Instead, I ran like a spoiled little girl, off to the middle of nowhere to find myself. Jesus Christ, Casey, how self-indulgent can you get?"

"You don't have a self-indulgent bone in your body. It was time for you to leave. You'd stayed in Danny's shadow long enough. You needed to step out into the light. And that's what you did."

"Yeah? Well, the timing sucked."

"Yes. The timing sucked. But that wasn't your fault. It was long past time for you to go solo. You did what you had to do."

"And then, there was you."

"I don't understand. What do you mean?"

He ran a hand through his hair. "I mean that there was a part of me that was waiting for your marriage to crash and burn so I could rush in and sweep you off your feet."

She pulled on her robe, knotted the belt, crossed the room and slid her arms around his waist. "And if you recall, my marriage did crash and burn. But I don't remember you rushing in like a white night to rescue me. Stop rewriting history."

"I'm not rewriting history. I'm just seeing it with new eyes."

"Those new eyes are lying to you. Look, Flash, I've known you for two decades. You would never do anything to deliberately hurt anyone. It's not in you. You're a good man, one of the best. I dare say there's only one man on the planet who comes near to you in my estimation, and that man would be my dad. He's not perfect, and neither are you. But you're both good, kind, moral, upstanding men who've spent your lives putting other people first. You would never have deliberately hurt Danny. You loved him. We both did."

"And isn't it convenient for me that he's dead now, and I'm sleeping with his wife?"

"You're sleeping with *your* wife," she said. "Where is this coming from? Why now, out of the blue?"

"It's not out of the blue. I've been wrestling with this for a while now. I'm having trouble getting past the guilt. But to answer your question, Phoenix and I left things on a really sour note."

"Ah. So that explains why you've been stewing for the past few days. What happened?"

"I'm not sure I should've done what I did. But I was pissed, and he was being a little prick, and I thought he needed some tough love. So I walked out and left him sitting alone in a restaurant in Brooklyn."

"*Brooklyn?* My God, Rob, that's like a foreign country."

"I know. But I did call Luther and tell him what I'd done. I left the ball in his court. I assume the kid made it back to his hotel in one piece. It's been a few days, and if anything happened, I would've heard by now."

"I still don't get it. What does any of this have to do with Danny?"

"You don't see it, do you? Ah, hell, you've barely spent any time with him. And it's a vibe, more than anything else. I guess I shouldn't expect you to see it."

"See what?"

"He reminds me so much of Danny. Maybe that's part of the reason for the itchiness between us. He rubs me the wrong way."

It was all beginning to make an odd kind of sense. "And that bothers you."

"Damn right, it bothers me! I wasn't there when I should've been for Danny, and then this kid comes along, and he looks like Danny, and he acts like Danny, and he's a mess like Danny. And somewhere inside me, there's this crazy idea that maybe, just maybe, I can redeem myself. Maybe, if I help this kid out, I can level out my Karma a little. Get rid of some of the guilt that's been such a heavy weight on me ever since Danny died."

She let out a hard breath. "Sweetheart," she said, "you can't change the past by changing the present. The past isn't something that can be resurrected."

"Maybe not, but you can balance the scales a little. The kid is headed down a bad road. I've tried to help him. Tried to talk to him. He refuses to hear anything I'm saying."

She lay her head against his chest, listened to the strong, steady beating of his heart. "I think," she said, "that this calls for two glasses and a bottle of wine. We'll get a little vino inside us, and then we can talk this out. You game?"

He shrugged. Tucked a strand of hair behind her ear. "Yeah, okay."

The kitchen tiles were cool under her bare feet as she crossed the room in the dark. She opened the cupboard and took out a couple of wine glasses, and that was when she saw the blinking light on her cell phone. Casey set down the glasses and picked up the phone, pushed a button to light up the screen, and saw that she had two voice mail messages. That was odd. Only a few family members had her cell number, and any of them would have called the landline instead of the cell.

Curious, she dialed into her voice mail. The first message was from Rob, checking on her whereabouts the day her battery had died. The second call had come in yesterday, while the phone lay dead in her purse. "Casey?" said a cheery voice. "This is Deb Levasseur. I'd like to see you. Sometime this week, if possible. Can you give my office a jingle and set something up? Thanks! Hope you're having a restful Labor Day."

What the hell? She listened to it again, but the message didn't change. Deb Levasseur, her OB/GYN, had called her on a holiday to ask her to schedule an appointment. And Deb had called her cell phone number.

The cell phone number she'd never given to Deb.

Everything inside her went still. There was only one reason Deb would have called. And only one person who could have given her that number.

She didn't want to believe he'd betrayed her that way. But she knew, without even confronting him, that he had. Her sweet, well-meaning, overprotective husband. Rob, the perennial fixer-upper, who could never leave anything alone, but had to grab it between his jaws and shake it, like a pit bull with a piece of meat. It was the way he was wired, and she loved him in spite of it. But right now, she was so furious with him that she couldn't remember why she loved him.

She set down the cell phone. Left the bottle of wine and the glasses on the counter. Right now, she was more likely to beam him over the head with that bottle than drink from it. She'd told him, in no uncertain terms, that she wasn't ready to ask for professional help. She'd told him that she would deal with her psychological issues on her own. Yet he'd ignored everything she said, and he'd gone to Deb behind her back.

That little Karma issue he'd been talking about? After what he'd pulled, it would take him seventeen lifetimes just to work his way back to where he'd been this morning.

Slowly, deliberately, hating what she was about to face, she marched up the stairs and down the hall. She paused before the open bedroom door, took a breath to calm herself, then stepped inside and closed the door quietly behind her.

Rob came in from the bathroom, towel in hand. He looked up and saw her face, clearly read the proclamation of war in her eyes. "What?" he said, all innocence.

"I just discovered a voice mail message on my cell phone," she said. "From Deb Levasseur."

He paled. He didn't say a word, but he didn't have to. The color draining from his face confirmed what she already knew. "Damn you," she said. "What did you tell her?"

"Babe, you have to underst—"

"What the hell did you tell her?"

He closed his eyes, swallowed. "Everything," he said, and his shoulders sagged. "I told her everything."

"How could you? How could you betray me like that, after I told you I'd handle it myself?"

"You're not handling it!" he shouted. "You're nowhere near handling it!"

"So you went running to my OB/GYN. What were you thinking?"

"I was thinking I'd like my wife back. And I went to Deb because I didn't know where else to go. You sure as hell haven't been any help to me in that arena. I trust her. You trust her. I thought she could set us up with someone."

"Us? Set *us* up?" She ran a hand through her hair. "Damn it, Rob, this isn't about you! I don't need some stranger poking into my head and trying to put a Band-Aid on my boo-boo. It's my damn boo-boo, and I'm entitled to it! You don't have any idea what it feels like to be pregnant, and then suddenly you're not pregnant any more, only you don't have a new little baby to hold in your arms, just empty space. You have no idea!"

"No," he shouted, "and you have no idea what it feels like to watch your wife go slowly insane! Chasing ghosts through New York City traffic, having nightmares and crying jags for no reason, taking crazy trips down memory lane! It's like having a two-year-old in the house, one that needs to be watched constantly. I can't handle it anymore!"

"You can't handle it anymore because you know I'm right!"

"No! You're not right! You're being a spoiled, self-involved little brat! You want what you want, no matter how it affects me, or Paige, or Emma. You have this fucking obsession about having another baby, even though you know it could kill you. If you gave a rat's ass about us, you'd realize that it would destroy us—all of us—if anything happened to you!"

"It's not an obsession!"

"I don't understand. What the hell happened to that smart, beautiful, reasonable woman I married? She's gone, and this woman that took her place? I don't know her. I don't even *want* to know her!"

"If that's how you really feel, there's a door right over there. Maybe you should take it! You have no empathy whatsoever. No understanding of what I've been through. You just don't care!"

"What about me? Have you even thought about me in all of this? You lost a baby. I lost a baby *and* my wife, and I've been struggling ever since to find her and get her back. You're the one with no empathy. It might surprise you to know that I have feelings, too. You've disappeared so far inside yourself that you don't even see me anymore. How do you think that makes me feel?"

"You're missing the point!"

"No. You're the one who's missing the point. I've always been told that marriage was about compromise. But you refuse to compromise. You refuse to even acknowledge my viewpoint, because it doesn't match yours. I love you. I've always loved you. But right now, I don't like you very much!"

"Why are you being such a jackass?"

"Because that's who I am, babydoll." He bent and picked his shirt up off the floor, shrugged into it, haphazardly buttoned it. "And for some inexplicable reason—" He shoved bare feet into his sneakers. "—even though you keep stomping all over my heart, I can't seem to give up on you. Sometimes, I wish I could, but I can't. What kind of damn fool that makes me, I don't know. But right now, I don't want to be anywhere near you. So I'm leaving. I'll be back when I've cooled off. In the meantime, you might want to think about your priorities." He paused, hand on the doorknob. "Because right now, they are seriously fucked up!"

He slammed the door behind him, stomped down the stairs. The front door closed with a thud. A minute later, the Explorer's engine roared to life. Then he was gone, down the driveway and out of sight. She stood at the window, fists curled in fury, and watched his tail lights until they disappeared from view.

The man was wrong. He was wrong on so many levels that she couldn't count them all. Her desire for another baby was not an obsession. It was a need, a physical ache, a maternal yearning so strong she couldn't control it. Did that qualify as an obsession? He'd called her self-involved, and that was the most hurtful thing, because it simply wasn't true. Her family was the most important thing in her life. She adored Emma and Paige. She even adored him, when he wasn't acting like a self-righteous, abominable ass.

There wasn't a grain of truth to anything he'd said. He'd simply said all those terrible things because he was furious with her. She'd caught him sticking his nose into something that wasn't his business, and she'd called him on it. Rob MacKenzie didn't like to be wrong. He thought he knew everything. And most of the time, he did. Most of the time, he was right. But not this time. This time, he was dead wrong.

This time, he was the village idiot.

But he was her idiot. And because of that, she dropped her face to her hands and cried.

Rob

HE'D been driving aimlessly for an hour. Too fast, but that was nothing new. It should have helped to cool his anger, driving fast through the velvety darkness, with the windows open and the radio blaring, the night air threading fingers through his hair.

Except that it hadn't. The fury was still there, festering in his gut, twisting and knotting his insides until they felt like a box of snakes. That damned Irish temper. The MacKenzies weren't known for mincing words or for backing down. They were jackasses, and proud of it, with hair-trigger tempers that could ignite with little provocation. He'd inherited that temper from a long line of MacKenzie forebears, and he'd passed it on to Paige. The jury was still out on Emma; his youngest daughter was strong-willed, but she seemed to have a cool head and even temper.

It would probably make her journey through life one hell of a lot easier than his.

Rob gripped the wheel harder, his shoulders aching, his muscles taut with tension. Arguing had been futile. They hadn't resolved a thing. His wife might not possess the famed MacKenzie temper, but Casey was about as malleable as a chunk of granite. The woman refused to back down, refused to admit that he was right. He loved her, but at times, he wanted to throttle her. This was one of those times.

Tires squealing, he took a hard right turn onto yet another anonymous blacktop road. He was hopelessly lost. These twisting back roads made no sense to a boy raised on the streets of South Boston. He'd lived in Maine for three years, but he still didn't have a clear picture of the lay of the land. It all looked the same to him. Trees, trees, and more trees, interspersed with fields and pastures and crumbling nineteenth-century barns. Casey, who'd grown up here, knew intimately every acre of land from Jackson Falls to the New Hampshire state line. He could spend the rest of his life here and never absorb what came so naturally to her. What was the saying he'd heard? *Just because the cat has kittens in the oven, it doesn't make 'em biscuits.* He was an outsider. No matter how long he lived here, no matter that his wife and his daughter had both been born here or that he paid substantial property taxes, he would always be viewed with suspicion.

The road curved to the left. He stepped on the accelerator, felt the quick response of the engine, the rush of adrenaline as he steered into the darkness with no idea of what awaited him on the other side of that curve. It chapped his ass that she didn't give enough of a damn about him, about Emma or Paige, to listen to reason. He wasn't the villain in this piece. He was just a guy who loved his wife, a guy who was trying to build a decent life with her.

A guy who didn't want to lose her.

He rolled into the straightaway and started down a steep hill, wheels humming against the pavement. They'd always been so connected they could finish each other's sentences. But the last few weeks had created a rift in the tightly-woven fabric of their relationship, had opened a vast gap between them that he had no idea how to breach. And, damn it, he was tired of fighting. He just wanted his life back.

The radio was playing an up-tempo Tom Petty song, a little too bouncy for his foul mood. His attention temporarily diverted from the road, Rob punched buttons until he found WTOS, the Mountain of Rock, where George Thorogood was belting out a song about being bad to the bone.

There. That was more like it.

When he returned his attention to the road, the doe was standing directly in front of him, frozen in time and place, her eyes glowing in the reflection from his headlights. Rob hit the brakes so hard the car fishtailed. He gripped the wheel with both hands and veered to the right to avoid her. His right-front tire dropped off the pavement to the soft shoulder. The deer bounded away into the woods. Cussing, still moving too fast, he yanked the wheel to the left and over-corrected.

Time seemed to slow as, tires screaming, the car lost control. He had a single instant of clarity, a single instant of knowing he was going to die, a single snapshot of Emma's face in his mind, before he reached the opposite shoulder.

And the car went airborne.

PART III: THE HEALING

Rob

IT was the rain that woke him. A cold, fine, needle-sharp rain that fell on his face like microscopic shards of glass. Puzzled, he opened his eyes to darkness. He slowly lifted a hand and recognized as raindrops the tiny, sharp-toothed objects drilling into his skin.

He blinked. The darkness remained. No light. No sound. His head ached, and his thinking moved at a glacial pace. Where the hell was he, and how had he ended up here? Moving at the speed of sloth, he patted the hard surface he lay on, and was even more puzzled to recognize it as damp grass. Had he gotten drunk and passed out in the yard? It had been more than a decade since he'd been that drunk. Casey would have his hide.

Pain throbbed behind his eyes. He reached up a hand to rub his temple, and it came back sticky. Squinting into the darkness, he could just make out the white blur of his hand, his fingers tipped with something so dark it blended into the night that surrounded him.

Blood. He was bleeding from his head.

He struggled to pull information from his brain, but it was like jogging through molasses. He was somewhere in rural Maine, lying on wet grass, in the rain, bleeding. That much he knew. But he had no idea where he was, no memory of how he'd gotten here, no idea how long he'd been here.

Think! he ordered himself. *Think, fool!* The answer was locked somewhere inside him. If he thought hard enough, he should be able to find it. He closed his eyes, tried to focus. Images swam behind his eyelids, but it was impossible to tell which were real and which were fantasy. Concentrating hard, he tried to nab one of them as it drifted by.

Bad to the bone.

Where the hell had that come from? He squeezed his eyes more tightly shut, but all he saw was a blank, impenetrable wall.

Ridiculous. This was ridiculous. He couldn't very well lie here all night in the rain, with George Thorogood lyrics running through his head. He had to get up on his feet so he could figure out where he was and what kind of mess he'd gotten himself into.

He drifted, unable to hold onto the thought long enough to will his body to follow the signals his brain was sending. *Gotta get up,* he told himself. *You can do it.* Eventually, he managed to brace both hands against the grass. Taking a deep breath, he gathered all his resources, and pushed upward.

Pain lasered through him, white-hot pain that sucked the breath from him, screamed inside his skull, and wrenched a sob from deep in his throat. He dropped back to the ground, gasping, disbelieving. Through a haze of indescribable pain, he muttered, *"Fuck."*

Somewhere inside that haze, Casey's face floated in the air above him. His love, his life, his woman, with her soft voice, her cool hands. She would make everything better. Casey always made everything better. He just had to figure out how to get home to her. Then everything would be all right.

He exhaled a hard breath, tried to stop the chattering of his teeth. He'd had no idea that September nights in the foothills of Western Maine could be this cold. Especially in the rain. He wiggled his fingers, pleased to note that they still worked. He should be wearing a jacket. Why the hell wasn't he wearing a jacket?

For the first time, it sank into his befuddled brain that he was in trouble.

Casey

IT took an hour before her anger dissipated, leaving behind emptiness and regret. She didn't want to fight with Rob. How was it that two so-called adults could be so hard-headed and obstinate? Why couldn't they sit down like rational human beings and talk out their differences? Why did their disagreements always seem to escalate into shouting matches?

It took another hour before she started to think about what he'd said. Could there be any truth to it? Was it possible that he was right? At some point, her train had clearly derailed. Had she really been so self-absorbed that she'd failed to consider how that derailment was affecting her family? If so, then she'd gone farther around the bend than she realized. And if that was true, she owed her husband a huge apology.

It wasn't until the third hour that she started to worry.

Because he'd been gone for far too long. Rob was generally the world's most laid-back and easygoing guy. But when his feathers were ruffled, that temper of his became a fire-breathing dragon. After the screaming was over, he always went off by himself to restore his equilibrium. He'd done it for as long as she could remember. But it wasn't like him to stay gone this long. Not without calling. Not since the night two years ago when he'd driven off in a blizzard, leaving her to stew for hours before she finally tracked him down at his sister's house, where he was drowning his sorrows in a bottle of Jim Beam.

He'd never done that to her again.

If that hoodlum hadn't stolen his cell phone, she could have called him. Chances were good that, even as furious as he was, he would have answered. Because underneath the fury, he loved her. He wouldn't want her to worry.

But without the phone, there was no way to reach him. When the clock reached the three-hour mark, she decided it was time to call Rose. If he'd gone over there, and if he and Jesse were commiserating over a bottle of Beam, calling home could have slipped his mind. So, as much as she hated it, at half-past midnight, Casey dialed her sister-in-law's house.

A groggy Rose answered. "Hey," she rasped when she recognized Casey's voice. "What's up?"

"I woke you, didn't I?"

"Meh. Don't worry about it. Sleep is overrated."

"I'm so sorry. I'm looking for Rob. I thought he might be at your house."

There was a moment's hesitation. "Rob? No, hon. We haven't seen him." Rose paused. "How long has he been gone?"

"Three hours, give or take."

"Where'd he go at nine-thirty at night?"

Casey rubbed absently at her temple. "We had a fight. A whopper. He did what he always does. Stomped around like an angry little boy, yelled at me, then drove away to cool off."

"You do realize that the infamous MacKenzie temper can involve a lengthy cooling-off period?"

"Of course, but...three hours?"

"Maybe you should buy him a punching bag to hang in the basement. It would save on gas. *Ouch.*"

"What?"

"Jesse just elbowed me. He doesn't think I should be making jokes when my brother is missing."

"He's not missing. He's just misplaced. There's a difference." Casey gnawed on her lower lip. "I was so sure he'd gone to your house. Now, I'm really starting to worry. Where else would he go in this rinky-dink little town?"

"He's probably driving around, still trying to work off that head of steam. The brat. Did you try Colleen? He's not hanging out with Harley, is he? Lately, they've been joined at the hip."

"At this hour? I highly doubt it. Harley's up at four every morning to milk cows. He's probably been asleep since eight-thirty."

"Look, he probably drove further than he expected, and now he's on his way home. He hasn't called because we live in western Maine, where there isn't exactly an abundance of pay phones."

"I wish I had your faith, but you know me. I'm a worrier."

"So am I, underneath the snark. He is my baby brother, after all. Call me when he gets home. I don't care what time it is."

Casey dropped the phone into its cradle on the kitchen counter and turned. Paige was standing in the doorway to the dining room, wearing a Wonder Woman sleep shirt that fell halfway down her lanky thighs, her long blond curls falling loosely around slender arms.

"Dad's not home yet?" she said.

"He's not." A chill blew across the back of her neck, raising gooseflesh on her arms, and Casey rubbed them for warmth.

"He left three hours ago."

She should have known her stepdaughter would keep track of the time. They'd made enough noise, yelling at each other, to wake the dead. Paige could probably tell her the precise minute that Rob had walked out the door. The poor kid had lost her mother at the age of fifteen. The idea that she could conceivably lose her father, too, had to be terrifying.

"Maybe we should go look for him."

It was a crazy idea, and a stupid one. He could be anywhere. Casey latched onto it anyway. Making a split-second decision, she said, "I'll go look. You stay here with Emma."

"But—"

She already had her car keys in hand, was already fishing her fall jacket out of the coat closet. "He might call," she said, tugging on the jacket and pulling her hair free from the collar. "Somebody needs to be here to answer the phone."

Casey didn't say aloud what they were both thinking: that the aforementioned call could come from the police. It was a possibility she wasn't ready to face. He was out there somewhere, and she would find him.

"Where will you look?"

"There aren't many obvious places in this town. I'll swing by Harley's, and Bill's. He's pretty tight with both of them. Take a drive through downtown. Maybe he pulled into a parking lot somewhere and fell asleep."

"Right." That was all she said, but Paige's tone left no question about her opinion.

"I'll be back in an hour, give or take. If the phone rings—"

"I know. Answer it."

A soft rain was falling, and clouds scudded across the face of the waxing moon as she unlocked the Volvo wagon they'd bought after Emma was born. At the time, she'd been driving the Mitsubishi Eclipse she purchased after Danny died. She'd never grown attached to the Mitsubishi; the car was merely

transportation. It had been Rob who, after a lengthy study of
Consumer Reports, had decided a Volvo was the safest car they
could buy for the purpose of chauffeuring their newborn daughter
to her pediatrician appointments and to story hour at the library.
Casey had found it by turns both amusing and charming, the
transformation of her laid-back rock musician husband into a
somber, responsible family man. But she hadn't argued when he'd
suggested trading the Mitsubishi for something a little more
substantial. She'd bought that car to replace the destroyed BMW
that Danny had died in. Every time she looked at the Mitsubishi, it
reminded her of the devastated young widow she'd been, and the
negative vibes were unnerving. Besides, she wanted to move on
with her life, not wallow in the past.

It had been a relief to dump it.

The damp night air cooled her, and she shivered as she slipped
onto the cold leather seat. Barely September, and already the nights
were cool and unforgiving, the restless rustling of early-turning
maple leaves a portent of what was to come.

She spent a couple of minutes warming the car, then took
Ridge Road to where it curved and intersected with Meadowbrook
Road. Ever vigilant, scanning the roadsides for any sign of
something amiss, she hung a left onto Meadowbrook, her Volvo
smoothly riding the bumps of the unpaved gravel road. She passed
Meadowbrook Farm, where she'd grown up. The barnyard lay in
silence, her sister's car and Harley's pickup truck parked side by
side like an old married couple. A half-mile beyond the farm, at the
foot of McKellar's Hill, she turned right onto River Road, and left
the gravel behind.

Set back from the road behind an unmowed meadow of
nodding wildflowers, Rose and Jesse's house was a hulking form
in the pale moonlight, a lone second-story window dimly lit. The
only vehicles in the drive were those that belonged there: Jesse's
truck, Rose's new car, Luke's rusty old beater. Rose and Jesse had
started married life three years ago with a houseful of teenagers.
Now, Luke was the only one still living at home. His choice of
work over college hadn't pleased his mother and stepfather, but
Rose had told her that after last winter's fiasco with Mikey, they'd
decided to give Luke some space to make his own decisions.

Beyond Jesse's property, the road took a sharp turn, clinging snugly to the dark, winding riverbank, and she monitored every foot of guardrail, looking for a break, for a length of crumpled metal, letting out a sigh of relief when she found neither. Another left took her to Hardscrabble Road and past her brother Bill's tidy yellow ranch house. It lay in peaceful slumber. No sign of Rob.

That pretty much took care of the obvious places.

She followed Meadowbrook Road to the state highway and turned toward town. The state had rebuilt the highway a decade ago, bypassing downtown Jackson Falls and turning it into a ghost town. Most people who drove this northeasterly route were headed toward the Canadian border, or to one of the big ski areas. Few of them even knew that just off the highway lay the center of the little river town that was nothing more to them than a name on a map.

She took the turnoff through town. It was exactly a mile from one end of the bypass to the other, and the old highway through town was dotted with small businesses. The IGA sat dark, its parking lot empty, its roadside sign advertising a sale on ground chuck and local produce. At the Big Apple convenience store, a customer was pumping gas into a dark green Subaru. She quickly scanned the parking lot, but Rob's Ford Explorer wasn't there. Lola's Steak House was dark and deserted, the Jackson Diner well lit, but every booth was empty, and she wondered how they managed to stay in business.

At the bowling alley, a police cruiser with just its parking lights on sat facing the road, waiting for some poor sucker to come along driving faster than the posted speed limit. She thought about pulling in, asking the officer if he'd seen her husband, but it was too soon to go there, too soon to make Rob's disappearance official.

Downtown Jackson Falls consisted of a single block of late-nineteenth-century brick buildings that housed a shoe store, a five-and-ten, a real estate office, the local veterinarian, and a handful of other small specialty stores that came and went, depending on the current business climate. The town's lone traffic light, at the intersection of Main and Bridge, flashed yellow. Just beyond the light sat the library, with its tidy green lawn and towering elms, and the grammar school she'd attended through sixth grade. A side street led to a small residential neighborhood that lay between downtown and the new bypass, just a half-dozen cross streets lined with Victorian houses, and a dusty trailer park that had seen better days.

She proceeded through the light and took a left after the school, winding her way through side streets until she reached the trailer park. Rob had a friend who lived here. Mike Turcotte played drums, and sometimes they jammed together. Maybe Rob had stopped by for a beer or three. Her husband wasn't a big drinker, but he was a sociable sort, and among the men she knew, sociability generally included lifting a few brews.

But he wasn't at Mike Turcotte's little trailer. Mike's Harley sat in the yard, his helmet draped over the sissy bar, and all the trailer windows were dark.

It had been a long shot anyway. Casey turned the car around, left the trailer park, and headed back toward downtown. Just south of the bridge, the river plunged forty feet through a cavernous canyon of boiling white water that smoothed out three hundred feet downriver. There'd once been a textile mill here. Most of the adult population of Jackson Falls had worked there. It had burned in a spectacular conflagration the year she turned eleven, plunging the town into an economic recession from which it had never really recovered.

She turned off Main Street, drove into the parking lot behind the stores, and parked along the riverbank. A half-dozen vehicles were scattered throughout the lot, most likely tenants who lived in apartments above the stores. None of the vehicles was Rob's. Casey got out of the car and stood at the riverbank, hands in the pockets of her jacket, watching the river flow past.

And thought, *Damn it, MacKenzie! Where the hell are you?*

Rob

YOU know," Danny said, leaning forward from his perch on a nearby boulder, "you always were a bit of a drama queen. But this is going a little too far, even for you. I assume you've heard of overkill?"

"You're dead," Rob said. "What the hell do you know?"

Danny gave him the infamous Fiore grin, the one that carried fifty thousand watts of dimpled splendor. The one that, when he was alive, had enticed females of all ages to toss their lacy unmentionables up on stage. Even dead, the son of a bitch still looked better than Rob had ever looked. Danny pulled a pack of Marlboros from his shirt pocket, upended the pack and shook out a cigarette. Swapping the pack for his Zippo, he flicked it open to light the cigarette, then closed the lighter and returned it to his pocket. Tossing that perfect hair back from his face, he took a deep draw on the cancer stick. Exhaled the smoke and said, "Don't tell me we're going to let a little thing like that come between friends."

"Doesn't make you any less dead."

"I hear you're sleeping with my wife these days."

"She's not your wife. You're dead and buried. She's my wife now."

Danny shrugged, blew out a cloud of smoke and waved his hand in a dismissive gesture. "Semantics. Nothing more than semantics."

"What do you want, Dan?"

"Me? I don't want anything. I'm not the one in a pickle, my friend."

"Yeah? Well, I didn't ask you to come here, so you can just go back to wherever you came from. You're not real, anyway, so what difference does it make?"

Danny drew on his cigarette, held it out, and studied it. "So this is what you want? This is how you want to go out, in a blaze of glory? A car wreck, like I did?"

"Fuck you, Fiore."

Danny grinned. "That's more like it. Good to see you still have a little fight left in you."

"I have plenty of fight left in me."

"Then why the hell are you still here? Lying helpless, like a turtle on its back? Get up off your ass, MacKenzie, and do something. Don't just stay here and wait to die."

"That might be a little hard to do right now, with a broken—" He waved his arm for emphasis. "—whatever. But trust me when I say that I have no intention of dying."

"Then act like it!"

"Who the hell are you to tell me how to act?"

"I'm your goddamn best friend! That's who I am!" Danny tossed the cigarette to the ground and scraped the hair back from his face with one hand. "And you're not done living yet, not by a long shot. You have a beautiful wife—" Danny winced. "—my wife, as a matter of fact, and a family that loves you. Not to mention a performing career that—"

"My career's over. I retired from performing. I'm producing now. I'm happier working behind the scenes."

"That's the biggest load of bullshit you've ever tried to feed me." Rubbing his thumb over his lip, Danny studied him thoughtfully. "Did you really think you could bury yourself up here in the middle of nowhere, sit around some empty studio, practicing guitar chords, and forget where you came from? Not a chance in hell. We did it together, MacKenzie. We starved together, and we played together, any place they'd let us get on stage, and we made it to the top together, because the only damn thing that mattered was the music. I knew you when you were a scrawny kid who didn't know his ass from his elbow. Until he picked up a guitar, and then he became a god. You belong on stage. Your talent's too big to confine to a recording studio."

"I was never a god. You were the star, Fiore. I was just window dressing."

Danny snorted. "I hope to Christ you don't really believe that, because if you do, you're deluding yourself. You were always the one with the talent. Always! You need to get back out there."

"It's too hard without you. And it's been too long. People's memories are short."

"So? Remind them."

"I have a family now. I can't go back on the road. Don't you remember the way it swallowed us up?"

"Stop making excuses. Do it your way. You have the money, the pull, the reputation, to write your own ticket. It's a changed world, Wiz. The world we knew is gone, but this one's bigger and broader and better. You can go so much further than I did. Sure, I could sing, but mostly I was a pretty face. Somebody the girls could fantasize about. You, though—you have a talent that'll just keep growing and growing. It'll take you into your old age. Another ten years on stage and I would've been a has-been. But, you—another ten years and you, my friend, will be a legend. Hell, you're already halfway there."

"Pretty words, Fiore."

"True words. Listen, Wiz. There's one more thing."

The nickname was one that Danny had christened him with when they first met. Short for guitar wizard, it was a term of affection and tremendous respect. They'd always been each other's biggest fan, and to hear it again, after all this time, touched a chord in his heart. "Yeah?" he said softly. "What's that?"

"Don't disappoint her like I did. Don't make her go through that kind of pain again. It would destroy her."

Rob closed his eyes, swallowed. "I have no intention of doing any such—" His eyes fluttered open, and he realized he was alone.

Danny was gone.

He was delirious. It was the only reasonable explanation. He'd imagined the whole thing. Danny had been a hallucination, a component of his delirium. Nothing more than a projection of his own feelings.

Steeling himself against the pain, Rob rolled onto his side, and with a strength he hadn't realized he possessed, raised himself on one knee and slowly, agonizingly, dropped onto his belly. He gasped, lungs burning, eyes squeezed shut against the searing pain that stole his breath away. Then lay there, breathless, until the worst of the pain receded. Slowly, gingerly, he opened his eyes.

And saw the cigarette butt, still glowing red, lying on the damp grass.

Casey

PAIGE met her at the door, her face ashen with worry. "Nothing?" she said.

"Nothing. I checked every place I could think of, and I drove up and down the state highway for a few miles in either direction." Casey took off her coat and tossed it over a chair back. "Then I realized how pointless it was, considering how many miles of road there are within Jackson Falls alone. I could drive all night and not cover them all."

"Aunt Rose called. Just to see if he was home yet. She sounded worried."

Casey crossed her arms over her chest and rubbed her forearms for warmth. "I don't know what to do. I'm trying not to panic. But this isn't right. He wouldn't be gone this long without calling unless something was wrong."

"Maybe he broke down and he's stuck in the middle of nowhere."

"He'd call. He'd walk to the nearest house and use their phone."

"At—" Paige glanced at the clock on the wall. "One o'clock in the morning?"

"Think about it. This is your father we're talking about. No fear, not a shy bone in his body, just a lot of brass. Polished brass, but brass nevertheless. He absolutely would walk up to a stranger's door at one in the morning and wake them up to use their phone. And you know what else?" For the first time, her composure slipped, allowing the panic to settle into her stomach. She tried to control the hitch in her voice, but couldn't. "He'd manage to talk his way in and make them think he was the one doing them a favor. Because that's the kind of guy he is."

The phone rang. She snatched it up, and her sister said, "Did you find him?"

"How did you know?"

"Jesse called us. Is he home yet?"

"No. I looked everywhere. I don't know what to do, Col. I'm so scared."

"What you're going to do is call Teddy."

"Teddy hates Rob."

"Jesus Christ, Casey, your husband's missing, and your cousin's a cop. Don't be an idiot. Call Teddy. Harley and I are on our way over. He's already called Billy to do the morning milking. We'll find him, hon."

She wasn't a particularly religious woman, but when she hung up the phone, she prayed. To God, to the universe, to whoever was in charge of these things. She couldn't go through this again. She couldn't be a widow again for the second time before the age of forty.

She couldn't lose Rob.

Don't even go there. He's fine.

But her mind went there anyway. The idea of facing the next fifty years of her life without Rob MacKenzie by her side filled her with a fear like none she'd ever felt. For the first time, she understood why he'd been dead-set against her getting pregnant again. If the possibility of losing her had been half as terrifying for him as this was for her, she really had put him through hell.

I'm sorry, babe. I'm so very sorry.

She refused to allow herself to fall apart. That wouldn't help either of them. She had to hold herself together for his sake. If he was out there somewhere, in trouble, they had to find him. All the rest of it, the apologies, the regrets, the compromises, they could deal with later. The only thing that mattered now was finding him.

Her hands were trembling so hard, she could barely find the buttons on the telephone. But her long-time friend, iron determination, helped those shaky fingers to dial Teddy's number anyway.

Rob

IT was the weirdest thing. At first, he'd been cold, so cold. But he wasn't cold anymore. It had stopped raining at some point. Maybe five minutes ago, maybe five hours. His clothes were still wet, his skin still clammy, but he wasn't feeling the cold anymore. He'd been drifting in and out of consciousness ever since Danny left, but even when he was awake, he wasn't lucid. Not really. His brain was fogged, his thinking glacial. *Car wreck.* That's what Danny had told him. But damned if he could remember it. No matter how hard he tried, he had no memory of how he'd wound up here.

Bad to the bone.

Why did that damn song keep running through his head every time he tried to remember? If his brain would kick-start itself into working order, maybe it would come to him. But his brain had stopped functioning a long time ago, and he didn't think it was coming back.

On the road above him, a car passed, its tires swishing on the rain-slicked pavement. He could hear it, but he couldn't see it, just the sweep of its headlights as it passed. He wasn't in pain anymore. Did that mean he was dying? He didn't mind it so much, dying. Not if it felt like this, warm and cozy and simple. He liked simple. Simple suited him.

Get up off your ass, MacKenzie, and do something. Don't just stay here and wait to die.

Danny'd said that, too. But what the hell did he know? Rob closed his eyes, and a flash of memory sparked behind his eyelids. His hand, fiddling with the radio. He struggled to remember more, but it just wasn't there. So he concentrated on something else. Tried to figure out what was the last thing he remembered.

It came to him slowly, twisted and mixed-up and crazy, like the kind of wild dream you'd have after eating a heavy meal too close to bedtime. He watched it like a movie inside his skull. The two of them, faces contorted, mouths moving soundlessly. Their words, instead of coming from their mouths, appeared in cartoon bubbles above their heads. Red. He struggled to read what they said, but couldn't make them out. But the words were red. The color of love. The color of passion. The color of anger.

They'd been fighting. He and Casey had fought before he wrecked the car.

The tiny portion of lucid mind still left to him experienced an instant of panic. Had they been fighting in the car? Was his wife lying, dead or dying, somewhere in the wreck?

No. He'd been alone in the car. He wasn't sure how he knew it, but he did. He let out a hard breath of relief, and with that breath, the truth, bold and brassy and inconvenient, wormed its way into his fuzzy brain. It was annoying, and not at all what he wanted to hear. Dying out here would be so easy. Comfortable and simple. He'd just drift off to sleep and never wake up.

He couldn't think of a better way to go.

And a part of him wanted that. Craved it, even. If he shuffled off this mortal coil, the planet would keep on spinning. His daughters, his beautiful daughters, would be fine. Paige was a grown woman, as strong and solid as an oak tree. She would bounce back, and be stronger for the experience. Emma was so young, she wouldn't remember him anyway. Being without a father would feel normal for her. He'd go out quietly, painlessly. Dying was so much easier than living. Living was a struggle. Life was hard and painful and screwed up. Nothing ever turned out the way you thought it would. It was a roller-coaster ride without any seat belts. All you could do was hold on and hope you survived the ride. Compared to that, dying sounded downright appealing. It would be so easy to leave it all behind: the struggle and the pain and the bullshit.

Except for one thing.

He couldn't leave Casey.

She was the only thing that tied him to this mortal life, and his love for her was stronger than death's siren call. As much as he wanted to take the easy way out, he couldn't. He'd promised her sixty years, and he still had fifty-seven of them to go. Fifty-seven more years of waking up beside her every morning, of falling asleep beside her every night. They would raise Emma together. They would have a long, happy marriage, filled with love and laughter, joy and pain, tears and anger, because that's what real life was like. And when the time came to leave her, he'd be an old, white-haired man who would look back on his life and his marriage and think, *Well done.*

He raised a hand to shield his eyes from the white light that blinded him. Why the hell was it hurting his eyes? In all the near-death experiences he'd heard about, nobody had ever said anything about the light being painful.

On the road above, a door slammed, then another. Voices. Two voices. A man and a woman. Were they angels sent to accompany him home? If they were, he wasn't going with them. He'd fight like hell to stay here. No way was he going with any angel into any tunnel that had a light so bright it hurt his eyes. No way was he going anywhere that would take him any farther away from Casey. As long as he still drew breath, he would find a way back to her.

Footsteps crunched on gravel. Then the woman let out a tiny shriek. And the man said, "Jesus H. Christ."

Even in his befuddled state, that was enough to confirm to Rob MacKenzie that they weren't angels.

At least not the kind with wings.

Casey

HE was right," she said, staring out the window of the truck. "My priorities are screwed up."

Her brother-in-law Harley, his hands at ten and two on the steering wheel, wisely said nothing.

"We had a terrible fight tonight. That's why he left. We've been at odds for weeks." She paused, wet her lips. "I'm desperate for another baby. He's afraid to try again. I've been in a very dark place ever since the last miscarriage. So wrapped up in loss that I didn't see what I was doing to him. I've faced so many losses in my life." She turned and looked at Harley. "Sometimes, it feels as though my life has been nothing but loss. My mother, Katie, Danny. Three unborn babies. And this last one sent me over the edge. I don't know why. But the possibility of losing Rob puts all those other losses into perspective. Because as bad as they were, nothing could compare to losing him."

"He's a good man," Harley said.

Her eyes filled with tears, and she didn't bother to try to hide them. Not tonight. Not from Harley, who, aside from Rob, was the person she trusted most in this world. "I'm so scared, Harley," she whispered. "I don't think I could breathe without him."

He'd been missing now for six hours. She and Harley had spent the last two of those hours driving around back roads, scouring the ditches for any sign of a crash. Her cell phone gripped tightly in one hand and a flashlight in the other, she'd examined bridges and gulleys, woods and fields. But there was no sign of her husband. Jesse was out searching the roads on the other side of town. Colleen and Rose, who'd both been married to Jesse and weren't exactly the best of friends, had nevertheless stayed at the house with Paige. Even her cousin Teddy, who'd never tried to hide his animosity toward her husband, had put out an alert and was out there in the dark, in his police cruiser, doing the same thing she was. That was what family did. They took care of each other. They banded together, setting aside their differences. They'd done that for her, for Rob. Because they were family, and because she wasn't the only one who loved him.

In her hand, the phone rang, and she recognized Teddy's number. Her breath dammed up in her chest, she looked to Harley for guidance. "It's Teddy," she said. "I'm afraid to answer it. I'm afraid of what he's going to tell me."

Harley rested a hand on her knee, squeezed it, and said, "You have to answer it, sweetheart. One way or the other, good or bad, you have to know."

The phone kept on ringing. She took a breath to compose herself, nodded, and answered. Her voice trembling, she said, "Teddy?"

And her cousin said, "We found him."

* * *

At the hospital, they wouldn't give her any information, except to say that yes, her husband was here, yes, he was being treated, and no, she couldn't see him yet. She would have to wait for the doctor to get the answers she sought.

So she waited. With Harley's comforting hand on her shoulder and fear rendering her almost comatose, Casey sat silently, her head in her hands. Too drained, too exhausted, to even think clearly. Rose and Jesse arrived, solemn and silent. Had she ever known Rose to be silent? Every so often, one or the other of them would get up and approach the reception desk, demanding to know what was going on. The response was always the same. *No news. The doctor will let you know when there's something to report.*

Two hours passed. Then three. She'd just dozed off, her head lolling on the back of the hard, uncomfortable chair, when a male voice said, "Mrs. MacKenzie?"

She jolted awake, blinked her eyes, and shot to her feet. "Yes?"

The man in the white coat was tall and slim, with wire-rimmed glasses and a stethoscope dangling from his neck. He extended his hand. "I'm Dr. Wright."

His handshake was cool, dry, and brief. "Your husband," he said, "is suffering from hypothermia, a broken pelvis, and a fairly significant concussion. Not to mention a host of contusions and abrasions. We had to stitch a particularly nasty cut on his head, and his nose is broken. When he came in, he was very confused. That was primarily due to the hypothermia, and it appears to be resolving as we've gradually raised his body temperature. It took us some time to stabilize him. Hypothermia's a tricky thing. It has to be treated with kid gloves or it can turn fatal."

Casey closed her eyes and swallowed hard. Opened them and said, "His prognosis?"

"He'll recover. But he won't be dancing the night away anytime soon."

"May I see him?"

"Absolutely. He's been asking for you. Just remember that he's on some pretty strong painkillers, so he's groggy. And don't be alarmed by his appearance. It looks a lot worse than it is."

At sight of her husband, Casey's breath caught in her throat. Even with the doctor's warning, she hadn't been prepared for this. Cocooned in blankets, he lay resting quietly. His left eye was puffy, bruised, swollen closed; stitches climbed his temple and inched like a centipede along the line of his jaw. Blood crusted his hair; his cheek was splotchy with multi-colored bruises, dried blood, and some kind of yellowish antiseptic. His nose, that beautiful, perfect nose, was twisted and swollen. There was an I.V. attached to his arm, a machine monitoring his heartbeat, his blood pressure, his body temperature.

A nurse bustling about the treatment room gave her a brief smile and said, "You can talk to him. He's not asleep."

Casey crossed the room, pulled up a chair, and sat. She gingerly laid a hand on his chest and said softly, "Hi."

He opened his good eye, focused it on her, and his smile arrowed straight through her heart. "Hi," he said. "Are you real, or another hallucination?"

Not sure what that meant, Casey gently brushed her knuckles against his cheek, startled by the coolness of his skin. Leaning her head close to his, she said, "I'm real, and so very glad to see you."

"Me, too." He closed his eyes again and swallowed. "You here to take me home?"

"Not until the doctor says it's okay, sweetheart. It might be a few days."

"It's jus' as well. They cut my damn clothes off. My favorite Zeppelin shirt, gone forever. You'll have to bring me some clothes, 'cause I really don't want to leave here bare-assed. Specially since I think that nurse over in the corner was trying to cop a feel."

Glancing at the plump, middle-aged nurse, who smirked at his salacious suggestion, Casey raised an eyebrow. "He's a little loopy from the meds," the woman said.

"Don't kid yourself," Casey said. "He's always like this."

The woman laughed and exited the room, leaving them alone.

"Brat," she said tenderly.

"Thass me. I messed myself up a bit, didn' I?"

"You did. You have a concussion and a broken pelvis. Not to mention hypothermia." She didn't dare to tell him what his face looked like. Rob wasn't a vain man, but even he had his limits.

"I'm Humpty Dumpty," he said, "and they put me all back together again."

She drew in a deep breath. "And I'm so glad they did. You don't know what my life has been these last few hours. I've been looking for you and looking for you. Everywhere I could think of. Up and down miles and miles of road. Because I knew you were in trouble. I knew you wouldn't just leave me and the girls like that. I knew you'd come home to us if you could."

"All I wanted was to get home to you. Jus' like Dorothy, I kept clicking my heels together, but nothing happened. So glad you rescued me."

"I didn't rescue you, babe. You were halfway to Rangeley, down a ravine, twenty miles from home. A young couple coming home from a late night out in Portland discovered you. When I find out who they are, I'm going to send them a thank-you card. I may tuck a ten-thousand-dollar check inside. Have I mentioned that you never do anything halfway, MacKenzie?"

"Goddamn Irish drama queen. I'm sorry."

"Don't be sorry, babe. Accidents happen."

"Not the crash. The fight. I don't have a right to squash your dreams. If what you really want is another baby, we'll keep trying. The fighting's not worth it. I just want us to be together."

"No," she said, "you were right. I've only been thinking about myself. I already have everything I could ever want. A husband I adore. Two beautiful daughters. A lovely home, a charmed life. I don't need any more than that, and once you're well, we're going to take care of the issue permanently. I'm also calling Dr. Deb first thing in the morning." Through her exhaustion, she realized it was already morning. "I'm going to ask her to recommend a therapist."

All around them, machines beeped, voices murmured, carts clanked. "If I tell you something," he said, "will you promise not to freak?"

She touched her hand to his cheek. "I promise."

"I wanna go back on stage. Back on the road. I know I said I never would, but there's a part of me that's missing. I've done a lot of thinking about it, and I really need to do this."

"I know."

"You know?"

"I realized it the night you and Phoenix sang together onstage. I wasn't sure you knew it, though. I've been waiting for you to bring it up."

"Why the hell didn't you tell me?"

She stroked his cheek tenderly. "Just like Dorothy, you had to figure it out yourself."

"I'm ready to write again. Will you help me? Can we write a new album together?"

"I'll consider it. Depending on what I get in payment."

"My heart. Always and forever. And fifty percent of the royalties."

She smiled, for the first time since she'd discovered Deb's message on her voice mail. And, threading fingers through his, she said, "That's an offer I can't refuse."

epilogue

Charlotte, North Carolina
Two years later

BACKSTAGE, the anticipation was palpable. His band members were so revved up he could taste it. They'd worked their asses off, and they'd earned the right to be excited. This was their big night, the result of two years of hard work and careful planning. He and Casey had spent a year crafting the songs for that first album, and their work had paid off. The record was shooting up the charts. He'd put together a band he was proud of, a band comprised of serious musicians, people he'd known for decades. There were thirty thousand people out there tonight, all of them waiting for him. It was thrilling, humbling, terrifying. Life as he'd known it was about to end. Fronting a band with a massive hit record would mean no more anonymity. People would remember his face. Especially now, with the distinctive crooked nose he'd broken in the crash. Casey said it was sexy, but that was just her way of telling him she loved him no matter what he looked like.

He'd never told her what had gone on during those hours he lay out there in that cold September rain. She didn't know about Danny's visit. Didn't know how close he'd come to giving up, didn't know he'd made a conscious decision to live because of her. Some things just couldn't be explained. He still didn't know whether Danny had been a hallucination or if he'd really been there. It didn't matter any more. What mattered was that after the night he'd almost died, he'd finally been able to let go of his guilt. Finally stopped blaming himself for Danny's death. Finally stopped believing he wasn't deserving of Casey's love. That night, Rob MacKenzie had turned his life around. He'd found his way, his reason, his path.

And he hadn't deviated from that path since then.

He had so many reasons to be glad he hadn't died on that grassy embankment on that chilly September night. So many things in his life to be grateful for. His beautiful, amazing wife, the wife who'd been willing to turn her life upside down to accommodate his inexplicable need to travel to the ends of the earth, playing one-night stands for strangers. After his accident, she'd spent months in therapy with a doctor in Lewiston who'd helped her unlock the grief she hadn't allowed herself to feel after Katie died. The multiple miscarriages, Dr. Emerson explained, had brought all that repressed grief bubbling to the surface and multiplied it exponentially. It had taken time, and work, but these days, she was the old Casey, cheerful and sassy and stronger at the broken places.

There was Emma, who was three now, beautiful and bright, solemn and curious, every bit her mother's daughter. And Paige, who was pulling a 4.0 average at Berklee, majoring in performance. She'd formed her own band, and was playing gigs in and around the Boston area. His daughter had her head on straight, and he predicted great things for her.

Then, there was Phoenix. His nemesis, the kid who wouldn't listen to a damn thing he said. Three days after he wrecked the car, he'd looked up from his hospital bed when he heard a stir in the corridor outside his room. There, standing in the doorway, wearing a trench coat, dark glasses, and the most ridiculous fedora he'd ever seen, was Phoenix Hightower.

"Hey, Phee," he'd said. "Come on in. *Mi casa es su casa.*"

Phoenix said something to Luther, who hovered outside, then he stepped into the room and closed the door. He pulled up a chair and sat. Took off his glasses, folded them up, and tucked them into the pocket of his trench coat. Studied Rob's appearance for a moment, then said, "It appears that you got yourself banged up quite nicely, old man. You look ghastly."

"How bad is it? You can be straight with me. They won't let me have a mirror."

"A wise decision, I'd say."

"I'm touched, Phee. That you're here. I wasn't sure you were still speaking to me after I ditched you in Brooklyn."

"Yes, well, I briefly considered a lawsuit, until I realized that you were the first person since I started this mad carousel ride who'd ever walked away from me. It was quite startling. And quite illuminating. As an added bonus, the cab ride back from the end of the earth gave me time to think about what you'd said."

"And?"

The kid leaned forward, clasped his hands between his bony knees. "My name is Russell Happer. I was born in London and raised in a dodgy part of town. My mother was a heroin addict, my father a common thief. When I was twelve years old, they got into a drunken fight, and she stabbed him twenty-three times with a kitchen knife. After she went to prison, I was sent to live with my Aunt Annette, in a little town in the Cotswolds. It was…unpleasant. After the third time I ran away, Aunt Annette stopped trying to find me. So at fourteen, I found myself on my own on the streets of London. I did what I had to do to survive. Theft, prostitution, singing on street corners for money, where I was discovered by a record executive. That's the only part of the official biography that's true, although it didn't happen at a school talent show. It happened on a street corner where I was singing to make enough money to buy my next meal."

Phoenix straightened, stretched out his legs, and said, "There. Now you know the real Phoenix Hightower. And if you ever tell any of this to anybody, I have friends who would easily make short work of you."

That confession was still one of the high points of his life. The minute Phoenix had finished his obligation to Ariel Records, he'd signed on with Two Dreamers. They'd already started writing the music for the kid's Two Dreamers debut album. No more teenage pop. Phee was ramping up to sing some serious stuff. Mostly R&B, old style, but with a modern touch. And next summer, if all went well, they'd be touring together.

But Rob's biggest reason to be grateful was propped on his hip right now. Davey, their little surprise package, their miracle baby, conceived on the morning he forgot the condom. Life, it seemed, really was what happened while you were making other plans. He'd been terrified when Casey told him she was pregnant. Deb had monitored her with religious fervor for those nine months, and Casey had sailed through the pregnancy, with no complications, and delivered a healthy, eight-pound baby boy.

Who, right now, was smelling a little aromatic. "I think he needs changing," he said, handing his son over to his wife.

"Lousy timing. Where's Kelly?" Casey scanned the hectic backstage area, spotted the nanny engaged in conversation with one of the roadies, and waved her over. The fresh-faced nineteen-year-old rushed to her side, and Casey held out the baby. "Can you change him for me, sweetie? I'd do it myself, but Rob's due on stage in four minutes."

"Of course, Come on, Davey Boy, let's get rid of that stinky old diaper." Baby in her arms, Kelly walked away, blond ponytail bouncing as she headed in the direction of their tour bus. Then she turned, waved, and shouted, "Good luck, Mr. MacKenzie!"

"That kid," Rob said, waving back, "is a godsend."

They'd found her working at the Jackson Falls Dairy Delight. A schoolmate of Paige's, she'd been thrilled to give up her summer job to travel on tour with the MacKenzie family in the luxury coach they'd had custom built. The tour bus was a fully functioning home on wheels, with plenty of room for all of them and every amenity they could have asked for. As soon as this tour thing had become real, he and Casey had made a pact. Three months out of each year, they would travel as a family, living on the tour bus. The other nine months, they'd spend at home, as private citizens, out of the limelight. They'd hired a foreman to take care of the sheep ranch in her absence, so she could travel with him. If he was going to be on the road, he wasn't leaving Casey or the kids behind. They were his life; the music was just what he did with that life.

Out front, the buzz from the crowd was getting louder. His tour manager raced by, said, "Two minutes," and kept on moving.

"Time to go," he said, and swung Emma up into his arms. "Give Daddy a kiss, Miss Emmy Lou Who. I'll see you after the show."

He kissed her noisily and handed her to Casey, who propped Emmy expertly on her hip, reached up her free hand, and straightened his collar. "I love you," she said, and kissed him with all the passion she could muster while holding a squirming three-year-old. "Emmy and I will be out front, watching the show. Knock 'em dead, hot stuff."

He fell in line with the rest of the guys, turned at the last minute and blew them both a kiss. Emma blew one back. Out front, the crowd began to roar, and then the announcer said, "Hello, Charlotte! How you doing tonight?" The response from thirty thousand people shook the rafters. "Tonight, it's my great pleasure to introduce to you, in their world concert debut, the band whose first album, *Ricochet*, just went platinum. Ladies and gentlemen, Rob MacKenzie and Rocket!"

The roar became an avalanche of sound.

And Rob MacKenzie turned and walked boldly, confidently, in the direction of his second life.

THE END

AUTHOR BIO

Laurie Breton started making up stories in her head when she was a small child. At the age of eight, she picked up a pen and began writing them down. Although she now uses a computer to write, she's still addicted to a new pen and a fresh sheet of lined paper. At some point during her angsty teenage years, her incoherent scribblings morphed into love stories, and that's what she's been writing, in one form or another, ever since.

When she's not writing, she can usually be found driving the back roads of Maine, looking for inspiration. Or perhaps standing on a beach at dawn, shooting a sunrise with her Canon camera. If all else fails, a day trip to Boston, where her heart resides, will usually get the juices flowing.

The mother of two grown children, Breton has two beautiful grandkids and two precious grand-dogs. She and her husband live in a small Maine town with a lovebird who won't stop laying eggs and two Chihuahua-mix dogs named River and Bella who pretty much run the household.

12396143R00153

Printed in Great Britain
by Amazon.co.uk, Ltd.,
Marston Gate.